Forbidden Waves

◦Book One◦

H. M. Huntress

First edition: November 2023

Forbidden Waves by H. M. Huntress
Cover designed by Getcovers.com

Please be advised this book contains explicit content, darker themes, and talk of pregnancy and inability to bear children. It is not intended for readers under the age of 18.

This book is dedicated to all the amazing friends
I've made on TikTok and Instagram.
Without you - this book would not exist.

Thank you.

Here is a Spotify playlist of songs which remind me of *Forbidden Waves*! *Please note this playlist is subject to change at any time*

Scan the QR code with the camera on your phone to listen now!

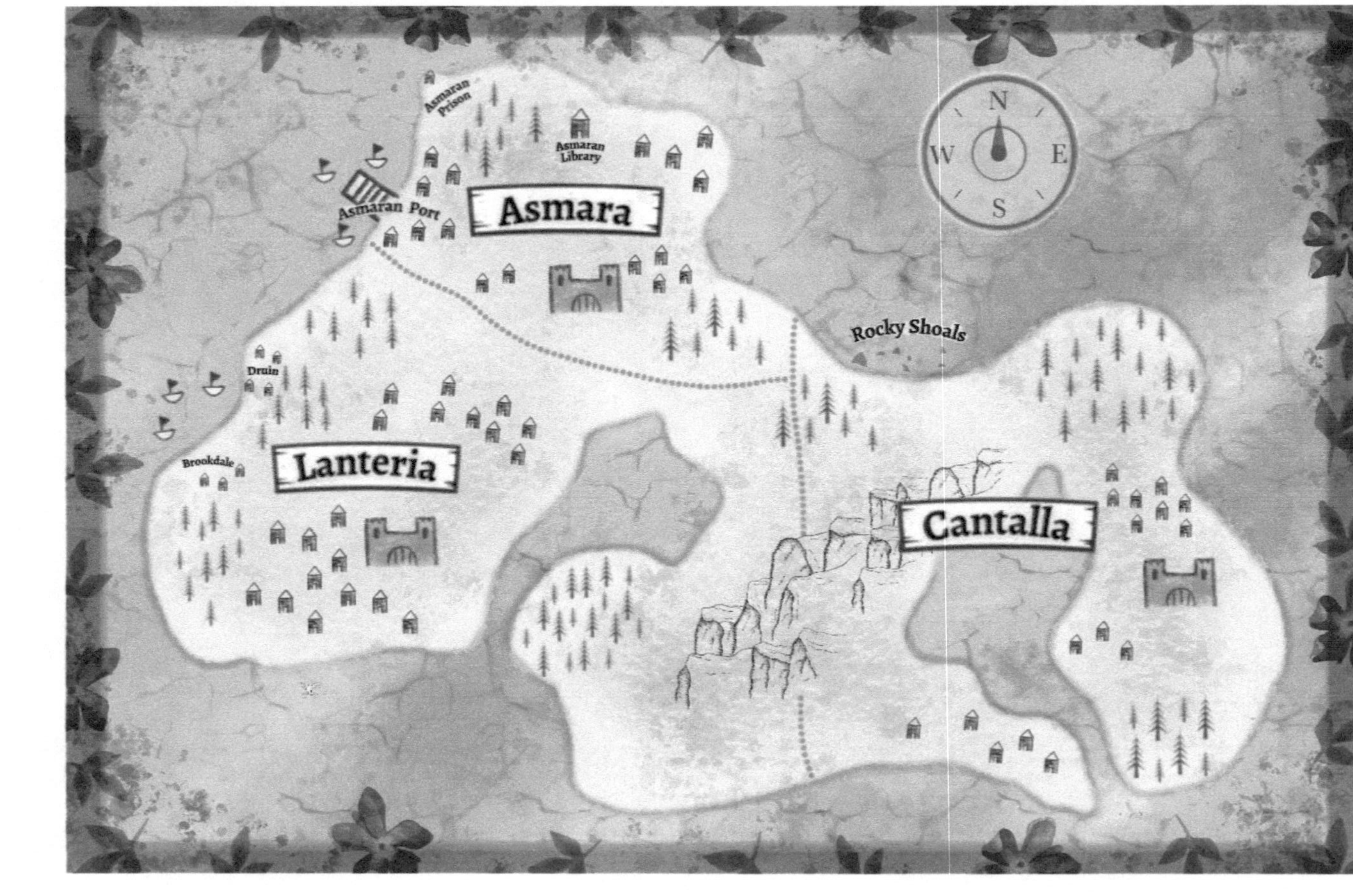

Asmaran Prison
Asmaran Library
Asmaran Port
Asmara
N
W
E
S
Rocky Shoals
Druin
Brookdale
Lanteria
Cantalla

Pronunciation Guide

Character Names

Aeros – Air-os

Aurelia – Aw-rell-ee-ah

Humer – Hew-mer

Khali – Kaw-lee

Lia – Lee-ah

Neros – Nee-rose

Ourania – Oh-rane-ee-ah

Terrian – T-air-ee-in

Places

Thalassia – Tah-lass-ee-uh

Finn

One by one we all lined up to be slaughtered. I gazed at the monstrous woman hovering above me on a wave of her own creation. *The siren queen,* I thought, grinding my jaw and hoping to break free from her enchantment. Her true name was one of the most well-kept secrets of the sea.

My crew and I kneeled before her as she sang a beautiful melody directly opposed to her ghastly appearance. Claws tipped her elongated fingers, and she tapped them against the mast to punctuate her words. From behind, her long, stark white hair would fool any man into thinking her a regular mermaid, or a woman. But her needle-like teeth and pitch-black eyes immediately flagged her as a siren. A threat. When sirens got too close, the smell of rotting seaweed overwhelmed the senses.

"Don't give in!" I cried out to my crew, though most of them were already enrapt in the queen's song. My first mate, Jamison, didn't seem to be among the group. Hope sparked in me that Jami may have avoided the queen's notice.

Fighting against the magic restraining me, my muscles screamed as I tried my hardest to move, to do *anything.* I seemed to be the only one not entirely entranced by the queen, but every second of her song pulled me further into her thrall.

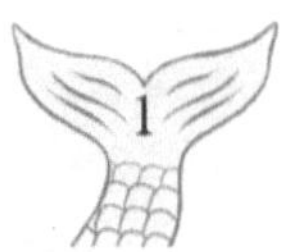

"Do not bother trying to break free," the queen stopped singing and spoke to me. The sirens who remained in the water continued her melody. "You have already lost." With a flick of her wrist, the queen flung one of my men overboard into the frothing sea below. Ear piercing screeches of delight filled the air, and I closed my eyes, cringing away from the sound. Nausea swelled in me as I pictured Marco being pulled beneath the surface...torn apart...

I fixed my eyes back on the queen. "What do you want from me?" Rage overflowed into my words.

The queen's black eyes somehow became darker.

"It's not you I seek." Her words slithered over me like tentacles.

"Who then?" I asked.

A thud sounded to my left and her gaze whipped to the spot where a beautiful, green-haired woman stood, wearing nothing but a grimace as she faced the queen.

"Set them free," the newcomer demanded. The ship rocked, slowly at first, but it became progressively more rigorous and sent a few men rolling across the deck, along with some barrels. I remained in place, but the distraction broke the siren's spell.

Jumping to my feet, I ran for my sword, which had slid across the deck as it rocked.

Two more women climbed up over the railing, landing on the deck with ease. I turned back to the siren queen, who seemed to be having a standoff with the green-haired woman.

"Light it, Nix!" one of the other women said behind me. I realized too late what they were doing and whirled to see a spark headed for a barrel of gunpowder.

"Time to go!" the woman I assumed was Nix yelled, and the few remaining crew followed her lead and dove over the side of the ship.

I stood, rooted in place. This was the moment I would go down with my ship. Watching the last of my crew members jump, I lowered my sword. The siren queen screeched behind me, followed by a large splash.

"Sorry, but I can't leave you here." The green-haired woman grabbed my arm. I tried to rip it from her grasp, but she was strong and pulled me toward the side of the ship.

"Don't make me die here with you," she said, glancing back at the spark which had almost reached the barrel.

"Move you idiot!" Jami cried as he came running up the stairs from belowdecks. He practically tackled me over the railing and into the water.

At the same time we went over, a deafening *boom* filled the air, and an explosion tore through our world. We hit the water not a moment too soon.

I floundered for a second, trying to get my bearings as water rushed into my mouth and down my throat. As I did, I realized Jami had stopped moving, his eyes glazed over. My eyes burned from the salt water, but I kept them pinned on Jami. Before I could grab him, two slim arms wrapped around my waist and hauled me backward, away from my ship. I tried to fight at first, but in the water, my limbs were heavy and my movements sluggish, so I gave into my fate.

It wasn't until we resurfaced for air that I saw someone else had Jami in tow, though my vision blurred, and I couldn't tell if he was okay.

"Jami," I tried calling him, but my voice came out raspy.

My back collided with the beach and my savior, or abductor, depending on how you looked at it, rose above me as

she shifted back into human form. *Of* course *they were mermaids, no one else would be quite so…vibrant.*

"Captain!" A low, sharp voice broke through my haze. A head of bright, green hair swam into my vision, followed by unblinking, violet eyes. "Stay with me, Captain," the voice came again, out of her mouth. Her unevenly shorn hair brushed over her shoulders.

"Captain!" A familiar voice reached me, and I turned my head toward Jami, reaching out my hand to him.

"Viv," the woman before me called out to someone I couldn't see. "Can you take over here? I'm going to check in on the others." Her bright green hair faded back into the haze, and brilliant, golden eyes replaced the first woman. Blinking slowly, I focused on the new woman. Close-cropped brown hair that swooped over her eyes came into focus next. She wore a scowl as she looked down upon me and crossed her bare arms tightly over her leather clad chest. The brown leather sleeveless corset top seemed like an interesting choice for a mermaid, but I said nothing. This was the woman who had blown up my ship.

"If all the tales I've heard of the *fearsome* Captain Finnian are true, he'll be fine," Viv said to someone behind her who came into view over her shoulder. The way she'd said fearsome made me think she was mocking me, but I ignored that.

"Depends on the tales you've been told," Jami said. "I've got a few that might prove otherwise."

I tried smirking, but it turned to a frown when it made my face ache. Reaching up, I touched my cheek to find it tender. Sliding my hand up to my forehead and back down, I realized blood dripped from a wound that must have been inflicted by some debris from my ship being blown to smithereens.

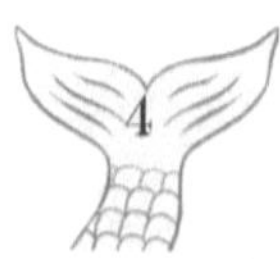

"Finn," Jami addressed me, taking my focus away from my wounds.

"Jami," I said.

"As I said, he'll be fine; he's being dramatic," Viv snapped and rolled her eyes. "I've seen worse," she added, lifting one shoulder, and letting her scowl slip.

Anger welled up in me as she seemed so cavalier about having destroyed my livelihood, and my home.

"Where are we?" I managed to get out. I touched the sand beneath me and heard water crashing on rocks nearby. The scent of the sea overwhelmed me, making me queasy. *That's unusual,* I thought. Normally that scent made me feel at home.

"He's all yours," Viv said to Jami before walking away. I watched her with intrigue, wondering where in the world she had come from.

"A beach in the south of Lanteria," Jami reminded me.

Right. I knew that. I'd been looking at a map right before we'd hit the first swell caused by the sirens.

Jami's jaw clenched as anger flashed in his eyes, mirroring my own I assumed as rage burned in my gut.

"We lost a lot of men. Though, most of them were dead before any damage was done to the ship," Jami said, waving his hand to our remaining crew spread across the beach.

"What of Marley, and Cole?" I asked, searching the beach for them.

"Fine. A little beat up, but no lasting damage," Jami answered.

My relief was short-lived. "Tilly and Mac?"

Jami shook his head. "We can go over the casualties later. You need to rest now. The mermaids will take care of our remaining crew until you're back on your feet."

"The mermaids are the ones who destroyed our ship," I said through gritted teeth.

"Those same mermaids saved our sorry asses." He nodded toward the green haired woman and Viv. "They got as many of us out as they could, but there were too many sirens to fight. If they'd tried, they all would've been killed," Jami explained.

"Where were you when the siren queen had us under her spell? I didn't see you." I rubbed my head as if that would do anything for the pain blossoming as the adrenaline faded.

"For some reason her song didn't affect me." Jami seemed concerned by that, but he kept talking, and I couldn't ask more about it. "I was trying to figure out a way to help everyone, but then the mermaids showed up."

"What is her name? The one with the green hair?" I asked, assuming she was the one in charge since the other ten or so mermaids did as she directed on the beach.

"Lia."

Lia

Hurrying from person to person, I made sure everyone who could be helped was receiving it. I paused on the beach, scanning the small group of men we'd been able to save. None of the dead would wash up here, they'd all have been devoured by now. I shuddered as an image flashed in my mind of men being torn apart, limb by limb, before being feasted upon. There were so many dead. *Too* many.

I'd been strung out for weeks attempting to save as many pirates and sailors as I could with my sisters. My limbs ached to relax, and a migraine had settled above my left brow. As the pain peaked, faces became hazy, and colors blurred together into indistinguishable blobs. The misty sea air only further confused my senses. The sun wasn't strong enough that afternoon to pierce through the fog forming after the stormy night.

"Lia," Viv called to me. Viv never used my full name, Aurelia, which I preferred. My mother was the only one who called me that, and it made me cringe whenever I heard it. "Take a break, we've done what we can."

Viv, along with the other women we called our sisters, weren't really related to me, but we'd all been together so long

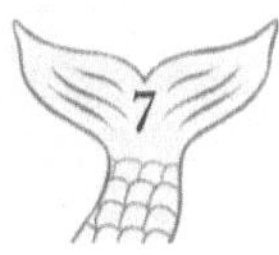

we saw each other as family. Viv was more than a sister, though. She was like my other half. If we'd been born to the same mother, we'd have been twins.

"How's the captain?" I asked, ignoring Viv's concern.

"He's fully awake and talking. I left him in the care of his first mate." Viv took hold of my arm and pulled me toward a flat rock, forcing me to sit. "Take a break," she repeated. I attempted to smile but grimaced instead as my migraine pulsed. Closing my eyes, I leaned against Viv who remained standing. Somehow, she didn't look nearly as exhausted as I felt. There were bags under her eyes, but otherwise, she looked ready to take on the world.

"How many are there?" I asked her, and she knew exactly what I was asking. *How many dead...how many did we save...*

"Thirty men and women dead. Fifteen are alive, although two..." Viv paused and sighed. "Two of them probably won't make it."

"We saved thirteen..." My voice shook. It was the worst we'd done so far. We usually saved at least half of the crew. This time had been different though. The siren queen herself had been present at this attack; usually she didn't bother. I didn't try to make sense of why the queen had changed things up yet again. Instead, I looked down the beach, away from the blood-stained sand from the injured and dying, to where the captain sat with his first mate. From afar, they looked like they could be brothers.

"Jami needs tending as well," I said, remembering the gash I'd seen on his leg before I'd been distracted by Finn. The infamous Captain Finn, whom I'd recognized immediately, had dark brown hair that he'd left untied to brush his shoulders. I'd met Jami briefly after dumping him on the shore before diving

back into the water. He'd tied back his long, dark, brown hair at the nape of his neck.

I tried to stand, but Viv kept me in place with a firm hand on my shoulder.

"I'll tend to him," she said. I sighed and nodded as Viv walked away. My damp, wavy hair brushed against the back of my neck as I leaned my elbows on my knees. On an impulse after the last attack, I chopped my hair to my shoulders. Precious seconds had been lost from having to repeatedly brush my hip length hair out of my vision when I came out of the water, costing more sailors' lives.

Closing my eyes, I rested my head in my hands. The waves crashing on the shore lulled me into a meditative state, despite the migraine. A low, throaty, growl jolted me from my reverie and my eyes snapped open. Where the captain had previously been, a lion stood, shaking out its mane. *The fearsome lion shifter pirate,* I realized. *So at least that story is true.*

As usual, Viv appeared unfazed as she attended Jami nearby. If anything, she seemed annoyed as the lion shifter circled her and Jami, laying down beside his first mate.

Shifters weren't uncommon; my sisters and I were proof of that. Despite my adventures over the past hundred years, I'd never seen a lion shifter before.

Though mermaids were a form of shifter, sirens were not. They couldn't leave the water and always remained in their one form. For that, I was grateful. I couldn't imagine fighting them on land as well as in the water.

As if taking a cue from their captain, the remaining crew on the beach shifted into their animal forms, other than Jami and the two gravely injured men. Shifters healed more efficiently in their shifted forms. There was a large snake, three wolves,

three foxes, two hawks, and an owl. A stag limped toward the water to wash its hooves of blood. Bandages littered the beach from all my hard work. I sighed, realizing all my tending could have been avoided if the crew had shifted sooner. As if to punctuate the point, pain flared above my eyebrow making me wince.

No remains of their clothes could be seen, which meant they had been magicked to shift with them. I had my own magicked clothes that shifted into barrettes, or jewelry, but I hadn't been wearing those today. We'd all left our clothes on the beach before entering the battle and had lost time in doing so. I'd be sure to ditch any unmagicked clothing items for the foreseeable future.

I stood and made my way over to Viv who was finishing wrapping Jami's wound.

"Do you have another form?" I asked Jami as I reached them. Viv glared up at me, but I ignored her. I'd noticed another difference between Jami and Finn: their eyes. Jami's bright green eyes could have rivaled my hair, and Finn's were a dark, stormy gray color.

"Alas, I am not a shifter. I was the only one among the crew who wasn't," he said, wincing as Viv tied off the bandage around his leg. We'd cut off the bottom half of his breeches to use as a bandage.

"Why keep you around?" Viv asked, her eyebrow quirking up.

Jami laughed. "Finn and I have been inseparable since we were both eight. Nothing could change that, not even a brush with the siren queen apparently." Jami's gaze fell to the lion who had fallen asleep beside him. Finn's breathing had evened out and with each exhale, a soft growl escaped. Viv's gaze followed

Jami's and her eyes softened as she watched Finn in his lion form.

"We have you to thank for that, Lia," Jami said, drawing the attention back to himself. "If you hadn't shown up, we would have all been lost to the siren queen."

"I'm sorry we weren't able to save more of your crew," I said, my heart clenching as I closed my eyes and the screams of the dying reached me once more as if they kept echoing through the air around us.

"Lia," Viv murmured as she grasped my hand. When I opened my eyes, Viv was at my side and Jami stood before me. "You need to rest," Viv reminded me yet again. I nodded and as I turned, a wave of dizziness washed over me and my eyes fluttered shut. The sensation of falling lasted only a moment before strong arms embraced me and I was lifted from my feet, pressed against a warm chest with a steady heartbeat that calmed my nerves.

"Don't," Viv started to object to Jami's holding me, but something stopped her.

"Lia wore herself out helping us and our crew. Let me return the favor," Jami argued.

I kept my eyes closed, too weary to open them, but I could hear everything going on around me.

"There's a house up there," Finn said, clearly having shifted back from his lion form. "I'll go ahead and ask if they'll let us stay for a few hours."

Viv tutted in disapproval, and I had to stop myself from laughing.

"And what if they recognize you, oh fearsome one?" she asked, the disdain in her voice crystal clear. "*I'll* go ahead and talk with them."

I cracked open an eye to watch her stride away toward the house, her head held high and a cocky swish to her hips. I couldn't help my giggle.

"Oh, so you *are* awake?" Jami asked, a teasing lilt to his voice. "And here I thought I was being the heroic sort, carrying your unconscious body to safety."

Opening my eyes fully, I looked up at him. "The truth is, I could walk if I wanted, but I like to arrive in style. What better way to get somewhere than in the arms of a handsome pirate?" I walked my fingers up his chest, noting the blush growing on his cheeks as he smiled.

"Fair enough," he said.

As he walked, I could feel his slight limp from his injury, and I bounced slightly against his chest. I could see a peek of a tattoo where his doublet was unlaced.

"Since you're not a shifter, will your leg not heal as quickly?" I asked.

"No. I take the usual amount of time to recover. Any magic that comes from the ability to shift skipped over me, even though both my parents were shifters," Jami explained.

"Does it bother you that your family can shift, and you can't?"

"Ten minutes in and already getting to the heavy hitting questions, aye?" He chuckled. "When I was young it bothered me, but I've grown used to being a non-shifter human."

Finn was silent beside us, but I could tell he was overthinking something from the way he kept shoving his hand through his hair and sighing loudly.

When we caught up with Viv, she was chatting with a young woman who I guessed was the owner of the house. Her copper hair was pulled back and her sleeves rolled up as if she'd been working in the freshly planted garden. Sweat and dirt

mixed in her brow, and I sighed at the thought of having such a mundane task to take care of rather than what I was currently up against.

Finn remained out of sight for the time being, in case Viv was right and the woman recognized him. Not everyone would want a pirate with a gruesome track record staying in their house, or anywhere near it.

"I thought something strange was happening out there," the woman was saying. "The siren queen is horrible! Of course you can rest here awhile. My husband always used to let wayward travelers stay when they were passing through, and I shall carry on his tradition."

I could hear the grief in her voice, and I wanted to ask when her husband had passed, but I didn't want to upset her. She appeared far too young to be a widow. Instead, I kept quiet and let Viv do the talking.

"You are too kind," Viv said, grabbing the woman's hand with both of hers. "We won't stay long and will replace any food we eat."

"Oh!" the woman exclaimed. "Food! I should head into town and get some for tonight. It's been so long since I had guests, I'd love to make you dinner."

"I'm not sure," Viv started, but the woman cut her off.

"Oh, I insist. I'll go now." She turned away, but then turned back again. "I'm Mel, by the way. Help yourself to anything inside."

Once she was gone, Jami brought me into the house, led by Viv, who found a bedroom for me to rest in. Pictures lined the walls, filled with paintings of the sea and fishing boats, which made me think Mel's husband may have been a fisherman.

"Now, out," Viv said, shooing Jami from the room. Turning back to me she said, "I'm going to check in with Nix and Bree, but I'll be right back."

"Take your time. I'm going to rest my eyes," I told her as I closed my eyes.

Once she left, I attempted to sleep, but the screams of the dying had been burned into my mind and replayed as I lay in silence. It didn't help I had blood caked on my clothes and body.

Rising from the bed, I glanced around the room, noting a bath in the corner. Thankfully this house had running water, so I filled the bath, stepping into it fully clothed.

The water turned a light shade of pink as the blood washed off me and I choked back a sob. Pulling my knees to my chest.

An image of the four gods and goddesses hung beside the tub. Neros, goddess of the sea, Terrian, god of the land, Aeros, god of the sky, and Ourania, goddess of the heavens all looked down on me. The weight of their eyes forced me to press my forehead against my knees, blocking out the image, and allowing myself a moment to breakdown. Where had any of those gods been as we watched the sirens tearing apart the men and women from the ships we'd attempted to save? I had no faith left for the gods who had turned a blind eye to the siren queen's tyranny.

By the time Viv returned, I had drained the tub, refilled it, stripped out of my soaked clothes, and bathed as a usual human would. The entire time, my skin had prickled, yearning to shift to my mer form, but the tub wasn't big enough.

I'd found a slip in the dresser beside the bed and pulled it on before curling up back on the bed. It was much comfier than the corset I wore. It wasn't something I wore out of

necessity, or propriety, but for someone who had always been lacking in the curves department, I liked them. That was how Viv found me. Put back together and finally resting.

"You look more like yourself," she said, as she stripped down to bathe as well. "Nix and Bree are taking care of the others. None of our sisters were too badly injured, just shaken that the siren queen finally made an appearance."

That gave me some relief, at least. I didn't know if I could have handled any more bad news.

"I hope we can be out of here and on the road by the time Mel returns," Viv said. "If we want any chance of taking on the siren queen, we need to gather an army as quickly as possible. After today, who knows what she has planned next."

"I know, you're right," I agreed. The road ahead of us would lead to more death, and I needed to prepare myself for the possibility that not everyone I cared about would make it out alive.

"At least the gods are watching over us," Viv said, pointing to the image beside the bath.

I scoffed. "I don't know how you still believe in them. Magic and our own actions are the only things that have been saving the lives of the people the sirens have been attacking."

Viv pushed the bubbles around the water, staring down at them. "I can't stop believing in the gods," she whispered. "But I understand why you don't."

I sighed and said, "I won't hold out hope for their help. This war is *our* fight, and I will do whatever it takes to win it."

Finn

"Finn." Jami walked up beside me in the tall grass covering the cliff we stood on, overlooking the beach the mermaids had brought us to. "What will we do now?" he asked.

I sighed. "Now?"

Our ship and most of our crew had been lost that day. The thought of returning to the water anytime soon was out of the question, even if there weren't the glaring problem of the siren queen. The breeze brought the smell of salt and seaweed to us, making me flinch.

"What was that?" Jami asked, concern pulling down the corners of his mouth.

"I don't know that I..." I stopped, not wanting to burden Jami with my new fears. "Nothing. I don't know what that was."

Jami narrowed his eyes at me, but he knew better than to push me on the subject.

"I think it's unwise for us to return to the water until the siren queen is dealt with," Jami said.

I gave him a grateful look for changing the subject and nodded in agreement.

"But how does one *deal* with the siren queen is the question," I said. There wasn't much we could do from land against the siren queen who couldn't leave the sea.

I noticed ripples further out in the water and my breath hitched as I clenched my fists at my sides. Nothing appeared.

"Maybe we can ask Lia for help," Jami suggested, recapturing my attention.

Without answering, I turned my back on the ocean and started toward the house. Most of our men sat outside in their shifted forms, but the two who had been gravely injured were inside with Lia and Viv. The other mermaids rested alongside our crew. The owner of the house had yet to return from fetching food in town.

"I don't trust them," I finally answered, a bite to my tone. "Why bother helping us? What do they have to gain?"

Jami stopped, reeling back slightly. "What do you mean? They saved us from the siren queen because they knew it was the right thing to do. They are not the monsters, here."

I turned back to him. "They blew up my ship!"

"If they hadn't, we'd all be dead!" Jami said.

"You're being too quick to trust them. Everyone has ulterior motives in this world, it would be ignorant for us to believe them immune to that."

"Right, sorry, Captain," Jami murmured.

I scoffed. He knew how much I hated being called Captain by him. We were practically brothers; we didn't need the titles. His lips pulled up in a grin.

I didn't want to agree with him, but he was right about one thing: the mermaids could have left us to our fates. Instead, they had risked their lives to save strangers.

"I won't cast judgment on them yet. It wouldn't hurt to talk to them," I said, trying to keep a level head. I wasn't about

to call them allies yet, since normally anyone who tried to 'help' me was trying to steal from me or undermine me in some way. It came with the territory of being a well-known pirate captain.

"Why do I feel like you only want to ask for their help to keep them around a little longer?" I asked, eyeing Jami.

His jaw clenched as he pursed his lips.

"They know the ocean better than anyone, and I thought they may have insight into the siren queen, that's all," Jami said, his voice too tight.

Smirking, I said, "Wise of you," baiting him, as usual.

"You think I didn't see the way you looked at Viv? I could just as easily be pestering *you*," he snapped, making me laugh. Jami joined in and we both clutched our sides from the ridiculousness of our argument.

The only reason I'd looked at Viv was because she'd been the one who'd blown up my ship. I wanted to keep an eye on her in case she made any other rash decisions.

"Come on," I said, leading the way into the house.

Jami hesitated on the threshold and his gaze caught on the mermaids outside. I turned to watch them as well. They kept to themselves, and I wondered if any of them would have helped save us if Lia hadn't led them into battle.

I realized what a ridiculous thought that was and headed inside. Of course they wouldn't have. What was the point of a leader if not to lead? If Lia had chosen to stay out of the fight, so would the rest of her group. Now I just needed to learn why she'd made the choice to help us and if I needed to worry about her intentions.

We walked through the cluttered kitchen to the hall where the bedroom was. I didn't feel too bad tracking in sand and dirt on my boots since it already covered the floors. I lifted my hand to knock when the door opened, and Viv stepped out.

She placed her hand to her chest as if I'd startled her, but she recovered quickly and crossed her arms over her chest, widening her stance.

"What do you want?" she asked, narrowing her eyes as her gaze shifted from me to Jami.

"We'd like to speak with you and Lia, if she is awake," I said.

"She's resting. Can I take a message?" She smirked and irritation flickered through me. Her smirk disappeared as the door behind her creaked open and Lia's face appeared in the doorway. She wore nothing but a slip which clung to her body at every curve.

"What's going on?" Lia asked, matching Viv's stance.

"Oh, um, we can come back," I stammered, while Jami appeared speechless as his eyes scanned the room, finding *anything* else to look at. Viv turned and ushered Lia back into the room.

"Wha-oof," I heard Lia grumble as she tripped over her own feet. Viv righted her and shut the door behind herself. "I'm not modest, Viv," Lia's voice could be heard through the door.

"Oh, trust me, I know," Viv said.

I pulled Jami to the side.

"Wipe the drool from your chin, you look ridiculous," I teased him.

He rolled his eyes and leaned against the wall. "I don't know why I let you treat me this way. Maybe I'll find myself a new captain who doesn't insult me so much." He lifted his chin.

I patted him on the back before saying, "You wouldn't last a day on any other captain's ship."

Jami opened his mouth, as if insulted, then pursed his lips and cocked a brow. "You're probably right."

"If you keep it up, I'm sure every shifter in a mile radius will smell your arousal." I was grateful to be in my human form so I wouldn't have to suffer.

"Shit. I always forget about that," Jami groaned.

It was an inconvenient truth that when in our animal form, shifters had a heightened sense of smell, along with all our other senses. Though it had helped me on many occasions, it could also make things awkward.

"I'd say you should just fuck her and get it out of your system, but something tells me she's not that kind of woman. *And* something tells me that probably wouldn't do the trick," I said.

"Don't say that shit," Jami snapped, making me chuckle, which only caused him to scowl again.

After nearly twenty years of friendship, I knew Jami better than he knew himself. It meant we had no secrets between us, and that wasn't always ideal. But it also meant we could tell each other anything without fear of judgment.

The bedroom door creaked open once more.

Viv exited first, her arms crossed again, emphasizing the impressive tightly coiled muscles of her arms despite her slight frame. Viv and Lia were similarly built, but Viv was a few inches taller.

Lia emerged from the room, fully clothed, back in her tight leggings and tank top from before. I could tell that, for Jami, it wasn't much better than the slip she'd been wearing by the way he tensed up as she walked toward us. I nudged him with my elbow, making him grimace.

"Careful," I warned and noticed Jami's throat bobbed as he swallowed.

"What did you want to talk about?" Viv asked, narrowing her eyes, clearly wary of us. I wasn't entirely sure if

that was because we were pirates, or if there was something more to it. My mind flashed to her blowing up my ship, and I gritted my teeth.

Taking a deep breath, I said calmly, "First, I wanted to thank you for all you did to help me and my crew. If it weren't for you and your friends, we would have all been killed." The reminder of all we had lost that day had a heavy weight settling onto my shoulders.

"No need to thank us," Lia said, lifting her chin. "It's what we do."

"Well, I do have some questions for you about that," I said.

Viv scoffed and shook her head. My gaze traveled over her, and I blinked slowly as I appraised her. Her nostrils flared and Lia sidestepped to stand between Viv and me.

"We know you owe us nothing and you can refuse to answer our questions if you choose," Jami spoke up. "We simply wish to know if you have any information regarding the siren queen and the unrest that has been happening at sea."

Lia's gaze flicked to Jami, and the tension eased from her body, but she remained in front of Viv.

"Maybe it would be easier to talk, just myself and Lia," I suggested, my jaw tightening. Jami put a hand on my shoulder.

"No," Viv snapped at the same time Lia said, "That might be best."

Viv grabbed hold of Lia's hand. "You're not going anywhere alone with him."

"We won't leave your sight," Lia promised before removing Viv's hand from her own and striding out of the house. We all followed behind her as she made her way to the cliff Jami and I had stood on earlier. I glanced at Viv one last

time before following Lia out there. My distrust was reflected to me in Viv's eyes.

Lia

The wind picked up, revealing the sun as it cleared away the fog and brought with it the chill of the sea air as we stood on the cliff. I tucked my hair behind my ears, trying to keep it from tickling my cheeks as it lifted with the breeze.

Turning to Finn, I said, "Sorry about that, Viv is a bit..." I paused, trying to think of the right word.

"Overprotective?" Finn finished for me. I shook my head, that wasn't quite it.

"She has her reasons. Not all men are as..." I trailed off, again at a loss for words. "Well, that's Viv's story to tell."

"I'm sorry," Finn said, his eyes darkening as he turned his gaze toward the sea.

"Let's talk about the sirens." I changed the subject from Viv.

"Yes." Finn cleared his throat and returned his focus to me. "The sirens seem much more...bloodthirsty lately."

"I believe everyone has noticed that. I've heard the siren queen is searching for something to increase her power." I relayed the information I'd gleaned from our last stop in Aneria. I'd overheard a siren questioning the captain of the last ship

they'd taken down before ripping his heart out with her claw tipped hand. I shuddered at the memory.

Finn's eyes widened in disbelief. "Increase it? Is she not already powerful enough?"

"She's not as strong as she once was. Her power fades as the years pass, and eventually a new siren will rise to take her place. But it seems the queen wants to forestall the natural order of things." I wondered if that would create a divide among the sirens if she forced her hand to remain their queen. I hadn't noticed any dissonance among them yet, and I couldn't take the chance of getting close enough to ask.

"What is it she searches for? Can we find it ourselves and use it against her?" Finn asked the very question I'd asked myself when I'd first learned of the queen's quest. However, everyone I'd asked so far had no answer.

"That's just it - no one knows of any such object or power. The only spell books in existence already belong to her, besides the few that remain with the witches of Asmara. But I've seen those and there's nothing in them to help." Though, I'd make sure to read them all again if it meant finding a way to stop the siren queen. "Your ship is the seventh attack in the last two months. We've only made it in time to intervene for four of those attacks."

"So, is there no way to stop her? No way to make the sea safe again?" Finn asked. I could have sworn I saw relief in his eyes, but he turned his head away, toward the sea.

"Not necessarily. The only reason the sirens keep gaining the upper hand is because they always attack at random when no one is prepared. If we could gather enough people in one place to fight back–"

"You mean to start a war." Finn's tone was not accusing, but his brows bunched.

"The sea stained with blood is evidence it's already begun, and I intend to finish it, *Captain*," I ground out. "If you wish to aid me, I will fill you in on the rest of the information I've gathered. Otherwise, we're done here." We had no time to waste. Until the siren queen was defeated or brought to heel, I wouldn't be able to return home.

"Have you not requested help from the royal armies yet? King Galvin," he paused, sneering at the name before continuing. "King Danforth, or King Oberrin may have some stake in this as well."

I scoffed. "None of them wanted anything to do with a war amongst sea creatures, as they put it. They said the siren queen's attacks weren't affecting them yet, so they had no reason to upset her and turn her sights on them." It had enraged me when I'd first interacted with them, but I'd since come to realize it was only a matter of time before they understood the true impact this war would have on their kingdoms. The only problem was we didn't have time. If the siren queen found whatever she was looking for, the sea would be lost and never again safe for any non-sirens.

Finn ran his hand through his hair. "Alright, then. I'll need to talk with Jami, but I have a feeling I know what he'll say. I do have one question for you before I agree to traveling with you."

"And what might that be?" I asked.

"Why save us?"

Staring at him for a few seconds, I considered my answer. Based on the pinch in his brows and the way he kept his hand near his holstered weapon, I knew he didn't entirely trust me. It was fair, I didn't entirely trust him either. So, I only gave him half of the truth.

"We aren't ones to stand by while people are suffering. Pirates or not."

He studied me as I'd studied him before saying, "Fine. Let's go talk with the others."

As Finn had guessed, and much to my delight, Jami was immediately on board to join forces.

"Absolutely. We'll do whatever it takes to return to the sea," he agreed. He cleared his throat and wiggled his nose as if trying to mask the excitement he displayed, only making me like him more.

Finn groaned from where he stood leaning against the side of the house, only a few feet from Viv.

"Good. We start now," I said, ignoring Finn's clear dissent at Jami's easy answer. "We'll leave for Asmara in the morning. That is where we will start our search for reinforcements."

"You said you'd already been there looking for answers on the power the siren queen searches for," Finn pointed out, and I turned to him.

"I said I'd read their texts, not that I'd been there recently," I clarified.

"For good reason!" Viv stepped away from the wall and approached me. "We haven't been back there since...since..." Viv brows pulled together, and she bit her lip. Concern nagged at me. Viv had grounds to fear returning to Asmara, but we couldn't put it off any longer.

"Breathe, Viv," I murmured, drawing an interested look from Finn. "He's behind bars, he can't get to you," I continued, placing my hands on Viv's shoulders.

"Should we be concerned about visiting Asmara?" Finn asked, and Viv whipped toward him.

"No," she said, lifting her chin and donning her invisible armor once more. A pang of sympathy went through me for her, knowing what it was like to hide a piece of yourself for so long.

"That's right. I'll let our sisters know," I said. "And, Captain," I started, but Finn put up his hand to stop me.

"Call me Finn. My ship and most of my crew are gone, I'm no captain." The disgust in his voice made me realize how much guilt Finn truly felt over the whole situation.

"That's not true, Finn," Jami said, gripping his upper arm. "You will always be our captain. We just need to find a new ship."

"Either way," I said. "You need to know, your two crew members inside, neither of them is going to make it if we move them. They'll need to remain behind." My chest tightened as I thought of them, wondering if they would survive the night.

"I'll talk with Mel and see if she can look after them until..." Finn stumbled over his words and cleared his throat. Jami squeezed his shoulder.

"I will gather our remaining crew and see who is willing to continue on with us," Jami said. "None of them can return home, considering they'd need to travel across the sea and that's become nearly impossible."

Out of the eleven remaining crew members, besides Jami and Finn, they all agreed to join our army. Only two of them, though, would be making the journey to the kingdom of Asmara while the rest stayed behind in the kingdom of Lanteria. One of the crew members chose to stay with the two who had been gravely injured and would send word of their fate. I told them to send the message to The Flight Deck Inn in Asmara where I planned on having us stay.

There were twenty mermaids, other than me and Viv, but only three of them would be traveling with us. The others would remain in Lanteria and search for reinforcements, keeping an eye on the sea to ensure there were no more attacks nearby.

In total, nine of us would be traveling to Asmara. With less people, the trip would go much smoother and faster. The trek, even on horseback, would take us at least a week with no stops. In our shifted forms, it would take half that time, but unfortunately, Jami couldn't shift, and the sea was unsafe for us mermaids.

"We need to go into town to find horses and provisions," I said, approaching Jami and Finn from the house. Mel was inside, serving dinner to a few of the crew members. "Now that we know the siren queen is nearby, we can't risk going back into the water."

Nix had found us an inn so we wouldn't overwhelm Mel with people for the night.

Our entire group walked into town, drawing attention from every passerby. In the center of town, there were numerous tents set up, filled with all different kinds of wares being sold by vendors.

Jami, Finn, and their two crew members, Cole and Marley, diverged from our larger group and found their own horses and provisions. Marley reminded me a bit of Viv. She wore her hair short like Viv's, though hers was a dark red color, and she had a similar *don't mess with me* attitude.

Viv and I waited beside a fountain as our sisters gathered our provisions for us. Nix had insisted that we rest, and she was a hard one to refuse.

"Why are we trusting them again?" Viv asked, her eyes trailing Finn as he moved from one tent to another.

"Because we need as many allies as we can get, and they fit the bill for able-bodied fighters," I said, half-joking. "If we're going to be traveling with them, we need to learn to trust them."

"I don't have to trust them, just tolerate them," Viv said, but she couldn't hide the frown pulling at her lips. I put my arm around her, seeing through her mask.

"They aren't *him,* Viv." I pulled back and my gaze bore into her. She looked away as tears threatened to spill down her cheeks. "I won't let anyone hurt you, ever again. Not like that."

"I know," Viv said.

"So, you'll give them a chance?" I asked.

"I guess, but I feel like you're not telling me something," Viv said.

"The siren queen went after their ship for a reason," I said. Viv waved her hand for me to go on. "I have a feeling there was someone on it who knows more about whatever magical item she wants, and she would have made sure they were left alive."

Viv tapped a finger against her lip. "I knew you were hiding something. Which one do you think it is?"

"I've no idea. Hopefully it's one of his crew that is coming with us so they'll be safely on land and away from the queen."

"Or they're dead and the secret died with them," Viv pointed out.

"Don't be so morbid, please," I said, shaking my head. "Just, keep a close eye on the pirates while we're traveling to see if you can figure out if any of them know more than they're letting on."

"Yes, Princess," Viv teased.

"And don't call me that," I snapped, scanning the area to make sure none of the pirates were around to hear. It wasn't that

I cared much if they knew who I was, but I didn't want to have to deal with the fuss.

"Yes, Princess," Viv repeated, dancing out of reach as I swatted at her, both of us laughing.

Jami

I smiled as I watched Lia and Viv in the square together. They laughed as if they had no worries, and it warmed my heart. There had been too much weighing on me today.

As Finn and I made our way around the vendors, a few of them recognized Finn and either refused to sell him anything or gave him whatever he wanted free of charge so long as he didn't shift and try to eat them. I barely contained my laughter. Marley had come up with the rumor of him tearing a man to pieces for refusing him a drink and spread it anytime we were in port.

Not all the stories of Finn's treachery and ruthlessness were false, but a lot of them were made up by our crew as jokes to keep ourselves entertained.

Pausing beside a jeweler's tent, Finn trailed a finger over a simple, silver, chain necklace, and I couldn't help but recall his mother wearing a similar one the entire time I knew her. I flipped my lucky coin between my fingers as we browsed the stall.

"We need to be careful with these mermaids," Finn said low enough so only I would hear. "We may both have the same

end goal, but that doesn't mean they won't risk our lives to get there, and I won't hesitate to do the same."

"What are you talking about?" I sighed, knowing this was all Finn's inability to trust coming to the surface again.

"I will have my revenge for our lost crew, whatever the cost."

"You're sounding a bit like your dear old pa again," Marley said as she popped up, snatching the necklace Finn's hand lingered near and slipping it into her pocket. I glanced around to be sure no one had seen, but no one reacted.

"Don't say that," Finn hissed. "You know how much I hate that man."

"I call it like I see it," Marley said, shrugging before strolling away and disappearing easily into the crowd. Her small size, which she made up for with her brutishness, made it convenient for her to slip in and out of places without being noticed.

"Will you go to King Danforth and ask for his assistance against the siren queen?" I asked, keeping my voice low. Finn didn't want his association with the king of Asmara to be well known, even though King Danforth had an understanding with almost all the pirate captains on this side of the world.

"I'll send him a missive once we reach Asmara," Finn said. "Until then, we don't speak of him."

I tapped my finger against my lips before clapping my hand on Finn's shoulder. "Come on. We've got everything we need, let's catch up with the others."

By the time we met up with the mermaids again in the stable at the inn, the rest of their group had returned to Mel's, leaving Lia and Viv with the three who would be traveling with them. Lia introduced them as Bree, Nix, and Korra. I studied them as we prepped our horses for the morning.

"You're short a horse," Nix pointed out. Her long, pitch-black hair had been braided back. Bree and Korra also wore their hair braided, but Bree's hair was brown like Viv's while Korra had pink hair. I had to wonder why some mermaids had such vibrant colored hair while others did not.

"I'll be traveling in my shifted form," Marley responded to her. "When you have wings, why bother with horses?"

"That's something we used to be able to say about being mermaids," Bree said, pursing her lips. Bree had the same pale complexion as Lia, while Nix and Korra were much darker skinned. Though it seemed Lia was the leader of their group, they reminded me of our dynamic, in which everyone was of equal standing even if some had actual labels, like *captain.*

"Can you take this, Nix?" Lia asked, holding out a canteen toward her. Nix grabbed it and Lia finished tying her bag onto her horse's saddle. We all carried a bag now, filled with food, spare clothes, and other essentials purchased with money borrowed from the mermaids. I didn't ask where all the money came from. Being a pirate, I had plenty of guesses.

"All set," Finn said, tying off his own bag. "Now I need a drink."

Marley slipped around the horse and handed him a flask. "Always prepared, Cap," she said, giving him a two-fingered salute.

"Don't call me that," Finn said before taking a swig from the flask.

I walked away as they started bickering about who the flask belonged to. This came up every time Marley pulled it out, and I was surprised she'd bothered this time. The flask truly belonged to me, but I never told them. I'd won it in a gambling den the first time we'd been in Asmara and the poor soul I'd been betting against had already lost everything but his gold

tooth. He'd been about to rip that out and put it on the table, but I'd asked for the flask instead. Nothing about what it would take to get that tooth out interested me enough to let him see it through.

"We're headed to bed," Lia said, hooking her thumb toward the inn. "Let your captain know we'll head out at daybreak." She peered around me and I followed her gaze, smirking at how Finn played keep away the flask with a now pissed off Marley.

"They're idiots," Cole muttered as he passed us on his way out of the stable. He'd tied his beard in the front similar to how I tied my hair back. It was the first time he'd ever had a long enough beard to do it.

"Got it, daybreak, I'll let him know," I answered Lia, shaking my head at the scene. "Thank you again, for today. Saving us I mean." Rubbing the back of my neck, I tried to hide the blush I could feel blooming on my cheeks.

"Don't mention it. See you in the morning."

Before I could think of something better than '*you too,'* to say, she'd already gone, and I was left standing with the horses.

Despite the chaos of Marley and Finn's antics, we made it to bed at a reasonable hour and were up bright and early to start our journey. We mounted our horses and headed back toward the coast. It would lead us to our destination, while allowing us to keep an eye on the seas in case more attacks occurred. Marley traveled in her shifted form as a hawk.

Lia, Finn, and I led the way, while Viv and Bree rode at the back of our group. When we reached the dirt road along the coast, relief washed over me as the familiar scent of the sea hit

me. I noticed Finn stiffen, though, and meant to ask him about it but Lia started talking.

"I could go for a swim right now," Lia said as her horse trotted up alongside mine. "I'm sure you love it as well."

The embankment along the road was all that separated us from the sandy beach and wide expanse of ocean. It was hard to be so close but not be out setting sail.

"I don't swim," I said too quickly, drawing a curious stare from her. "I mean, I can, I just prefer not to," I clarified.

"Oh, I assumed all pirates loved water to spend each of their days out on it. Mind me asking why you don't?"

I blinked and I was back in that old clawfoot bathtub in the woods as my brothers held me down.

"Jamesy, the nothing boy," Charles jeered as Roland pushed down on my head again, submerging me in the ice-cold water.

Blinking again, I was back on the road, staring at Lia. She smiled, waiting for my response.

Clearing my throat, I said, "Old wounds."

Lia's smile slipped, but instead of her gaze turning to a pitied look, she leaned closer and said, "We all have those. Someday they won't hurt so much."

Leaning back again, she resumed riding as if we'd been discussing the weather. I bit my lip, trying to keep from saying anything stupid, even though I wanted to confess my love right then and there. I hardly knew Lia and yet something about her had me head over heels from the moment I'd laid eyes on her. Every word she said only deepened my desire to know her. *Truly* know her.

Fuck, I thought, glancing at Finn who rode right behind me. He wore a shit-eating grin that told me he knew exactly what I was thinking about.

"Fine day, ain't it?" he said, cocking his head and his brow at me.

I rolled my eyes and returned my focus to the road. My horse maneuvered around the divots and pits in the dirt road well enough without much guidance from me and soon we were picking up speed.

We began a pattern of riding faster for a while, and then slow to let the horses rest before picking up the pace again. Marley would check in every now and then, letting us know if anyone was coming or if she saw anything suspicious at sea. Thankfully, she'd seen no signs of the sirens.

"How do you know people will be willing to help us in Asmara?" Finn asked Lia when we'd slowed down again.

"I assume you've been there considering it's one of the only ports left that tolerates pirates," Lia said, giving him a pointed look.

Finn stuck his tongue in his cheek and said nothing, though I knew it took effort on his part. I was impressed, really, by his restraint.

"So, you should know that Asmara is filled with all sorts of shifters. Viv and I used to frequent their port often, before-" she stopped herself short, pursing her lips and rolling her shoulders before continuing. "I have friends there who I know will be willing to help us."

Finn didn't respond, but I could see the wheels turning in his mind as his jaw worked back and forth. I wasn't sure what it would take for him to trust the mermaids.

"Oh!" Lia pointed to the sky. "The first star."

I glanced up, noticing the singular star in the darkening sky. The sun had yet to drop below the horizon, but night would soon be upon us.

"Are you going to make a wish?" Lia asked, turning wide eyes to me, her grin contagious.

"I never have before," I said, almost embarrassed by that even though I was a grown man who had never believed in wishing on stars.

"What, you don't believe in magic?" she teased, waving an arm around as if magic surrounded us. Which, if you counted the shifters I kept company with, it technically did.

"Not that kind of magic, no," I said. You could get almost anything you wanted with the use of magic, and yet some things just weren't possible.

Lia sighed. "Well, I made my wish. Certainly makes it more likely mine will come true, since you won't make one." She side-eyed me with a smirk on her face.

"I guess I can't argue with that," I chuckled. "If I say it out loud, does it ruin the magic?" I asked and she shook her head. "Alright, then I'm wishing for at least twenty more minutes of your company."

Wrinkling her nose, Lia laughed. "I feel like that's cheating. Wishing for something you know is going to happen. But I'll allow it."

I put a hand to my chest. "Oh, are *you* the one who grants the first star's wishes?" I asked in mock shock. "I'm honored to meet you."

Lia threw her head back. "Yes! It is I! The great wish granter from the sea!" she said, making us both break out into a fit of laughter. Looking behind me, I realized Finn had dropped back to ride with Viv.

Viv

Riding at the back of the group, I watched Lia with Jami. It wasn't that I didn't like Jami or Finn, I just didn't trust them yet. We'd barely known the men a day and now had to travel with them. I yearned to be back in the water, which would be a much faster way to travel to Asmara.

My gut clenched and my scars tightened at the thought of the kingdom in which I'd been held captive for two excruciatingly long years, nearly twenty years ago by a physician named Marcus Humer. Cold crept up my spine and goosebumps pimpled my arms as I was dragged into a memory of my time spent there.

I was shoved through the single door into a dimly lit room with no windows. A long, metal table sat in the center of the room and beside it a flat topped, waist high cabinet stood. Potions, drugs, and horrific tools littered the top of it and filled the concealed shelves inside. I had been in this room too many times and could name every single item in that cabinet.

"Hey, you okay?" Finn's voice pulled me out of my reverie. I jerked my head toward him.

"Fine," I said, my voice terse.

"At least the fog cleared for us," Finn continued talking, distracting me from the engulfing memory. Slowly, my goosebumps faded and the cold ebbed away.

"So, what brought you and your sisters to Lanteria?" Finn asked, raising a red flag for me. Strangers only asked questions when they were suspicious of you or wanted information to use against you.

"What brought *you* to Lanteria?" I flipped the question on him, raising a single brow as I eyed him. I couldn't tell what his motivations were or what type of man he was yet, and that unsettled me. All I knew of him were the stories and rumors told in the ports we'd visited, and none of those painted him in a favorable light.

"Fair enough." Finn dipped his chin toward his chest.

I returned my gaze to the group ahead of us, assuming Finn wouldn't be answering the question either.

But he proved me wrong. "We were headed to make port in Asmara, since they're still welcoming toward pirates," he explained with a smirk.

"I forgot about that," I admitted. "It's been a while since I've been to this continent." I had avoided it as much as possible since I'd escaped my hell in Asmara.

"Where is it you call home? Thalassia, I assume?" Finn assumed correctly, though it wasn't a large leap to make. Almost all mermaids lived in, or at one point in time, called Thalassia home. It was the only underwater mermaid civilization in the world, aside from one much smaller underwater kingdom in the south, that only housed about two hundred mermaids at any given time.

I decided to throw Finn a bone and give him an answer. “Yes. My sisters and I call Thalassia home. What about you and your crew?”

“Most of us are from Sylvane, but a few of our crew come from other kingdoms.”

“It’s beautiful there,” I said, recalling the snow-capped mountains, evergreen pines, and constant dusting of glittering snow coating everything. The kingdom of Sylvane lay far north of where we were now, in a much colder climate. A drastic difference to the warmth and palm trees in Lanteria. “I made a solo trip there a few years back, I hope it hasn’t changed too much. It is one of my favorite places to visit.” I thrived in the cooler temperatures.

“Well, maybe someday I’ll have the pleasure of showing you my favorite places back home,” Finn said, grinning.

A lump rose in my throat and I shook my head. “I have no plans to return there,” I lied. For some reason, my self-preservation kicked in anytime a stranger so much as hinted at getting me alone. The last time I’d let someone in and trusted them to ‘show me around,’ I’d wound up in a cage.

Finn’s eyes darkened and he cleared his throat. “Right, of course.” He straightened his shoulders, and I wondered if his own defense mechanisms were taking over his mannerisms. The thought of that had some of the ice around my heart melting, just slightly. *He’ll only hurt you, remember what happened last time you let someone in,* I chided myself.

“I’m going to check in with Jami.” Finn pulled ahead and Bree returned to my side.

As I watched Finn, he slowed his horse beside Cole’s, saying something to him and making them both laugh.

Bree’s laugh caught me off guard.

“What?” I asked.

"That went well," she said.

I scoffed. "I don't know what you're talking about."

Shaking her head, Bree said, "We're going to be traveling with them for a bit, you may as well *pretend* to like them."

"Why should I? I don't trust them, and I'm not going to act like I do. It's clear Finn doesn't trust us either, so there's no love lost." I didn't need any more friends. I had my sisters and that was enough.

As the sun slipped below the horizon, I stared out over the water, watching as the orange and red hues danced across the waves.

"It's sights like this that make me forget all of our monsters for a few seconds," I murmured.

Reaching over from her horse, Bree held her hand out to me and I took it, letting her lend me some comfort.

"I'll always be with you to fight off the monsters so you can enjoy a thousand more sunsets like this one," she said. "We *all* will."

I held onto her hand for a few more seconds before releasing it.

Marley swooped down low in front of Finn, transforming back into her human form on the side of the road.

"There's an inn ahead! It's right before the next town," she called out so everyone could hear her. "We may as well stop there for the night."

I smiled in relief that we would be able to stop soon. My thighs were chafing and my entire body was sore from riding all day.

The inn was small but had a grand porch with rocking chairs lining it. An older woman with glasses and slippers on her feet watched us as we approached on foot, leading our horses.

She pointed a crooked finger at Lia and scowled. "We don't allow your kind here," she said, her shaky voice laced with hate. "Don't want no trouble," she muttered. Her eyes narrowed on Korra's pink hair.

Anger bubbled in my gut. "We only need a place to stay for the night, and we'll be gone in the morning," I said, but the woman shook her head and pointed to a sign next to the front door.

No mermaids, snake, or bird shifters.

"Bird shifters?" Marley chimed in.

"They shit on everything," the woman grumbled.

Marley looked like she might storm over to the woman and knock her out of her chair, but Cole held her back with an arm across her chest.

"She's not worth the trouble. Come on," he said, leading Marley away from the inn. "We can camp out on the beach."

Everyone turned away, except for Lia. I watched her as she studied the woman for a few more seconds, and then left with everyone else. I handed my reins to Nix before hurrying to Lia's side. It wasn't as if it was Lia's fault we were turned away, but she had been the one the old woman had singled out because her green hair was a stark reminder of what she was. Like any other gene, a mermaid's hair color was only an indicator of their bloodline, nothing more.

"That woman is horrid," I said as I slid an arm around Lia and leaned my head on her shoulder. "People who hold such prejudices against us aren't worth our time."

Lia sighed. "I know. It baffles me that there are people like that in this world. I always want to think of some grand comment to change their mind and make them see the error of their ways, but I know it takes more than that."

"At least now we get to sleep on the beach, under the stars," I said, trying to make our alternative sound more enticing.

Lia smiled despite the pain I saw in her eyes.

When we were far enough away from the inn that we wouldn't have to worry about interacting with the owner or its patrons, we stopped and turned down the banking. We tied the horses to a long piece of driftwood.

It was warm enough that a fire wasn't necessary, but we made one for the light it provided and to cook some of the food we had in our packs.

Kicking off my boots, I flopped down beside the fire and dug my feet into the sand, relishing the feeling of it. If I couldn't be in the water, this would be the next best thing.

"I'm already sick of being on land," Marley said, pulling her flask from her saddlebag. Cole had his own that he already swigged from. "I've never been turned away from a place for being a hawk shifter."

"I'd like to say the same, but we've been turned away multiple times for being mermaids," I said. "They're usually a bit more subtle about it than that woman, though."

"I'd be happy to go back there and burn the place to the ground," Marley offered.

I snorted a laugh, caught off guard. "That's unnecessary and wouldn't really help our cause much. But thanks anyway." It didn't happen nearly as often anymore, but sometimes people turned us away or avoided us because mermaids were too closely associated with sirens. Though the sirens hadn't been as troublesome in the past hundred years, they had a nasty reputation from their past that they were only perpetuating with their recent attacks.

Marley shrugged and changed the subject, saying, "It's been a while since I've spent the night on a beach."

I watched her and Cole closely, trying to determine if either of them had anything special about them that would warrant interest from the siren queen.

I hadn't given Cole much consideration before, but he was quite attractive. Though, he wasn't nearly as muscular as Finn. He was much softer around the edges and wore his beard long while his dark brown hair was shorn close to his head.

"Last time you slept on a beach it was because you got too drunk and couldn't find your way back to the ship," Cole said, dropping down on the opposite side of the fire to me.

"Only to find she'd been a hundred feet from it the whole time," Finn chimed in, pulling a flask from his own saddlebag.

"It sounds like you all have fun together," Lia said as she sat beside me.

"'Course we do," Marley said, putting her arms out on either side of her and spinning in a circle. "Otherwise, what good would living be?"

Bree, Korra, and Nix all sat around Lia and I. Jami remained by the horses, feeding them, and giving them water.

Laying her head in my lap, Bree stared up at the sky while I played with her hair.

"I'll never get tired of watching the stars," she said.

"They may tire of you watching them," Nix teased. "You ever think of that?" She poked her head over my shoulder and rested it there, staring down at Bree.

"There was also a time when Marley got lost following the North star, because she was actually following a firefly," Cole said, making us all laugh.

Nix pulled back from me and stood, shifting the sand, and making me sink a bit further into it. She joined Marley.

"Care for a drink?" Marley offered the flask to Nix. "It's a Captain Finn special." She winked at Finn who lifted his flask and shook it.

"Meaning I accidentally mixed Marley's wine with whiskey *one* time, and now it's all she drinks," Finn said, chuckling.

Nix shrugged a shoulder and took the flask, taking a sip, spluttering, and spitting it back out on the sand.

"That good, huh?" I asked, smirking.

Nix wiped her mouth with the back of her hand. "How do you drink that?" It's disgusting," she asked through her laughter.

"I don't really know, but it makes me happy." Marley did another spin as if to make her point.

Jami walked over, standing behind Finn.

"There's something in the water," he said, pointing to where a shadow bobbed a couple hundred feet out in the water.

It disappeared beneath the surface, and somewhere far to the right, a splash had Finn jumping to his feet.

"Maybe we should have someone keeping watch while the rest of us sleep," Lia suggested.

Finn cleared his throat and ran a hand through his hair. "Good idea."

Marley and Nix volunteered to take the first watch and walked the shore, making sure nothing lingered in the water while the rest of us settled in to sleep. Jami and Bree offered to take the second watch.

Even though I trusted Nix and Bree to keep us safe while we slept, it took a while for me to settle down. Lia and Korra were on either side of me, which helped calm my nerves, but my brain wouldn't stop circling around the idea that someone was watching us.

At some point I fell asleep, and when I woke, Bree had taken Korra's place and the sun was peeking out between the trees behind us. I let out a sigh of relief I'd made it through the night.

Finn

I hadn't been able to sleep. It wasn't just that we'd seen something in the water, but I still had my suspicions about the mermaids. Viv watched me a bit too closely sometimes. Not that I wasn't watching her right back, but I had reason to. She'd blown up my ship.

When I'd first dropped back to talk with her the day before, she'd seemed far away with a haunted look, as if lost in her own mind. Like a fool I'd taken it upon myself to provide her with a distraction, thinking she'd be grateful to think about something other than whatever haunted her. Instead, she'd seemed agitated and maybe a little annoyed.

So, today I'd decided to avoid her altogether and ride with Jami and Lia. They seemed to be having a much better time, as they both laughed animatedly.

"What's got the two of you so upbeat?" I asked, pulling on the reins to slow my horse beside them.

"Jami was telling me about the time you both snuck off into the mountains as kids and nearly got yourselves killed," Lia said.

"Was he now?" I turned to Jami, raising a brow and Jami shrugged in response. "Did he mention that he was the one who came up with the grand plan in the first place?"

Lia gasped and put her hand to her chest. "No, he did not!" A smile broke through her dramatic mask, and she giggled. "We all tend to forget those little details when we tell our stories, don't we?" She winked at Jami. I could have sworn Jami was going to faint from the way his eyes widened, his back straightened, and he seemed to be fighting for air. I fought back a laugh.

To distract Lia and save face for Jami, I cleared my throat and said, "It's true. We like to think the best of our past selves."

"Mmm hmm," Jami managed to get out as he recollected himself.

Oh, he's in deep shit, I thought, laughing to myself. I wanted to be upset with him for already throwing caution to the wind and forgetting all I'd said about being careful with the mermaids, but Jami had always been this way. Falling hard and fast while the girl had already moved on to the next man. I believed Jami and myself to be opposites in that way. While Jami could come on too strong, I always took my time and concealed my feelings for too long. On more than one occasion I played *too* hard to get, and the woman lost interest in me before I revealed my true feelings.

It didn't bother me, though. I wasn't sure I wanted to settle down with any woman. If I ever did that, being captain of a pirate ship would become much more difficult. I didn't need the added burden.

At the thought of returning to the sea, my palms dampened with sweat. I didn't want to return to the sea. For the

first time in my life, I'd rather remain on land. I shook my head. That was crazy.

Turning my head to stare at the water for a second, I winced as the waves crashed on the shore.

"You seem distracted," Lia said, bringing me back into the moment.

"Just thinking about my ship," I said, worrying at my bottom lip.

Lia's smile disappeared and her gaze dropped down to her hands. "Once we defeat the siren queen, I'll help you find a new one. A better one." The sincerity in her voice surprised me yet again. This woman had no reason to want to help me.

"Why?" I couldn't help but ask. I expected Jami to protest, or tell me I was being rude, but instead Jami stared at Lia with the same curiosity written on his face.

Lia glanced between us, her nose wrinkling as she pursed her lips. "Because you're helping me," she said after a moment. "I can't take on the siren queen alone, but I will if I must. Though, I know Viv will always be by my side, no matter how crazy my plans are." Love shone in her eyes as she spoke of Viv.

"You won't have to take the siren queen on alone," Jami said.

Water splashed to my left. It caught everyone's attention as a child's laughter reached us.

I called the group to a halt and dismounted. "We should have warned the townspeople to stay out of the water," I said, striding down the bank onto the beach.

Two boys, one blonde and one red-headed, played in the water while their parents watched from farther down the beach. I sensed someone behind me but didn't turn to see who had followed.

In the water, another head emerged from beneath the surface about a hundred yards out from the two boys. Pitch black eyes stared back at me, and a smile revealed the needlelike teeth that could tear flesh from bone. Horror hit as I sprinted toward the water.

"Get out of the water!" I yelled as I ran. The boys didn't seem to hear me, but the parents turned toward me, confusion on their faces. As they glanced back toward their children, they saw nothing because the siren had already dived back under the water.

I regretted changing out of my magicked clothes, which turned into a braided bracelet when I shifted, in favor of the newer, drier ones I'd bought in town. I didn't have time to worry about stripping down before shifting. I experienced the usual discomfort as my bones and muscles readjusted, but nothing would ever compare to the pain of my first shift. Now, it was almost as easy as breathing. In a flash, I was running on four massive paws, shaking out my mane as a roar ripped from my throat. In my lion form, I'd never felt more powerful.

My horror was reflected in the parents' eyes, though they assumed I was the threat and were running toward me. I ignored them, outpacing them easily, and as I reached the water, the blonde boy was pulled under.

Nausea churned in my stomach as the water lapped at my legs, but I pushed past it, focusing on the boy above the water. I heard splashing behind me and chanced a look back to see Viv transforming into her mer form and diving beneath the surface to go after the blonde boy.

From what I could tell, there were no other sirens, but I couldn't be sure. I'd kicked up too much sand to see clearly as I'd swam, and the thought of looking down now made my throat constrict from fear.

I made it to the red-headed boy and waited for him to grab onto me. The boy, unafraid of me, wrapped his arms around my thick neck and let me pull him back to shore where the parents were standing in shock. Jami had joined them, while Lia swam toward where Viv disappeared, and the rest of our group remained with the horses on the road.

"Where's my son?" one of the women seemed to have snapped out of her shock. Her eyes scanned the water as she waded into it. Jami grabbed her arm, remaining firmly on the sand, and pulled her back.

"The mermaids will bring him back," he said, but I could see the uncertainty in Jami's gaze.

When I reached the shore, the red-headed boy released his grip on me and ran, crying hysterically, toward his parents. He seemed to have snapped out of his calm haze.

Shaking out my mane, I turned back to watch the water for Viv. Fear clutched me that she'd resurface without the boy, but an even stronger fear that she wouldn't resurface at all nagged the back of my mind.

Lia dove beneath the surface and I heard a little gasp escape Jami.

We watched with bated breath as the surface of the water turned calm amidst the waves. The seconds ticked by without any sign of the mermaids or the boy.

Lia

Being in my mer form made my entire body alight with joy. It contrasted with the fear twisting my gut as I scanned the ocean surrounding me for Viv and saw nothing but sand and seaweed. A few fish swam toward the ocean floor, and I watched them dart away as I approached.

We'd only seen the one siren, but there was no telling how many more may lurk out of sight.

Viv? I reached out to her. We could only communicate with our telepathy underwater.

Seconds passed like hours as I awaited her response.

I'm fine. I've got the boy. Her voice in my mind instantly soothed all my worries. *I'm headed to shore.*

I still didn't see her, but I trusted her and swam to the surface.

Finn prowled the beach in his lion form.

Everyone turned their heads as I swam toward them, but their shoulders and faces fell again when they realized it was only me.

Nix, Bree, and Korra had left the horses behind and were at the edge of the water, as if they'd been about to break

my order and jump in. If something happened to Viv and me, someone would need to carry out our mission.

They backed away as they saw me.

As I neared the beach, I heard the father of the missing boy ask, "Are we supposed to just stand here? He'll drown if we don't do anything!"

The mother wailed at that.

He wasn't wrong. As I scanned the water again, Viv broke through the surface a few hundred feet to my left.

"Viv!" I cried out in relief. The mother did as well when Viv hauled up the boy beside her and swam with him to shore. I met her in the water, shifting back and taking the boy from her, with the father helping on the other side. Viv shifted and remained further away, wrapping her arms around herself as she watched us lay the boy down on the beach.

"He's not breathing," the father said, his hands aflutter as he tried to determine how to help his son.

I pushed him aside. "I can help," I said, kneeling beside the boy and brushing his blonde hair out of his face. He couldn't be more than ten years old, I realized with a pang in my chest. *So young and nearly taken from the world by an ancient monster...*

"What are you doing?" The mother kneeled on the other side of the boy, grasping his hand.

I hovered my hand above the boy's mouth and began pulsing my hand like a wave, focusing on removing the water from his lungs.

Shifters didn't have magic like witches. If we did, I could snap my fingers and replace the water with air in his lungs. However, I *could* manipulate water. It helped mermaids move through the water faster when we were swimming. In this moment, it would save this boy's life.

"What..." the father trailed off as water dribbled out of the boy's mouth and he began hacking. I sat back on my heels, relaxing as relief swept over me.

"Thank you!" The mother threw her arms around me, nearly knocking me off balance, before laying over the boy and squeezing him tight.

"Come on," Viv's voice was soft as she held out her hand to me. "We should get back on the road."

"We thought the sirens were only a problem farther out to sea," the mother of the red-headed boy said, placing the back of her hand against her forehead while clutching her son close. "How can we ever repay you?"

"No need. Just, stay out of the sea for the time being, even the shallows," I said, taking Viv's hand. The parents and children nodded eagerly, the children still in hysterics over their near encounter with death.

Viv pulled me to my feet and led me back toward the road. Jami and Finn were already back at the horses, though Finn hadn't shifted to his human form, and was keeping his distance from the others. The horses pulled back from the lion.

I noticed Viv's sodden pants and went to remove the water, but she stopped me. It was a pain having to deal with sodden clothing, but it was a waste of our magic to have to siphon the water out with what little magic we had in our human forms.

"What happened in the water?" I asked Viv as she wrapped her arm around my shoulders.

"I saved the boy," she said matter-of-factly.

"Yes, I know that," I scoffed. "Were there any other sirens out there?"

"No. Just the one." Viv took her arm from around me. "I took care of her." She walked ahead and I caught her hand.

"Viv," I murmured. "Talk to me." It wasn't as if we had never killed a siren before. Recently, it had become a common occurrence. Before that, we'd lived somewhat harmoniously with the sirens. Mermaids could safely go out alone in the water without being ambushed by them. That wasn't the case anymore. A mermaid could easily take on a siren if it was a fair fight, but they never made it fair. Now, the sirens were straying from their usual territory, attacking ships, unprovoked.

I didn't want to have to fight the sirens, but there was no avoiding it anymore.

"I'll tell you about it later," Viv said as we reached the rest of the group.

Finn shifted back into his human form and I paused. He was completely naked. My eyes drifted down as he grabbed a fresh pair of pants from his saddle bag and pulled them on.

"Enjoying the view?" Finn asked, smirking.

Unabashed, I shrugged and said, "I've seen worse."

Viv chuckled and hopped up onto her horse. "What she means is, she's seen better."

I looked to Viv and amusement lit her gaze. It didn't happen as often anymore, and it warmed me to know Viv was enjoying herself, even for a moment.

"Be kind, ladies. I have a fragile soul," Finn joked. He pulled his shirt on, much to my dismay, and going by the look on Viv's face, to hers as well. I quite enjoyed admiring his muscular physique.

"Don't listen to him, he's a hard ass," Cole chimed in, and I turned to look at him.

"You'd talk about your captain that way?" I asked with a playful tone. I wanted to get to know these people we'd be traveling with for the foreseeable future.

"It's not their words I'm worried about," Finn said, turning his head to look over his shoulder at us. "It's their actions."

I glanced back at my own sisters. I could agree with what Finn had said, but my sisters and I would never speak ill of one another regardless. It wasn't in our nature.

A smile pulled at my lips. "It's when their words and their actions match that you know you can truly trust someone," I said.

"Mmhm," Finn mused, but said nothing more on the subject. Cole chuckled and ran his hand down his beard.

I looked at Marley who had shifted and flew above us and considered that maybe these people could become more than travel companions to me.

We rode through the day and reached the next town as darkness descended. A sign welcomed us to Brookdale as we slowed our pace. Small stone buildings had been built on the outskirts of the town. In the center of town, the buildings and homes were closer together and taller. We stopped at the first inn we found and left our horses with the stable boys.

Finn led the way inside, Marley and Cole trailing after him. I stopped my sisters from following, beckoning them to my side. Jami hesitated but went with Finn, leaving us alone.

"I want two of us out here keeping watch at all times," I told them. "Keep an eye on the sea and alert the others if we see anything suspicious."

"Bree and I will take first watch," Korra offered. Bree nodded in agreement.

"Nix and I will take the second shift," Viv said.

I wanted to protest and take Viv's place, but I knew Viv resented being fretted over. It was hard to know how the fight

with the siren earlier had affected her since she wouldn't talk to me about it. I had to trust that Viv could handle it and if she needed help, she'd ask.

"Right. Let's head in then, shall we?" I took Viv's hand and squeezed it before leading her and Nix inside. Bree and Korra remained outside, as planned.

Patrons filled the inn's sitting area to the right, which was two couches and two armchairs arranged around a fireplace. The fire burned bright, and heat washed over me as we walked in.

To the left, there were a few small tables with two or three chairs each where people sat eating baked goods from a buffet table. Straight ahead, Finn and his crew stood at the front desk talking with the man behind the counter.

I could hear chatter around the room, but one word stood out to me and I honed in on that conversation.

"...sirens are keeping us from the water. It's been a whole month since I was able to get out there," a man said. He sat in one of the chairs next to the fire with a woman. "I've got to keep trying, or else I'll run out of money and lose the house."

My jaw clenched as I tried to return my focus to our group. I couldn't take on the burdens of everyone, no matter how much I wanted to. We were already trying to defeat the siren queen, which would solve this man's problem, and I'm sure many other fishermen and tradesmen's problems as well.

"Two rooms will be fine. Better than none," Finn was saying, which brought my attention to the counter. "The lady will be paying," he added when he noticed me walking toward them.

"Right," the innkeeper said, pushing two keys across the counter. Finn grabbed them and gave the man a two-finger salute.

"Your rooms are straight down the hall there, and to the left." The innkeeper pointed to a hall beside the desk with horrible green and yellow floral wallpaper.

Viv and I exchanged a look, and Viv wrinkled her nose, making me laugh. Jami glanced back, and I could have sworn I saw longing in his eyes, but he turned away again before I could tell.

Interesting, I thought, a smile playing at my lips.

I dropped a few coins on the counter from my stash. I'd had a witch make me a small, waterproof pouch to keep my coins safe in mer form for when we used to frequent Asmara. It came in handy now, and Nix kept it filled with her pickpocketing. It wasn't something I would normally condone, but she made sure to only take from those who wouldn't miss a coin or two.

Viv looped her arm around mine, and we walked down the hall after the pirates, Nix on our heels.

"I hope there's a bath in our room," Nix said, yearning in her voice. "I'm in desperate need of some contact with water."

Viv glanced back. "It will only make it worse, trust me," she said. "You can't shift in a bath."

Nix groaned in disappointment. "I'll find a way."

I understood her longing. We didn't usually go more than a few hours out of the water. Not because we couldn't but because we preferred being in our mer forms. It wasn't uncommon for shifters to feel more natural in their shifted forms.

We came to a halt as the group in front of us stopped outside a bright orange door. Finn stuck a key into the lock, opening it for his crew. I peered in after them and saw there was only one large bed in the room.

"I guess we're getting cozy tonight!" Marley joked, throwing herself onto the bed with her arms and legs stretched to take up the whole thing. "You boys can sleep on the floor."

Cole ran and jumped, landing beside her, and almost squashing her arm. "No way! This is the first real bed we've had since Kopenhag." He rolled around, and Marley curled in on herself, sighing in annoyance.

Jami strolled into the room and flung his bag to the floor, taking a seat in one of the chairs against the window on the far wall.

"Don't mind them," Finn said, handing me a key to the door across the hall.

"Marley is always welcome to stay with us if she'd rather. It will only be three of us here at any given time. I have Korra and Bree on watch outside until we swap," I offered.

Finn tilted his head in confusion. "Why? Do you think we're in danger on land?"

"No. I always want to have eyes on the sea. If I can stop any more attacks, I will." I ground my jaw with determination.

"That's very selfless of you," Finn commented, but I sensed his wariness. "Why make it your problem?"

"Why did you help save those boys earlier?" I countered.

Finn grunted some sort of understanding and stepped toward his room. "Have a nice night, ladies," he said and closed the door behind him.

I turned to our door and opened it with the key Finn had given me. As expected, only one large bed occupied the room. But that wasn't a big deal. My sisters and I were used to sharing.

Aside from the bed, there was a wardrobe on the wall opposite the bed, and a chair like the one in the other room, but no window. Much to Nix's chagrin, there was also no bath.

Viv

When sleep found me, it brought me back to the bottom of the ocean battling that siren.

All I could think about was saving the boy. He'd already been under for far too long. As I ripped him from the siren's grasp, she lashed out with her claws, barely missing my face as I jerked back.

"He's mine," the siren hissed. Unlike sirens, mermaids couldn't talk underwater and be understood, so I didn't bother to respond. Instead, I shoved the boy behind me, using some of my magic to create an air bubble for him.

The siren lunged at me, teeth bared. I dug my own claws, now extended, into her shoulders, keeping her at bay. Overpowering her, I flipped her and shoved her down into the sand on the ocean floor.

"The siren queen is coming for you. Let me take the boy and she shall have mercy on you," the siren said, licking her toothy grin as she eyed the boy behind me.

Shaking my head, I removed one of my hands from her shoulders and moved it to her throat. Her mouth opened as if to laugh, but I dug my claws in and tore her throat out before she

could finish. It was the easiest and most efficient way to kill a siren.

I turned back to the boy, throwing him over my shoulder, and swam as fast as I could to the surface.

"Viv," Korra said as she shook me awake. "It's your turn for watch."

Groaning, I rolled over and planted my feet onto the cold, wooden floor. Korra flopped into my spot, nudging me the rest of the way out of the bed.

I rubbed my eyes and pulled on my boots, knotting them twice. Nix waited for me in the doorway where light streamed in from the hall.

"You look awful," she commented as I joined her. "Bad dreams?"

"Something like that," I mumbled, yawning, and closing the door behind me.

Across the hall, the door opened, and Finn squinted into the hall, running a hand through his tousled hair. The sight of him in nothing but his low-slung pants, and so vulnerable as he watched us curiously, seeming half asleep, made my heart race.

Humer also made your heart race once, I reminded my stupid heart.

"Where are you going?" he asked, his voice rough from sleep.

"To make sure the siren queen isn't trying to kill us in our sleep. Is that alright with you?" Nix responded, striding away before he could even answer.

"I'll come with you," he said, making her stop in her tracks.

"Why?" I asked. "You don't trust us to keep watch?"

"No," he answered matter-of-factly. Stretching his arms behind him, I tried not to watch his pants riding lower. "Let me grab a shirt." He noticed where my eyes had dropped to. "Unless you'd rather I didn't."

Huffing, I crossed my arms over my chest and strode toward Nix, refusing to look at Finn again.

"Do what you want. We'll be outside," I said, grabbing Nix's arm and heading for the exit.

Once we were outside, we crossed the dirt road to the boardwalk leading down to the ocean. Sitting on the rock wall that separated the town from the beach, we stared out at the water.

"Think he'll really come?" Nix asked.

"Yes. He doesn't trust us and will do anything to make sure we aren't doing anything behind his back." It was exactly what I'd do if the roles were reversed, but I wasn't about to admit that. "I barely know him and yet I can't stand him."

The crunch of shoes on stone behind me announced his arrival.

"Glad to know we're on the same page," Finn said, and I bit the inside of my cheek, trying to keep from whipping around and snapping at him. I gripped the stone wall we sat on and took deep breaths.

"Your presence is truly unnecessary," Nix said.

"What, don't you trust me?" he asked, a lilt to his voice as he flipped the script on us.

Turning to him, I said as calmly as I could manage, "You've given us no reason to trust you, *pirate.*" *And if I let myself trust you, there's a chance you'll betray me,* I added silently.

"You're the ones who blew up *my* ship," he said through clenched teeth, clearly becoming as agitated as I felt. "I think if anyone has a reason to be distrusting, it's me."

I stood and faced him. "Would you rather we let your entire crew die? Let all of *us* die? Because that's what would have happened. And then the siren queen would have destroyed your ship any way and taken who she was looking for."

Finn's eyes cast downward as his mouth slightly opened and I realized I'd slipped up.

"What do you mean, *who she was looking for*?" he repeated. "Are you saying there was someone on my ship the siren queen wants?"

I turned quickly, sitting back down. "It's a possibility," I said. "But what do I know. It was your ship."

"You're not giving me anymore reason to trust you," he said before sitting on the opposite side of Nix. "I can't believe you have been keeping this from me when it could put my own people at risk. Do you know-"

Lightning dissected the sky, lighting up the area and scaring a bat as it flew overhead. Thunder followed a few seconds later, drowning out all other sounds for a solid seven seconds.

As if it had been waiting for a proper announcement, the skies opened, and rain pattered down all around us. Letting my head fall back, I relished the moment before Nix tapped my shoulder.

"Lia would want us to go back inside and not risk being struck by lightning," she teased, hooking her thumb over her shoulder toward the inn.

Finn had already started walking back, not bothering to wait for either of us.

Lia

Waking up without Viv beside me in the morning was weird. Everyone else had already vacated the room, so I was alone when I opened my eyes and it felt wrong. Mermaids were used to sleeping in packs, until they found their mates and would then switch to sleeping with them. So, we were hardly ever alone.

Rolling out of bed, I spotted a note in Bree's choppy handwriting on the side table.

Eating breakfast, come join when you wake.

I crumpled up the note and tossed it in the trash before heading for the mirror to straighten myself out. I couldn't wait until we found a place with a bath. This whole trek would be much more pleasant if we could all wash up occasionally.

Shaking out my bed hair, I ran my hands through it and fluffed it up again. It was hard getting used to the short length, and I wasn't sure if I liked how it looked yet, but it was growing on me. My own violet eyes stared back at me, the dark circles around them mostly gone.

"A new look for a new adventure," I told myself before turning away from the mirror and heading toward the common room.

Bree and Korra sat at a table near the front door of the inn. Along the wall was a buffet of delicious looking pastries and fruits, and I headed straight for it.

"Pick one of the muffins, they're to die for!" Korra said.

I deliberated between the cranberry or the blueberry for a moment and grabbed the cranberry muffin. It wasn't something I had often, and I figured it wouldn't be something I could indulge in again until we reached Asmara.

"Any word from Viv and Nix yet?" I asked as I sat down beside Bree.

"They came back inside because of a storm, but headed back out about an hour ago," Bree said. "There wasn't a peep from the ocean the whole time we were out there. It almost seemed *too* quiet."

"They're biding their time." I picked at my muffin. "Probably choosing their next target."

"What if *we* are their next target?" Bree asked.

I scoffed, trying to be convincing. I didn't want to worry Bree too much until I was sure the queen had been looking for someone on Finn's ship. "The siren queen won't waste her time on us. Clearly whatever she is looking for wasn't on Finn's ship, so why continue pursuing them?" I hated to lie to her, but it was for her own good.

"You're probably right," Bree sighed, leaning back in her chair and crossing her arms as she appeared deep in thought. "What if we tried to talk to one of the sirens?"

I stopped picking at my muffin and tilted my head to see Bree better. "You know as well as I do that that would only end in bloodshed."

"Not necessarily. Contrary to popular belief, the sirens *are not* mindless creatures."

"They are when it comes to their queen," I reminded her. "They will follow her orders even if it means their own demise."

"But-"

"Bree, I need you to promise me you won't try to talk to one of them. It's not worth losing you over." I stared into her eyes until she looked away and nodded her agreement.

"I know. It was a stupid suggestion," she murmured.

"Not stupid, just reckless." I reached out and squeezed her hand. "I promise I'll figure this out and get us home as soon as I can." We all had people back home we loved and missed, but Bree had a girlfriend, unlike the rest of us. She'd chosen to join our mission not only because she was our sister, but to ensure she and Molly could travel the seas safely together again. They'd had a close call with the sirens a week before Thalassia had been sealed off from the world.

"I don't expect you to do that alone," Bree said. "We're all here for a reason, and that's to support *you.*"

"I know. And I will forever be indebted to all of you. Once the siren queen is gone, balance will be restored, and we can return home." The thought of home had tears pricking my eyes. We'd left it a little over two months ago, when the attacks first started, and we wouldn't be able to return until we dealt with the siren queen. I'd been away from home longer before, but my choice to return had never been taken from me. It changed the game and made me more motivated to win this war.

"Let's talk about something a bit less doom and gloom," Korra suggested. "We have plenty of time to worry about the siren queen and her plans when we're on the road." She reached over and plucked a piece of my muffin from my plate,

popping it in her mouth. I couldn't help but laugh, thankful for her diffusion of the gathered tension.

"Let's talk about boundaries, Korra," I teased. "Like *not* stealing my food, for one." She stuck her tongue out at me and I responded with my own cross eyed, tongue out, face that made us both dissolve into laughter. Bree remained impassive, but she made no more mention of the sirens or their queen.

Marley wound up getting the bed.

Cole had made a valiant effort to remain on the bed, but she was vicious in her sleep. Without a hammock to keep her limbs pinned to her sides, she flailed as if she were fighting sirens in her dreams.

I was used to sleeping on the floor and preferred it sometimes. The cool hardness of the wood kept me from falling into too deep a sleep if something were to go wrong and I needed to be awake in an instant.

It was something I'd learned from early on. If you slept too deeply, people could sneak up on you. My older brothers taught me that.

"Anyone up for some breakfast?" Finn asked, opening the black curtain, and letting the morning sunlight in. Dust clouded out from the curtain and Finn coughed violently. Cole and Marley both hissed at the light streaming in, but I hopped to my feet.

Leaving the two sleeping pirates behind, Finn and I made our way to the front of the inn where we'd seen the baked goods the night before. Lia, Bree, and Korra already occupied one of the small tables near the buffet.

"Viv and Nix must have returned to watch duty," Finn said, his jaw ticking. I narrowed my eyes at him.

"Does that make you uncomfortable?" I asked.

"I don't trust them," Finn reminded me. "Who knows what they may really be up to."

"What ulterior motives could they possibly have?" I whispered as we neared the mermaids. "We could have chosen not to help them, and they still would have come on this journey. If anything, we're slowing them down."

Finn's mouth twitched. "Maybe."

"Good morning, ladies," I greeted the mermaids. "Did you sleep well?"

"Well enough," Lia said, smiling up at me and waking the butterflies. "And yourself?"

"Fine." I nodded to her before walking over to the buffet table and grabbing myself a cranberry muffin. Finn had already taken a muffin and a glass of some kind of reddish juice. Taking a chance, I grabbed a glass as well and joined Finn at the table beside Lia's.

"Was there any activity last night that we should be aware of?" Finn asked, picking at his muffin.

"None," Bree answered.

I took a sip of my juice and nearly gagged on it, spitting most of it back into the cup. "That's disgusting," I gasped.

Lia giggled and stood, sashaying over to me. She leaned down, lifted the cup to her lips and took a sip.

Tapping her cheek, considering for a moment, she remained hovering over me with her hands on the table. "Beet juice," she said, winking at me.

My heart all but stopped as I watched her, and my entire body heated. Pushing back from the table, she returned to her

seat and leaned back, draping her arm over the back of her chair.

What the fuck just happened, I thought as I fought to regain control of my senses. Every single nerve seemed as if it was going haywire, sending shockwaves through me as I fought back the urge to kiss her right then and there. I'd never been aroused by something as mundane as a woman drinking from my cup before.

Finn kicked me under the table.

I jerked out of my stupor. "Oof." I rubbed the spot on my shin that Finn had most likely bruised. "Shit," I mumbled.

Lia and her sisters chatted about travel for the day, but her eyes kept flicking to me. I couldn't help but watch her and wonder if she shared any of the feelings I now harbored for her.

Marley and Cole joined us at the same time Viv and Nix came inside. With everyone gathered, we decided it was time to set out for the day. We had a lot of ground to cover, and it was best if we limited our stops from there on out. Every day we spent on the road was another day the siren queen had to attack another ship.

"We should ride through the night," Finn said as we mounted our horses. "If the siren queen is truly so threatening that you're constantly watching the seas, then we can't afford to waste any time getting to Asmara."

I heard the edge in Finn's voice hinting at his suspicion of the mermaids, and apparently so did Viv.

"If you truly don't believe us about this, why are you even here?" She approached him, sizing him up as he sat atop his horse. "We don't *need* you, if that's what you're thinking."

"Viv," Lia warned. "He has a right to be wary of us. We've given him no reason to trust us yet."

Viv turned on Lia. "We saved his ass from the siren queen. I think we've given him plenty of reason, but fine." Casting a look over her shoulder she added, "Don't think I'll be saving you ever again."

This isn't going to end well, I thought as I pinched the bridge of my nose. *Those two are a volatile combination.*

As we rode, there was a clear division between the pirates and mermaids. Finn hadn't tried to hide his suspicion of them and they weren't trying to do anything to sway him. I didn't blame them, considering they'd already done the absolute most by saving us from the siren queen.

Finn didn't see it that way, of course.

"Stop looking at me like that," Finn snapped, making me realize I'd been staring at him. "It's weirding me out."

I laughed. "Sorry."

Once we increased our speed, there was no way we would have been able to hold a conversation. We rode through the night, as Finn had suggested, taking only a small break for the horses to eat, drink, and recoup. During that time, the division remained, though I snuck away for a moment to try and talk to Lia.

"Hey," I said, catching her attention as she refilled her canteen with water. She smiled when she saw me and all I could think about were her lips as she bit the bottom one.

"Is everything alright?" she asked, screwing the cap back on her canteen.

"Fine. I only wanted to check in with you and see if you or anyone else needed anything." I rubbed the back of my neck, knowing I was probably making a fool of myself. Obviously if they had needed anything, they would have dealt with it themselves.

"Nothing we need," she said, letting her gaze drop lower. "Want, is another question, but we'll save that for another time." Lifting her gaze to mine once more, she winked and brushed past me.

I remained rooted in place, unable to process what had happened. *Was she hitting on me? Or am I going crazy?*

"Jami!" Finn called, and I snapped back to reality. "Time to go."

The next couple of days everyone was much more focused on the journey.

On the second night, Marley thankfully found us an inn to stay at. It had started to drizzle and I had no desire to sleep in the rain.

Finn prodded me before I could fall asleep, though. "Hey, you awake?" he asked, knowing full well I was.

"What?" I groaned.

"Let's go find a bar, I need a drink," Finn said, and I perked up. After the long couple of days we'd had, I could use a good drink, or ten.

"You're not going without me," Marley's voice sounded right behind me in the dark room.

I almost screamed but swore instead. "Shit, Marley! Give a guy a warning!"

"Fine, everyone, let's go," Finn said. I heard the door open, and light filtered into the room, illuminating Cole still passed out on the floor. None of us bothered to wake him. He'd know where to look for us if he woke up; we were creatures of habit.

Outside, the air had cooled down quite a bit since the sun had gone down, though the drizzle had stopped. Marley

opened her arms wide, as if she were spreading her wings in her hawk form.

"I miss sleeping out on the water, under the stars," she said.

"It's only been a week since we did that," I pointed out and she ignored me.

"At least we won't have to walk far," Marley said, gesturing to the building next to the inn labeled *Pub*. "They keep it simple here. I like it." A few people walked into the pub and a few more trickled out.

"What are we waiting for?" Finn asked, starting for the door. We followed him in, and it was as if we'd stepped into a whole other world.

Dim lighting illuminated the crowds around the room. Raucous laughter drew my eye to the other side of the bar where a group of men played a game of darts. The air smelled of alcohol and something sweet, like honey. From outside, you'd never guess how many people were in there, but we had to snake our way to the bar to get through everyone.

After getting our drinks, we found a table big enough for the three of us.

"Do you think someone will recognize the captain?" Marley asked, smirking. "Should we wager on it?"

I glanced around the room, gauging what kind of people were in the pub. It wasn't that people recognized Finn everywhere we went, it was more often they recognized his name. But the nearer we got to Asmara, the higher the chances of people recognizing him from our many visits to the port.

"Don't be ridiculous," Finn scoffed. "We're too far out from Asmara."

"What's the wager?" I asked, ignoring Finn's protest.

“What do you want?” Marley said, tapping her fingers on the table.

“The bed,” I said the first thing that came to mind. It wasn’t that I really cared to have it, I just enjoyed messing with Marley.

“Fine. I’m wagering someone will recognize him in the next hour,” Marley said, putting her hand out toward me.

“And I wager in the next twenty minutes,” I said, gripping Marley’s hand and shaking on it.

“Wait – if it’s in the next twenty minutes, then you’re both winners, right?” Finn asked, shaking his head.

“It won’t be that fast, so I’m not worried about it,” Marley said. “Timer starts now.”

I opened my mouth to speak when Marley leaned forward, slamming her hand on the table.

“And you can’t tell anyone who he is,” she clarified. Considering I’d been about to do that, I slumped back in my seat and took a swig of my drink.

“Killjoy,” I murmured.

I had nothing to worry about, though, because five minutes later a woman strolled over to us from the bar. From the way she undressed Finn with her eyes, I assumed she knew exactly who he was.

Leaning against our table and leaning down to talk to Finn, her cleavage was on full display.

“My friend said you’re the famous Captain Finnian I’ve heard so much about,” she said, batting her lashes.

“Ha!” I pounded my fist on the table, startling the woman and making her glare at me for interrupting her attempt at seducing Finn. “The bed is mine!” I cackled as Marley pouted and folded her arms over her chest in defeat.

"Um, excuse me?" The woman turned back to Finn, dismissing us. "As I was saying-" But she couldn't finish because Finn stood and walked away. She turned to us, glaring as if we were the cause of Finn's rudeness, when in fact, I had no idea what had gotten into him. Usually, he was all over these kinds of opportunities.

I followed him with my gaze, trying to figure out where he was headed, when I caught sight of Viv leaning against the far wall. Her eyes were locked on Finn's as he approached her, and I shook my head.

Viv

I'd heard the door across the hall open and shut, followed by Finn and Jami's voices. I tried to ignore it and go back to sleep, but curiosity got the better of me and I followed them. Bree and Korra were on watch and let me know they'd seen them go into the pub next door, so that was where I headed. I had no plans of drinking, but I did want to keep an eye on the pirates.

Inside, the pub was packed wall to wall. I hadn't expected so many people, but it helped keep me concealed. I leaned against the wall beside the door and watched the others as they found a table and made themselves comfortable.

I glanced around the room, noticing a lot of people staring at Finn, but eventually, they all averted their attention elsewhere. I was about to leave when I noticed a woman approach their table. She headed straight for Finn, which didn't surprise me. Rolling my eyes, I pushed away from the wall and as I did, Finn's gaze landed on me.

I'd hoped to leave without them noticing, but that wasn't happening. He stood from the table, ignoring the woman right in front of him, and kept his eyes locked on me. Pretending I

didn't notice, I leaned back and crossed my arms, propping my foot against the wall.

Finn approached me, not stopping until he was well into my personal space. I tried my best to appear unphased.

"What are you doing here?" He placed his right hand to the side of my head and braced himself against the wall.

"Just curious," I answered truthfully, staring into his eyes unblinking.

"You know what they say about curiosity, don't you?" he taunted.

I narrowed my eyes at him. "Something about a dead cat."

He shook his head. "Something like that."

"Your reputation doesn't intimidate me as much as you wish it to," I said.

"Oh, no?" He leaned closer. I half thought he might kiss me, and realized I wasn't entirely revolted by that idea.

Stop it, Viv, I thought. *He'll only hurt you like the last man who found his way in.*

Finn continued, distracting me from my inner dialogue. "Did you hear the story of the man I tore in half for suggesting he might steal from me?" Finn's smirk turned down and I couldn't help but laugh at his attempt to scare me.

"I've lived long enough to know that stories spread around the ports are at most half true. So, I don't put any stock in them anymore." Putting my hand on his chest, I took a step toward him, closing the already too small gap between us and pushed slightly. "Don't mistake me for someone who will bow to a man simply because he expects it."

"Oh?" Finn's brow rose and he refused to budge an inch. "I think I'd rather enjoy the sight of you on your knees before me, now that you've thrown that idea out there."

Heat pooled low in my gut, and I thanked the goddess it was too dark for Finn to see the blush that had most definitely brightened my cheeks. *You always did fall too easily;* my inner voice sounded a whole lot like Humer this time and it unnerved me.

Shaking my head, I said, “Keep dreaming, because that’s the only place you’ll ever come close to that happening.” I slid along the wall and stepped out of the bubble we’d created. As I walked away, I felt Finn’s eyes on me, and I couldn’t help but glance back to find him biting his lip as he watched me leave.

Outside, the cool air did nothing to quell the heat building inside me. I wanted to run to the ocean and dive in, but that seemed like a bad idea. If Bree and Korra saw me, they’d ask questions I didn’t want to answer. And there was the whole siren ordeal.

“Have fun?” Bree asked as I walked past her back to the inn.

“No. Finn is infuriating,” I said, pausing as I turned to her. “You know how pirates can be.”

“Sure,” Bree said, winking. She knew me almost as well as Lia and saw right through me.

Finn

I watched Viv until the door shut behind her. It irked me that she'd spied on us. Yet, being so close to her had me wanting to reach out and touch her. When she'd placed her hand on my chest, it had been as if she'd shocked me, and it had taken everything in me not to follow her out of the pub.

Back at the table, the woman who had approached me had gone, thankfully, and I dropped down into my seat once more.

"What was that about?" Jami asked. "Why was Viv here?"

"Keeping an eye on us," I said. "I told you we shouldn't trust them." Though I'd meant it when I first said it, it didn't ring as true for me now, even though I knew they were keeping secrets.

"That only proves we need to show them *we're* trustworthy, as much as you want them to prove themselves trustworthy," Jami said. "You keep pushing people away and you'll never have anyone outside of your crew you can rely on."

"But he'll keep his reputation intact," Marley said with a smirk. "The most important thing, right Cap?"

I tapped my fingers on the table. "She's not wrong. It's easier to get things done when everyone knows who I am and not to try to double cross me."

"Or they'll be ripped apart, limb by limb," Marley said in a menacing voice, the same way she'd first told that story. It had never happened, but she was a great storyteller. I would admit to ripping a guy's arm off once, but that was after a rough night, and he deserved it.

It wasn't the only instance I'd had to dole out justice, even before I became captain. There was a time when my face had been plastered all over establishments with a warning, *Wanted; alive.* It had been another pirate captain, Captain Alvar, who desired revenge for me killing him first mate. But the man shouldn't have been caught trying to stir up mutiny against my old captain, Jorge.

"Being a lion shifter has its benefits," I said. "People are more willing to believe your stories after seeing me in my lion form."

"Lucky you inherited more from your mom than your dear old dad," Marley scoffed.

I flinched inwardly at the mention of my father. "Don't talk about him, Marley. I don't ever want anyone to know I'm related to that filth." If anyone ever asked, I told them my dad was dead. I kept hoping that saying it often enough would make it true, but it hadn't worked out in my favor yet.

Jami reached over and patted my arm. "Don't be so dramatic, Finny-"

"Don't call me that," I growled, sending Jami and Marley into a fit of laughter. The only time he ever called me *Finny* was to annoy the shit out of me, and somehow, I always fell for the bait. The nickname had been one given to me by a former fling and Jami had never let me live it down.

Marley hopped out of her seat, chugging the contents of her glass before slamming it back on the table. "Another round?"

Jami and I nodded.

A few more people approached me throughout the night, each hoping to win a spot in my bed, but I wasn't in the mood. My interaction with Viv kept me distracted and thinking about what she'd said the other night. If someone on my ship truly had answers about where the mysterious object was that the siren queen sought, then maybe I should be asking them more questions.

Watching Marley and Jami joke with each other, it was hard to believe that either of them would keep such a thing from me. We'd spent nearly every day together the last five years. It would be nearly impossible to hide such a momentous secret.

"Stop wallowing," Marley chided, knocking her chair against mine.

"I'm not wallowing," I countered. "I'm thinking."

"Well don't do that either, it never leads anywhere good." She and Jami laughed.

"Have either of you ever heard of a magical object strong enough that the siren queen would want it?" I asked, figuring there was no point keeping them in the dark.

Both shook their heads.

"If I had, I would use it. Make myself pirate queen," Marley joked, raising her chin, and bowing slightly as if she were royalty rather than a pirate.

"That's what I figured," I sighed and took a sip of my drink. "The mermaids are crazy."

Viv

The next night, we made a camp on the beach. It was high tide when we arrived, leaving a good stretch of dry sand between the water and the road. We all woke with sand in every crevice. I wished we wouldn't have to deal with that again, but we'd likely be camping on the beach at least once more.

I shook out my short hair, watching granules of sand falling from it. "Ugh," I groaned. As much as I loved the sea and the beach, I hated being coated in sand.

"Come on," Lia said, laughing as she took hold of my hand. "We'll have to find freshwater to bathe in so we can all relieve ourselves from the accursed sand." Everyone had already begun leading their horses back to the road. Lia and I joined them and started back on our trek.

As we rode, I watched Finn closely.

"What do you think it would take for him to trust us?" I asked Lia.

"Why do you care so much?" Amusement colored Lia's tone and when I turned to her, she wiggled her eyebrows.

"I don't. He can hate us for all I care." I honestly didn't care if he trusted us or not. It may make things difficult in the

future, but presently, it didn't affect me one way or another. "Why join us on our journey if he didn't trust us?"

"Did he really have another choice?" Lia pointed out. "They lost their ship and most of their crew. It was either help us defeat the siren queen or try to return home across the ocean, only to be attacked by her again."

I sighed. Lia was right, as per usual, but it didn't change the fact that Finn frustrated me. As if on cue, Finn dropped back toward us, his horse slowing while the others continued at their usual pace. I groaned inwardly.

"Speak of the devil," I murmured.

"Be nice, Viv," Lia warned, but there was no real threat in her voice.

"I'm always nice," I responded, and Finn overheard.

"I'd like to see that," he joked, grinning at us. I scowled in return.

"What do you want?" I asked at the same time Lia spoke.

"Do you need something, Captain?" She used his title even though he'd requested we call him Finn, and he cringed slightly. I wanted to high five Lia but settled for the feeling of satisfaction turning my scowl to a smirk.

"I wanted to apologize," he began, and I scoffed, earning a glare from Lia. "I deserve that," he said.

"I assume the only reason you're apologizing is because Jami asked you to?" I asked, pointing to Jami who watched us from the front of the group. He turned his gaze back to the road as he saw me pointing at him.

"He may have played a role," Finn admitted, much to my surprise. I'd assumed he'd be the type never to admit defeat.

"Your apology is accepted," Lia said. "Though I don't think I'm the one who needs convincing." Her sidelong gaze at me was not subtle in the slightest.

"Do you trust us all of a sudden?" I asked, staring down Finn.

"Not entirely. I want to know why you think the siren queen wants one of my crew," he said.

I could feel Lia's eyes burning a hole in the back of my head and refused to look at her. I knew I'd fucked up by revealing that tidbit of information, and I'd been too ashamed to tell her.

Clearing her throat, Lia said, "Since you already seem to be clued in, I'll say, we don't know for sure. That's why I didn't tell you sooner. But it's a logical explanation for why the siren queen was present at that attack when she hadn't been at any others. And why she said it wasn't you that she wanted."

"You heard that?" Finn asked, and I turned my head to look between them. I hadn't known about that part.

Lia nodded. "She could have meant she was looking for something else, but more likely it was some*one* else."

"I asked Marley and Jami if either of them knows anything about the magical object she's looking for and neither of them did. So, if she was looking for someone, I doubt it was either of them."

"Have you talked with Cole?" I asked and Finn's eyes fell on me. For the first time, we were talking as acquaintances might, not adversaries, and there was no disdain or skepticism in his gaze. My stomach did a flip and I cursed it. He didn't trust us, nor did I trust him, and I wouldn't lose sight of that so easily.

"Not yet, but I will."

"I'm going to have a chat with Jami myself," Lia said before shifting her weight and pulling her reins to the side,

leading her horse around the rest of the group so she could join Jami at the front.

I glared at Lia to no effect for leaving me alone with Finn. Everything she did was purposeful, so I knew she had some motivation for wanting to leave me alone with this man I couldn't stand. *Be nice,* Lia's words rang in my ears.

Nice my ass, I thought.

"I'd hoped to talk with the both of you more," Finn said, watching Lia go. I couldn't help but think of the way he'd watched me when I'd left the bar. Heat crept up my neck, making me sweat.

"And you did." I pressed my lips together to keep myself from saying anything else. Nothing that came out of my mouth around Finn would be considered *nice* by Lia.

"Hardly," he groused.

"What? Are you afraid to talk to me alone? You're the one who threatened *me* the other night." I raised my brow and the corner of my mouth. "I don't bite, Finn."

Finn's gaze trailed down my torso to my legs and back up. "I might not mind if you did," he said, an almost purring like sound in the back of his throat. "And I'm sorry about the other night."

Oh god, I thought, my face heating. *That took a turn.*

"You repulse me," I lied through my teeth. After seeing Finn naked the other day, I'd had plenty of daydreams about him, but none I'd ever act on or admit to. *Yes, Viv, keep him away,* Humer's voice echoed in my mind. *You're* mine.

Gritting my teeth, I ignored my thoughts and tried my best to focus on my conversation with Finn.

"Fair enough," Finn said, lifting a shoulder. "I'll be sure not to pine after you."

I narrowed my eyes at him. "Pine away, just know your feelings will never be reciprocated."

We continued our ride in silence for a few minutes, laughter reaching us from Lia and Jami. They seemed to always be laughing when they were together. A pang of jealousy shot through me, but I dismissed it.

I've made the choice to be alone for the last twenty years. If I wanted something more with someone, I could choose that too, I thought. Though, I wasn't sure if that was true. It had been so long since I'd been with a man, or woman, that I'd lost all sense of how to act around them when I *was* interested.

I could practice on Finn, I considered, but almost immediately shook my head and realized how ridiculous that was. *No. Never.*

"What's going through your mind?" Finn asked and I choked on my spit as I realized he'd noticed me staring.

After a coughing fit, and Finn laughing at my obvious discomfort at his question, I composed myself enough to answer him.

"I'm wondering why you're still here and not back with your first mate up front," I said, though I didn't even sound convincing to myself.

"I was beginning to wonder the same thing," Finn said, and with that, he left me alone, again.

Finn

Despite my better judgement, I'd tried to build a bridge with Viv, and she'd refused me. I wasn't sure why I bothered. Though, it did intrigue me why she was so closed off with me. I wouldn't push her though.

Returning to the front with Jami and Lia, I found them laughing again. They always seemed to be enjoying one another's company.

"I wasn't done talking to you," I said to Lia.

Lia cocked her head to the side. "Viv and I are practically the same person. Whatever you say to her, I'll learn about it later." Her smile was off putting, but I had a feeling she meant it that way. "Though you weren't talking for very long."

"Yeah, well, she doesn't make it easy for me to talk to her," I grumbled.

"And why should she? What reason have you given her to trust *you?"* She narrowed her eyes at me, and I understood what she was getting at.

"I told you both I was sorry! I was wrong not to trust you after you saved our lives from the siren queen." It wasn't entirely true, I still had some misgivings, but I would never be able to put them to rest if our groups stayed divided.

"That is a big step for him," Jami cut in. "It's not in his pirate nature to trust easily." He smirked and Lia's eyebrows rose.

"And you think it's in *our* nature?" she countered, straightening her back as she turned away from us. "Mermaids have been shunned by other shifters for thousands of years. I may not have been around for the shifter wars, but my parents were, and they told me plenty of stories. It wasn't until recently that people began accepting us as shifters, which we *are.*"

"Right, sorry," Jami backtracked. "I was only trying to back up Finn a little." He gave me a '*help me out here*' look.

"We know the struggles of the mermaids. We can't say we've experienced anything like that, but pirates have also been shunned by society," I said, trying to help the situation, but as soon as I said the words, I realized I'd only made things worse as Lia's head snapped back toward me.

"For good reason!" she cried out in disbelief. "Pirates steal from others! You *chose* to take the path leading to being shunned, we never did. It's simply who we are that scares people. We're too like the sirens, according to them. To fear one is to fear them all. You're lucky I look at a person rather than their label before judging, or we may have left you to the siren queen."

Even knowing as little about Lia as I did, I knew she probably would have saved us either way, but I didn't point that out.

Instead, I said, "Pirates only steal because there are some people in this world who have too much wealth. If we don't take from them, they'll go unchecked and accumulate mass amounts of gold and jewels. We redistribute that, making things a bit more *fair.*" Even I knew I was spewing bullshit.

"I'm gonna stop this right here," Jami said, putting his hands up in surrender. "Let's not pretend we have any idea what the mermaids have gone through, Finn. Lia's right, we chose to become pirates, knowing that we would thieve for a living."

I stared at him for a second, the need to continue this fight pressing against my mind.

Drop it, Jami mouthed.

Taking a deep breath, and clenching my teeth, I said, "You're right. I tend to talk in circles sometimes. Sorry, Lia," I offered her another apology and she nodded, but didn't indicate whether she'd accepted it.

Turning my head to the right, I stared into the trees, wondering if I should shift and go for a run to burn off the adrenaline from the confrontation still rushing through me.

"I appreciate a man who can admit when he's wrong," Lia said, and I turned back to see her flashing me a winning smile.

"Now, where were we, Jami?" she talked over me as if I were no longer present. "Oh yes, talking about your time working for the butcher."

I sighed and dropped back beside Cole and Marley. She'd opted to ride with him on the back of his horse for a few hours, taking a break from flying.

"She was right, you know," Marley said.

I groaned. "I don't need you to tell me that."

"You just wanted to defend yourself because you don't want to be seen as lesser," Marley pointed out and my eyes drifted to hers.

"I'm a pirate. Not a thief," I said. Though, I was beginning to wonder if they were one and the same.

Ever since I'd lost my ship, I yearned to separate myself from that life more and more. When I'd gone into the sea to

save that boy, I'd been so distracted by the adrenaline, it had only stopped me for a second before I dove in. Afterwards, when I thought of being back in the water, my stomach roiled, and my entire body seemed repulsed by the idea.

"Did you ever want to be something other than a pirate?" I asked Marley.

"I never considered it. I've always been a thief, for as long as I can remember. Stealing food for my family, stealing weapons when I decided I wanted to be more than a common thief, and now stealing gold and jewels for the fun of it." Marley's eyes lit up as she talked about her life. My eyes caught the glint of the necklace she wore that she'd stolen in Lanteria. It suited her nicely but brought a lump to my throat as I imagined a similar necklace around my mother's neck.

I shook my head, returning to our conversation. "It is fun, isn't it?" I said, thinking about the last time we'd pillaged another ship. *That* part I missed. The thrill of the fight, and the reward of whatever we found aboard each ship. I'd say I didn't care for hurting others, but that wasn't true either. It was a necessity and I'd accepted it early on as a hazard of the job. Some of my crew had savored that part, but it never worried me. They showed restraint when it mattered most.

The thought of my crew had my nails digging into my palms as my grip on the reins tightened. Only thirteen remained. Thirty had been lost to the sirens. I failed them all.

"Captain?" Marley asked, concern in her voice. "We'll get back out there." Her assumption that I was simply missing the sea didn't surprise me. Marley had never been one for grieving the dead. She understood that when you were a pirate, an untimely death was inevitable.

"It's okay to miss the others, you know," I said.

Marley's face twisted in confusion.

"I know, but I choose not to," she said, and I tipped my head back laughing. Cole joined in, after being quiet for so long. He wasn't usually too talkative when it came to the more serious topics.

"Oh, to have the ability to pick and choose when to grieve," I said. "If you ever choose to miss someone, I'll be here. Don't hold your emotions in, okay?"

"Aye aye, Captain." Marley saluted me with a crooked grin.

Lia

We camped on the beach again that night. After everyone else had fallen asleep, I took a walk. As confidently as I presented myself to the others, I'd begun to doubt my plan.

It was true I had friends in Asmara who would be willing to help in a fight against the siren queen, but we needed much more than a few of my friends. We needed an army that could fight in the water, and that would be much harder to find. Sure, we could shoot aimlessly into the water from ships and pray they hit a few sirens in the process, but unless we had enough people in the water fighting, the sirens would easily escape our assault.

As for whomever the siren queen was looking for on Finn's ship, I was not any closer to figuring out that puzzle, even with Finn's help.

Maybe we would be better off shifting our focus to finding the magical item she searched for and beating her to it.

"Lia?"

I turned to find Jami following me.

"Is everything all right?" I asked, my eyes automatically flicking to the sea where there seemed to be nothing amiss. I paused, letting Jami catch up with me.

He reached my side and the concern in his eyes surprised me. "I was about to ask you the same thing. Why aren't you sleeping?"

"I couldn't sleep," I admitted.

"Would it help if you talked about whatever's on your mind?" he offered, and the sincerity in his voice threw me off. Jami had been extremely open and considerate since the moment we met. At first, I thought it was a tactic to lure me in, but I was beginning to think it was his actual character.

"Maybe," I said. "I'm tired of walking, though." I plopped down into the sand and pulled my knees up to my chest. Jami sat cross-legged beside me. For a while, we sat in silence. Jami didn't press me to talk about whatever was on my mind, and the longer we sat like that, the more willing I was to talk.

"I'm worried about our army," I admitted, a weight lifting from my shoulders.

"We don't have an army yet," Jami pointed out.

"Exactly," I sighed. "Without an army we'll never be able to take on the siren queen and win."

"What happened to the Lia who told us she would take on the siren queen alone if she had to?" Jami nudged me with his shoulder.

"She realized how stupid that would be and is now reconsidering all of her life choices," I joked, and we both laughed. I put my hand down into the sand between myself and Jami. His hand covered mine and squeezed.

"No matter what, you won't be alone, Lia. All of us will be by your side, army or no army." He didn't remove his hand from mine, and I liked the feeling of us entwined in this way.

"You're too good to be a pirate," I told him, and he laughed.

"You're not the first person who has told me that," he said. "Finn tells me at least once a day."

"So why do you do it?" I stared at him unabashed. I'd never been one to shy from eye contact.

"Because I'm not too good to be anything," Jami said, his hand flexing and releasing mine. "I've lied, stolen, and killed, just like the rest of them."

"But you don't enjoy it, do you?" I asked out of genuine curiosity, not judging him one way or another.

"Not always, but there are times when it's enjoyable."

"Hmm..." I tapped my chin.

"Tell me about you," Jami prompted. "I hate talking about myself." He built a mound of sand between his legs as he talked.

"That doesn't mean I'm going to let you get away with avoiding it forever," I said, trailing a finger down his forearm and grasping his hand once more.

"Tell me why you're so invested in this fight, and maybe I'll share something more about me," he said, winking.

I pursed my lips and considered whether I wanted to trust my truth with him. The thought of sharing it with him made me excited, rather than wary.

"Well," I started, clearing my throat. "My sisters and I come from Thalassia, as you know."

"Mm, most mermaids do, right?" Jami asked and I nodded.

"But we cannot return there unless we defeat the siren queen," I said.

Jami gaped at me. "Why not? Are they making you fight her alone?" The anger in his voice made me smile.

"No, it's not quite like that," I said. "We chose to leave the safety of Thalassia to fight the queen so mermaids can be free to swim the ocean once more."

"Are they not free to now?"

"You've seen what it's like. The siren queen won't rest until she commands the sea. It's not safe for anyone." My eyes watered at the thought of home. "Thalassia sealed itself off to protect its inhabitants. No one can leave or enter until the seal is removed."

"Why would you take it upon yourself to bear the burden of defeating the siren queen? Why not leave it to everyone else?" Jami asked, and I saw the logic in his question. It was a question I imagined anyone who faced a great evil would ask themselves. To me, the answer was simple.

"Because I have to. Because no one else will." Though it wasn't the whole truth, it was the most important piece of it. "Because I am the princess of Thalassia and I have a duty to my people."

Jami

I stopped breathing for a second as I stared at Lia following her revelation.

"You're..." My mind reeled as I processed that I was in the presence of royalty. Not just any royalty either, but the elusive and secluded royalty of Thalassia. They were the true rulers of the sea before the siren queen started her hunt.

"Princess Aurelia of Thalassia. Daughter of King Lahara and Queen Marisa, heir to the throne," Lia said.

"Wow." Now that she'd said it, it made sense. She had seemed to be the leader of her sisters, and she truly was. She was their *princess.*

"Do you have any siblings?" I asked.

"Not for lack of my mother trying. Believe me, if I could be replaced, she'd do it in a heartbeat."

"I'm sorry. It may not mean much, but she's crazy for thinking you could be replaced." I squeezed her hand and she smiled.

"That means a lot, actually. Thank you." She leaned over and kissed my cheek.

Lia and I fell asleep talking. We'd changed the topic to a lighter subject: her describing Thalassia and all its wonders. It

sounded like a dream to behold, and I hoped that someday I'd find a way to witness it myself.

When I woke in the morning, Lia had curled herself against me, her head pillowed on my arm, which is what woke me. My arm tingled as I flexed my fingers, trying to bring life back to it without moving too much. Lia's breathing was even, as she continued to sleep, and I didn't dare move for fear of waking her. I relished the way her body felt against mine and wished we could remain like that all day.

"Lia!" Viv called and I groaned in annoyance.

Lia shifted in my arms, stretching her legs out, and arching her back so that her chest pressed flush against mine. Her eyes flew open at the contact, and a smile pulled at her lips as she realized how close we were. She rolled away, and I sat up, my good mood deflating.

"Thank you for last night," Lia said, sitting back on her heels as she turned to me once more and kissed my cheek. Before I could react, she was on her feet, jogging toward Viv.

"I'm here, Viv!" she yelled, waving her hand in the air.

I pushed myself to my feet, rubbing my hands together to remove the sand. There was no getting the sand from all the places it had worked itself into in the night.

I caught up with Viv and Lia as they made it back to the rest of the group. *Back on the road,* I thought, as we packed up our stuff and remounted our horses.

"Where's Bree?" Lia asked, making us all look around.

"She went for a walk before dawn and hasn't returned," Nix said, continuing to ready her own horse. "I told her we'd leave without her if she wasn't back in time."

"Motherfucker," Lia hissed. I couldn't help but smile. She didn't seem the type to swear often, and it gave me chills thinking of all the ways I could get her to swear for me.

"Jami," Finn chided. "Calm down."

"Dammit." I shook my head to clear it. "How do you always know?"

Before he could answer, Lia hopped off her horse, drawing our attention, and ran to the sea, shifting as she entered it and diving beneath the surface.

"What's going on?" I asked, searching the water to try to spot any signs of her or danger.

"Bree mentioned trying to talk to a siren the other day," Korra said. "She must have decided to act on her idea, even though Lia made her promise not to."

"I'm going after them," Viv said, dismounting her horse as well.

"Don't," Nix warned. "Lia can handle it. We don't want to draw too much attention if they haven't already."

We waited anxiously until, finally, they both resurfaced and returned to shore. They shifted in the water, soaking their clothes, but neither of them bothered to remove the water once they were on dry land.

Lia stormed ahead, her jaw set and her eyes blazing.

"I can't believe you would disobey me," Lia snapped.

The rest of us took a hint and turned for the road, but we could hear them clearly.

"What if the sirens want to take out their queen as much as we do?" Bree snapped back.

"I don't care if they want to be rid of her! That's not the point here! You deliberately disobeyed me and put yourself in danger." The concern in Lia's voice didn't surprise me considering how much she loved her sisters.

"I'm sorry," Bree grumbled.

Lia rode ahead of the group, leading us to our next destination, while Bree remained near the back.

Drama aside, it had become monotonous riding through each day with the same views. Oceans, a few trees, a cliff or two, and some wildlife. It helped that I had plenty of time to talk with Lia and Finn, but I wished we could take a break from riding, if only for a day.

I'd said as much to Finn when we paused riding to let our horses drink from a trough in a town we were passing through. He laughed outright and didn't deign to answer. Lia overheard me, though, and gave me a pitying pat on the shoulder.

"Maybe in day or two we can afford to take a break, but right now, we need to move as fast as we can." She pointed out to the horizon, but I saw nothing out of the ordinary.

"What is it?" I asked, embarrassed not to understand what she was getting at.

"There's a big storm coming. I can sense it," she explained.

Finn shifted beside me and twitched his nose.

"You may be onto something," he said. "My senses aren't nearly as keen in my human form, but there's definitely something in the air."

"We probably have a day before it hits in full force," Lia said. "So, I'd like to be in the safety of a tavern or inn when that happens."

"Got it," I said. Ever since I'd become a pirate, storms didn't bother me as much as they once had. We'd sailed through some serious weather on countless occasions. I could imagine the horses wouldn't be too happy about having to be out in the storm though.

Remounting our horses, we continued through the town, stopping to grab more food, before hitting the road again.

As we rode, I kept one eye on the horizon, watching for any signs of the storm Lia mentioned. Everything seemed so still, though. The water was calm, and the wind a light breeze. I shivered as I realized it was the calm before the storm. A perfect day at sea was usually followed by a horrific one.

We chose to ride through the night to cover more ground before the storm. In the morning, a drizzling rain had begun.

"The next town we come to, we will find a place to stay," Lia promised. "We just need to ride it out until then. Hopefully it will stay this drizzle."

I rode beside Lia, hoping to talk with her again.

"Could you use your power to keep the rain off you?" I asked, and she turned to me. Tiny droplets of rain coated her eyelashes, and when she blinked, they trickled down her cheeks. Her beauty fascinated me. Realizing I should be listening to her response, I snapped back to attention.

"...But I can't use it for more than a few minutes out of my mer form," she said, and whatever had come before, I would never pluck up the courage to ask. I nodded in understanding, having heard the most important piece of her response.

"It's interesting because most shifters have no magic other than the ability to shift into their animal forms. Only then do they have their heightened abilities," I said, thinking of how Finn was extremely powerful in his lion form, but as a man, he had the same limits as me.

"Well, mermaids aren't most shifters," Lia smirked. "We're far cooler," she mock whispered and winked.

"I guess snake shifters still have magic in their human forms too, though, right?" I asked, trying to remember what I'd been taught as a child.

"Their bite is always venomous, no matter their form, yes. And dragon shifters can breathe fire in their human form. There are a few exceptions," Lia said, biting her lip and casting her eyes down.

"What's that look for?" I asked.

"Just remembering an old boyfriend I had," she said, laughing at whatever memory filled her head.

I tried to hold back my scowl, not wanting to hear about any other man who had been with Lia. Instead, I pretended to be interested, for her sake, since she seemed to want to share the story. "Oh?"

"He was a dragon shifter named Ryder," she continued. "We didn't last long, he had quite the temper. But he would let me ride on his back sometimes when he flew." She leaned her head back, closing her eyes, as if reliving that experience. "I've never felt anything like it before."

I smiled as I watched her, glad I hadn't let my jealousy get the better of me. Seeing her this way, with the rain dripping down her skin and her face lighting up with the memory of flying, made me feel as if I knew exactly what she was talking about. "I think I have," I murmured.

"Hmm?" Lia dropped her head and turned her gaze back to me, amusement dancing in her eyes.

"It sounds amazing," I said. Rain came down harder and any part of us that had miraculously stayed dry so far was drenched.

"We're almost there!" Lia called back to everyone, and we rode faster.

The town came into view shortly after, but there was no sign this time telling us its name. It was a small, rundown town that wasn't on any map I had ever seen. We earned suspicious glares from the few people we passed by as we entered the town. Thankfully, the first building we came to was a small inn.

We left our horses with the stable boy and headed inside. The stable wasn't much of a stable, more of a big awning, but at least the horses would be shielded from the rain. The inn itself seemed to be well kept, at least, minus the paint peeling from the windowsills.

I prayed there would be at least one spare room with a bath so we could wash off the built-up grime we'd all collected. The rain had helped in some ways, but it had also created more mud which splattered us as we rode.

Inside and to the right was a man behind a desk. His head lay on his arms on the counter, and he snored as he slept. Straight back was the bar. There were only a few people sitting at the bar, and no one at any of the few tables in the room.

Everyone besides Finn and I had already huddled around the fireplace next to the desk with the sleeping man whom I assumed was the innkeeper.

Finn walked up to the desk and rapped his fist on it, startling the man from his slumber.

"Do you have any available rooms?" Finn asked and the man grumbled, rubbing sleep from his eyes.

"Rooms?" he repeated, turning to the wall of hooks behind him where there was only one remaining key. "One room," he grunted, grabbing the key, and slamming it on the desk.

"We'll take it," Finn said taking the key and replacing it with a few coins. The man picked them up, inspecting them,

before dropping them into the front pocket of his apron and laying his head back on the desk to resume his nap.

"Better than nothing, I guess," Finn mumbled as he rejoined me. "Come on." He strolled over to the fireplace, swinging the key from his finger and held it out to the others.

I watched as Marley scowled, but everyone else shrugged, relieved to at least have that much. We'd make it work, regardless of the space. Otherwise, we'd be out in the storm. Turning to glance back out the window on the front door, my eyes widened at the sheets of rain pouring down from the rooftop.

When I turned back, everyone was walking toward the door labelled "Rooms" at the back of the inn beside the bar. I hurried to catch up.

Viv

After settling in, Bree, Korra, and Marley decided to stay in the room while the rest of us headed to the bar for a drink.

Trailing after the others, I watched as water dripped from my clothes down to the wooden floors. I used my magic to remove the excess water from myself and sent it into a puddle off to the side of the hallway.

"Someone may slip in that," a man said, amusement in his tone, as he came up silently behind me. Smacking myself in the chest with my hand as I jumped, I whirled around and found a tall, lithe, man with curly black hair standing behind me.

"Sorry, didn't mean to frighten you." He dipped his head in apology and his bright blue eyes caught the light. "I'm Tobias." He held out his hand but when I didn't take it, he slid it back into his overcoat pocket.

"I know too many people already," I said, hoping to deter him from wanting to talk to me any longer. As I turned away from him, though, he chuckled and walked alongside me.

"Fair enough," he said. As we emerged at the end of the hall, I saw Lia, Jami, and Cole standing by the fireplace, so I aimed for them. Tobias matched my steps and turned with me. "Care if I join you?" he asked.

"Yes," I said, only making him laugh again.

"I like your bluntness."

"That's unfortunate." I was about to tell him to leave me alone when Finn walked up beside me with a drink in his hand.

"Back off, leopard boy," Finn growled. "And give her back her bracelet."

I gasped as I lifted my wrist and realized my silver chain bracelet was gone. I turned a furious gaze on Tobias.

"How did you know I was a leopard?" Tobias asked, impressed rather than annoyed. He swung my bracelet on his finger and dropped it into my outstretched hand.

"I know another cat when I see one," Finn said, taking a sip of the drink in his hand. His nose scrunched up and he shook his head. "Nasty stuff." I gaped at him as he took another swig regardless of his comment.

"So, you must be a...lion shifter?" Tobias asked as he looked Finn up and down. I cocked an eyebrow as I did the same, wondering what it was that gave Finn away as a lion.

"Don't act as if you don't know," Finn smirked.

"I confess, I recognized you the minute you walked in. *Captain Finnian,"* Tobias drawled. "One of the most feared pirates. But, it begs the question, what are you doing on land? A pirate isn't very fearsome without his ship, is he?"

Finn growled low in his throat, and it sent a shiver through me.

Lia came bounding over from the fire, dispelling the tension that had formed around us. "Tobias?" she cried excitedly.

He stared at her, bewildered for a moment, before recognition sparked in his eyes. "Lia?"

I looked between the two of them as Lia threw her arms around him. Lia had never mentioned a Tobias, or a leopard

shifter, to me. But, then again, Lia had a lot of friends I didn't know. As princess, she was often tasked with building relations between Thalassia and kingdoms on land.

"What are you doing in a place like this?" Tobias asked, stepping out of her hug with a grin on his face. I wanted to smack it off him. Finn seemed equally annoyed with the whole interaction, but he remained by my side as Lia and Tobias caught up.

"Want a sip of this?" Finn asked, holding out his drink to me.

I blinked in surprise. "Uh, sure," I said, taking the glass and sipping from it. Sputtering, I handed the drink back to him. "What is that?"

"It's supposed to be whiskey. I think it might be camel piss," he said, looking into the glass as he swirled it around. I burst out laughing, drawing Tobias and Lia's attention. Finn's eyes lit up as he met my gaze.

"How in the world would you know that?" I gasped out between laughs.

Finn ran his hand through his hair. "It's a long story, maybe I'll tell you sometime."

"What's so funny?" Lia asked.

"I'll tell you later," I said. "So, how do you know Tobias?"

"He helped me... Oh!" Lia turned back to Tobias, grabbing his arm. "This is Viv!"

My brows furrowed in confusion as Tobias turned to me, his eyes widening. Pity shone in them, and it clicked as my stomach dropped. Tobias had helped save me from Humer's laboratory.

Lia noticed the change right away and she cleared her throat, dropping her hand from Tobias' arm.

"But let's talk about what we're doing now," she said, changing the subject. "We're trying to build an army against the siren queen." Lia continued telling Tobias their plan, but I zoned out, my eyelids growing heavy.

Nails scraped along a metal surface somewhere in the distance. Smoke burned my nostrils, and my entire body had gone numb.

Screams and yelling reached me in bursts as I flickered in and out of consciousness.

"Viv," Finn's voice pulled me back into the moment. Blinking rapidly, I cleared the memory of the day I'd been rescued from my mind. Tobias had been there, I'm sure, but I didn't remember much of that day.

"Come sit by the fire," Finn said as he took my hand and led me toward an armchair. I let him help me.

As I sat down, the heat of the fire overwhelmed me and calmed my nerves.

"That feels nice," I murmured. Finn sat in the armchair beside me and offered his glass again. I took it and drank a large gulp, savoring the burning sensation as it grounded me in the present. "Thank you," I whispered as I handed the glass back.

"Anytime," he said, staring into the fire.

I watched him for a minute. There was no pity on his face as most people showed when they dealt with me. It wasn't that I had flashbacks often, those were becoming more common the closer we got to Asmara. After being held captive, to most people I knew, I became someone to be pitied and taken care of. For a while, I hadn't cared enough to take much notice of it, but now, it got on my nerves.

"Who is that Lia's talking to?" Jami asked, startling me. I'd forgotten he was there.

"Some leopard shifter," Finn answered. "Apparently they go way back." The ice in his drink cracked as he swirled it again.

Jami crossed his arms over his chest, puffing it out slightly. I smirked.

"Maybe you should go over there and introduce yourself," I suggested. "Lia likes men who are assertive."

Jami's eyes snapped to mine, and he groaned. "Am I being that obvious? I swear, I'm trying not to come on too strong, but she's just..."

"Amazing?" I finished for him. "Yeah, she is. And if you hurt her, I will drag you to the bottom of the ocean and leave you there."

Finn let out a low whistle. "Better watch yourself, Jami. Viv's got bite." He chuckled.

"I won't hurt her," Jami said. "I'm not sure she likes *me* yet."

"Oh, she does." I glanced over my shoulder at where Lia spoke with Tobias. "I'm honestly more worried she might hurt you, but that's her prerogative."

"I'll take any time with her I can get," Jami admitted, and I saw the love-struck, doe-eyed, look he gave Lia and knew he wasn't exaggerating.

"Oh, you poor idiot," I murmured.

Lia rejoined us without Tobias and settled onto my lap. I wrapped my arms around her, and she leaned her head back against my shoulder.

"Tobias is going to try to recruit more shifters for our army," Lia said. "He has connections all over the continent, and he said he'll send anyone who wants to help to Asmara."

"That's great, Lia," I said with more enthusiasm than I felt. Our venture seemed like an impossible one, but I had to believe in Lia's ability to do the impossible. She'd saved me from Humer, after all.

No one said anything more on the subject. We sat like that until my legs started to fall asleep and Lia decided she wanted a drink.

"I'll join you," Jami offered. "Need another?" He pointed to Finn's empty glass and Finn nodded.

"What about you, Viv?" Lia asked.

"Get me whatever you're drinking," I responded.

Lia looped her arm through Jami's, making his cheeks flush red, and drew him toward the bar.

"How long have you and Lia known each other?" Finn asked me.

I turned to look at him. "Forever."

"How long is forever?" he pried, and I pursed my lips.

"You're just trying to get me to reveal my age, aren't you?" I asked, and he put his hands up in surrender.

"Guilty," he said, a grin pulling at his lips. "Jami and I have known each other since we were eight years old. Coming up on our twenty-year anniversary." He winked, and I stifled a laugh.

"How did you meet?" I asked, picking at the skin around my nails. It was an old habit I'd started while in captivity. Anytime my anxiety started to rear its head, the picking would start.

Finn's gaze darkened and he rolled his shoulders. "I found him alone in the middle of the woods, half frozen to death in the snow."

My eyes widened and I forgot my nails. "What happened to him?"

"His brothers had left him there as a joke, but it nearly killed him," Finn's voice lowered, and he fisted his hands on his knees. "But my mother and I saved his life. We've been like brothers ever since."

"Wow," I breathed.

"What's got you two so glum?" Lia asked cheerily as she bounced back toward the fire, handing me my drink before plopping down on the plush carpet in front of the chairs.

Jami came into view, placing Finn's drink on the small table between the armchairs.

"Old wounds," Finn answered, and Lia's eyebrows shot into her hairline as her eyes flicked to mine. Finn followed her gaze, but he didn't ask the question that danced in his eyes.

"Not mine," I said, and Lia's shoulders dropped as if that disappointed her for some reason.

"Where did Cole get to?" Jami asked, scanning the room. "He said he was stepping outside for a smoke and never came back."

Finn rose from his seat, stretching his arms out before him. "I'll take a look outside, you stay here." Taking his drink from the table, Finn headed for the door.

"Should we be worried?" I asked, following Finn with my eyes.

"Nah," Jami said, waving my concern off. "He does this a lot. I just want to make sure he didn't get stuck outside in a mud puddle or something."

"Stuck in a mud puddle?" Lia asked. "Does that happen often?"

"You'd be surprised," Jami said, chuckling. "He's had his fair share of instances being stuck some place you'd never think it was possible to be stuck."

"I'd like to hear those stories," Lia pressed, leaning back on her elbows, and stretching her long legs out in front of her. I didn't miss the way Jami's throat bobbed as he watched her.

"I'm going to check on Finn," I said, leaving the love birds to themselves.

Passing the bar, I overheard a woman whisper to the woman beside her, "I've never seen them around before, but I heard one of them calling the rugged one Finn. Do you think he's *the* Captain Finn?"

I paused, interested in their conversation, and studied the strange artwork on the wall beside the bar to appear as if I wasn't listening in.

"As much as I'd like to ride that lion, he's a bit intimidating. Did you hear the story about how he ripped a guy in two with his claws for walking too close to one of his crew members?" the other woman said, her eyes widening as she told her story.

It was nothing I hadn't heard before, so I continued toward the door. I sipped my drink and cringed as the tartness hit my tongue. It was a bright green drink that tasted like a sour apple. *Of course Lia would choose something like this,* I thought, laughing to myself. It wasn't nearly as bad as Finn's drink, so I sucked it down before heading out into the rain.

Finn

Cole was nowhere to be found outside the inn. I groaned, realizing my almost dried clothes would get wet again.

"Cole!" I yelled, but there was no response. "If you're stuck in a fucking mud puddle again..." I grumbled, trudging out into the rain. It soaked me through instantly.

Heading to the stables first, I found only the horses and a sleeping stable boy.

This idiot better be in trouble, or else I'm kicking his ass, I thought as I headed back into the torrent of rain.

As I started toward the nearest building, a trickle of fear skittered down my spine. I tried to shake off the feeling, but it lingered, alerting me that something was *very* wrong.

"Cole!" I tried calling out again. A grunt came in response this time. Hurrying toward the sound, I rounded the side of the inn.

"Finn," Cole grunted as I came to the back of the building. He clutched a hand to his side as blood oozed from a wound there.

I cursed. "What happened?" I took Cole's free arm and put it around my shoulders, helping him to the side of the

building so we could sit at a picnic table, under the umbrella they'd thankfully left up, and have a reprieve from the rain.

"I was having a smoke, behind the building, cause the inn - agh," he groaned before continuing. "The innkeeper didn't want me smoking in front of his building, the old bastard. And I saw someone," Cole paused, coughing as he tried to catch his breath.

"Was it a man with curly black hair?" I asked, thinking of Tobias. Lia may have trusted him, but he'd tried to steal from Viv. I wouldn't trust him until he followed through with helping us gain support against the siren queen.

"No," Cole grunted, shaking his head. "Looked more like a woman, but they had their head covered. Something scared her off though and she disappeared. Like *gone*."

"Alright. We'll find who did this." I pulled my drenched shirt over my head and pushed it against Cole's wound. "Hold that there."

"Finn?" Viv's voice reached us, and I whipped around to see her running toward us.

"You shouldn't be out here," I said as she reached my side, but it came out harsher than I'd intended.

"And you're not the boss of me," she responded. Her jaw dropped as she saw Cole. She kneeled beside him on the bench, ignoring my protest that she get back inside.

"We need to get him back to the inn," Viv said. "Help me lift him." She took one side of Cole while I supported his other side.

We struggled back toward the front of the inn, half dragging Cole. We hauled him inside, alarming all the patrons who had gathered at the bar. Jami and Lia ran over as soon as they saw us enter.

"What happened?" they asked in unison.

"He was stabbed, clearly," I ground out, helping Cole into a chair while Viv ran to the innkeeper and asked if he had any medical supplies.

While we waited, my blood pressure rose, along with my temper.

"Get some towels and hot water," I snapped to Jami who reacted immediately, running toward the bar.

Lia sat beside Cole and reached out to take my shirt from his wound. In all the chaos, I forgot I was half naked. Not that it bothered me. Most shifters were used to being naked in front of people all the time.

As Lia lifted the shirt, I grabbed her wrist.

"What are you doing?" I growled, but she turned an unwavering stare on me.

"Helping. Let go of me," she growled right back. I hesitated but released her from my hold.

As soon as she removed the shirt, blood seeped from the wound again. She gripped the edges of Cole's shirt where the weapon had gone in and ripped them so that the entirety of the wound was on show.

"Here," Viv gasped as she skidded to a halt beside me, handing me a box of supplies. I slammed the box onto the table and dug through it. Jami reappeared with a bucket of water and towels.

"Give me that," Lia said, grabbing the bucket and dipping one of the towels into it to clean the wound. "This isn't quite ideal." She snapped her fingers. "Alcohol! Get me their purest alcohol!" she demanded, and Jami ran back to the bar.

I pulled a needle and thread from the box and groaned, "This will have to do."

Jami brought a bottle of alcohol over and handed it to Lia who splashed some onto Cole's wound. He screamed in pain, and I shot Lia a glare that she ignored.

"Give me the needle and thread," she said without looking up at me.

"I'll do it," I said.

"*Give me the needle and thread,*" Lia repeated, this time lifting her gaze to mine, and I saw the determination that flared in her eyes.

"Trust her," Viv said, placing a hand on my shoulder.

Sighing, I handed the needle and thread over to Lia who set to work right away. To Cole's credit, he only screamed once more before it turned to more of a whimper. I turned away, holding my fist against my mouth as I tried to quell the rage burning inside of me. Someone had attacked my crew. A coward who had run from the scene.

"I'll be back," I said, striding from the inn and back into the rain. I stood outside, letting the rain pound down on me, trying to determine which way the shifter might have fled, when a hand clamped onto my upper arm. It released me just as quickly, but I turned to find Viv standing behind me.

"You're not going to find them," she yelled over the rain. "If Cole didn't see them shift, they must be a small animal, like a snake or bird. They could be hiding anywhere."

"That means they could still be here," I yelled back. My eyes roved over the front of the inn for any holes that would fit a small animal. There were plenty. "What if they stick around to finish what they started?"

Viv wiped rain from her eyes, putting her hand up to attempt to shield them. "Then we'll be ready if they do." Her jaw ticked and I could tell she was almost as upset as I was.

"Why did you follow me?" I didn't understand Viv's motivations. If someone asked, I'd swear she hated me.

Looking away, she shrugged. "Because no one else was going to. Come back inside."

"You're not the boss of me," I said, repeating her sentiment from earlier, a smile pulling at my lips no matter how hard I fought it.

"Why do you do that?" Viv asked, sounding exasperated. She stepped toward me, and I reciprocated, so we were standing only inches from one another.

"Do what?" I asked, cocking a brow, which resulted in her rolling her eyes.

"*Test me,*" she answered. "It's like you're trying to find which buttons to press." The rain traced lines down her face, and I found myself wanting to touch her there, wipe away the rain, and...

She stepped back, her gaze turning cold. "I don't want to play games with you."

I ground my jaw and matched her stare. "I'll ask again, then, why did you follow me out here?"

She whirled on her heel and stormed inside. Taking a deep breath, I followed, only to get out of the rain. We both headed for the fireplace where they'd moved Cole. Lia had finished his stitches and he seemed stable, though pale as a ghost.

"He'll recover," Lia said as we reached her. "He lost a lot of blood, so he's too weak to shift, but once he can, he'll recover in no time."

"Why would someone want to hurt him?" I asked as I stared at Cole sleeping.

"Do you have enemies in this place, most fearsome pirate?" Lia eyed me knowingly. "Or debts owed?"

"I repay all my debts," I snapped. "Enemies are inevitable, though." I wouldn't be able to count all my enemies if I tried. There were too many to track. As a pirate, you burned a lot of bridges and pissed off a lot of people, especially other pirates.

Lia waved her hand out before her. "It could be as simple as revenge."

"I guess we'll chalk it up to that for now," I assented, though I wasn't entirely convinced that was what happened. As far as I knew, I'd never come across a shifter smaller than a fox. It was unusual because it took too much of a toll on a human's body to shift into something so small and they didn't live through a shift like that.

"I'm going to check on the others," Viv said, heading for the room. Lia nodded to her and watched her leave. I did as well, wondering if I'd finally broken through to her today. Normally she had walls up so high I could barely hold a conversation with her. She'd let me in earlier, before slamming the walls back up fast and hard. I had no idea what to think, but it certainly left me questioning everything I knew about her.

Lia

Viv disappeared down the hall and a part of me itched to follow her. I hadn't wanted to voice the concern, but it was possible the siren queen had been behind the attack. She had so many shifters on land working for her, it was hard to know who to trust.

When they brought Cole in, it crossed my mind that Tobias may have been behind the attack, but I pushed that thought away as quickly as it came. He'd helped save Viv from the hellscape Humer had kept her in, and he'd offered to help us again. I needed to trust him.

"You should probably put a shirt on," Jami said to Finn who had his fist under his chin and stared into the fire. He glanced down at himself.

"Oh, yeah. I keep forgetting about that." He dropped his arms to his sides and started back toward the room. I didn't miss the way his muscles rippled as he moved and the hair that trailed down from his navel below his waistline. My eyes flicked to Jami, and he was already looking at me. I smirked and gave him a small shrug.

Finn wasn't my type. I'd been with enough men to know that the dark, broody kind weren't as much fun as men like

Jami. Men who were more excitable and carefree. Besides, Viv had seemed to have a connection with Finn despite their bickering, and I would never cross that line, even if Viv didn't want Finn romantically.

"What's going through your mind?" Jami asked once Finn was out of earshot.

I sat down in the chair Cole didn't occupy and crossed my legs out in front of me. "Nothing of great importance," I said. "Why do you ask?"

"You always look like you have a million thoughts going through your mind at once." Jami sat on the rug before me, leaning back on his hands so he could look up at me. "I'd like to know what some of those thoughts are."

I covered my mouth, attempting to hide my smile, but Jami wouldn't be fooled. "Some are about you," I admitted, noticing his cheeks redden as he grinned.

"Oh really?" He tilted his head to the side. "Tell me more."

"Mmm," I mused. "Most of them have to do with the siren queen," I said, and his grin faded. "And how we are going to defeat her."

"I think about that a lot, too," he said, his eyes drifting to the window behind the front desk. "She could be attacking ships right now, and we wouldn't know."

"I think about my home," I continued, shifting the topic away from things we couldn't control. "And my parents."

"Tell me about them," Jami said, intrigue lighting his gaze.

"Well, I've already told you about so much," I said. We'd swapped childhood stories of adventures while riding. "But the beauty of Thalassia could never be explained without

seeing it. It's like nothing you've ever witnessed on dry land." My heart swelled as I thought of home.

The words flowed out of my mouth in excitement as I imagined it all. "There are buildings made entirely from shells, the most beautiful shells you could ever imagine." The colors swirled through my mind. "And the luminescent algae at night," I swooned. "It's like gazing at the stars, but up close."

"It sounds magnificent," Jami murmured.

"The castle was built into a rock formation, using the corals and sea life that had already grown there as décor and accents for the structure. The rest is made from gold and glass." I could picture it so clearly in my mind, it was almost as if I were there, but when I opened my eyes, the illusion shattered, and my heart sank.

"You miss it terribly, don't you?" Jami asked, leaning forward, and resting his elbows on his knees. "We'll defeat the siren queen so you can return home."

"I hope so," I said, trying my best to feel confident in that statement.

"It seems strange that the King and Queen of Thalassia, well, your parents," he corrected, shaking his head. "Wouldn't form their own army, seeing as they literally live in the middle of the war zone," Jami mused, tapping his fingers against his thigh.

I sighed, resting my elbows on my knees as I leaned forward. "We are their army," I whispered.

Jami's eyes widened and I continued, "Thalassia has never had need of an army before. No one who means them harm can get to them without drowning first. Or those who can make it, like sea shifters, can be held off by the defense bubble around Thalassia. Before they put the more permanent one in place that keeps us out now, they had one that would keep out anyone who meant them harm. It was hardly ever needed."

“What will they do if the siren queen manages to break through their barrier?” Jami asked, concern in his gaze.

“Thalassia may not have an army, but that doesn’t mean we don’t know how to fight. The citizens will fight off the siren queen for as long as they can.” Grief pressed against my chest at the thought of all my friends and family back home fighting for their lives.

But it wouldn’t come to that. I clenched my jaw and fisted my hands in resolve. I would do whatever it took to bring down the siren queen.

That night, Marley let Cole have the bed. He'd healed enough to shift and curled up in a ball in his fox form in the middle of the bed. Everyone had taken turns bathing in the tub, and it was finally my turn.

Thankfully this inn had running water, so we didn't need to pump it from a well like I'd had to do as a child. That was before my parents had come into a large sum of money and moved us to a house with all the amenities - running water, electricity, and even a housekeeper to do all the chores.

As I was about to sink below the surface of the bath to rinse my hair of the soap I'd scrubbed into it, someone banged on the door.

"We're headed to the bar," Finn called through the door.

"I'll meet you there," I yelled back before dunking myself. As I did, a memory resurfaced, demanding all my attention.

"Jamesy, the loser, the weak, the nothing *boy," my brother Charles mocked as my eldest brother, Roland, shoved me beneath the ice-cold bath water.*

He held me down so long; my lungs began screaming for air.

I broke the surface and sputtered; the weight of the memory having held me down far too long. Resentment simmered in my veins at the thought of my brothers. I hadn't seen or heard from them since leaving home ten years ago, and I planned to keep it that way.

Climbing out of the tub, I wrapped a towel around my waist and ran a comb through my hair. I'd lost the tie for it somewhere, so I left it down. It brushed against the bottom of my shoulder blades and sent a shiver through me. Anytime my hair grew past my ears, my brothers would shorn it off, making sure to do a hack job of it. I grew it out now to spite them.

I left my dirty clothes in the pile with everyone else's. We were going to wash them in the tub, so I figured I'd get the process started. I waited for the tub to drain from my bath before refilling it with clean, warm water. I dumped the pile of clothes into it, immediately turning the water murky again.

Scowling at the sight, I drained the tub, refilled it, and added soap. This time it remained much clearer as the bubbles began to build.

I left the clothes to soak and entered the bedroom to get my spare clothes. Cole, in his fox form, was curled on the bed, and to my surprise, Lia sat on the other bed, twisting her hands in her lap. I'd never seen her looking so unsure before.

"You're still here," I said, and her eyes flicked to me, widening slightly and I remembered all I wore was a towel.

She tucked her hair behind her ear and fluttered her eyelashes. "I thought I'd wait for you, and I'm glad I did," she said, biting her lip as she continued to stare.

I crossed my arms over my chest, and Lia's smile grew.

"I feel like you might be objectifying me," I joked.

"Oh, for sure." Lia stood from the bed and strode over to me. "But only a little." Standing before me, she lifted her gaze to mine, and I saw the anticipation in her eyes as she walked two fingers up my chest, following the line of the scar on my sternum that divided my two chest tattoos. Goosebumps rose on my entire body, and there was no hiding my arousal in the thin towel.

A low growl came from the bed, and I glanced over Lia's shoulder to see Cole's eyes narrowed on us.

I stepped back and ran a hand through my hair. "Let me get ready and we can go," I said, turning to grab my spare clothes from the chair I'd left them on. I couldn't look at Lia again as I headed back to the bathroom, but I could sense her amusement.

In the safety of the bathroom, I pulled my pants and shirt on, leaving the top of my shirt untied as always. I shoved my feet into my boots and tucked my lucky coin back into my pocket. When I remembered Cole being attacked, I thought better of leaving all my weapons behind and strapped my gun holster to my belt.

Stepping back into the room, I noticed Cole had fallen back asleep, stretched out with his tail hanging off the bed. I went to the window, checking it to ensure it was locked.

Lia hopped off her bed and headed for the door, opening it.

"Ready?" she asked, turning back to me before striding into the hall. I hurried to follow her, slamming the door behind me. A bark of protest from Cole sounded through the door, but I ignored it.

"I've never seen you with your hair down," Lia said as we walked down the hall. She lifted her hand to play with the ends of my hair. "I like it."

I made a mental note to never tie my hair back again. "You're the first woman to tell me that." I instantly cursed myself as her eyebrows rose. "I don't mean... There aren't other women. I haven't..." I stopped myself from babbling.

Lia giggled. "It's okay, Jami. I know you've been with other women, just as I've been with other people."

I sighed in relief. I'd never been great with words, and often fumbled them when it came to women, but Lia never made me feel bad about it. She always rolled with it and seemed to find it endearing.

"There's the others," I said, pointing to Finn and Viv at the bar. Marley, Nix, Korra, and Bree occupied one of the tables, which were now all filled. Apparently once the sun went down, this inn's bar was the place to be. I imagined it was the only bar in town.

I noticed some tension as I stepped up beside Finn and placed a hand on his shoulder. Finn turned a blank stare on me.

"Everything all right?" I asked. Finn rolled his shoulders and took a swig of his drink.

"Peachy," he ground out, stalking away from the bar to join the others at the table. My gaze flicked to Viv who shrugged and turned toward Lia who walked up on her other side.

"Are you playing nice with the captain?" Lia asked, playing with the ties on the back of Viv's leather corset. Looking at me over Viv, Lia found my gaze and jerked her head toward Finn. *Go,* she mouthed. So, I did.

Joining Finn at the table, I plopped down into the last remaining seat and stole Finn's glass, chugging it.

"Hey!" Finn groaned, reaching for the glass before giving up and settling back in his chair. "I'll just get another."

"I thought things were getting better between you two," I said, casting my eyes to Viv and back to Finn's.

"So did I," Finn murmured low enough for only me to hear.

"What happened?"

"Hell if I know," Finn said, shaking his head and rubbing his hand over his stubble.

"Sorry, guys, I'm not trying to eavesdrop, I swear," Bree cut in. "But cut her some slack, you don't know what she's been through."

Finn and I both turned to Bree, but she said nothing more as she sipped her drink.

"I don't think Viv's the type of woman who'd want us to cut her any slack," Finn pointed out and Bree laughed.

"You're right about that," she said, raising her glass to him.

"Maybe you should try talking to her again," I suggested.

Finn scoffed, "No way. I'm not putting myself through that again tonight." He snapped his fingers at Marley who whirled on him with a scowl.

"Yes, *Captain?"* The word dripped with disdain. Marley had no fear when it came to standing up to Finn, but I knew she'd follow him to the ends of the Earth if he asked.

"Get me another drink," Finn commanded, and Marley rolled her eyes. "Please," he added. Marley mock saluted him and headed for the bar.

"Make that two!" I called after her and she flipped me the bird. "At least I know she heard me," I said with a laugh. Finn remained in a foul mood.

Viv

Finn had gotten too close, and I'd panicked. Closing myself off to him, I'd been curt when he'd tried to have a conversation with me and refused to give him any straight answers.

It wasn't like I wanted to push him away, but old habits die hard. It didn't help that Humer appeared in my mind anytime any feelings for Finn arose.

"I'm sorry," I said, and Lia squeezed my hand.

"Don't be. You're always saying you're sorry, but I don't need your apologies. I love you, Viv, thorns and all." She lifted my hand and kissed it. "Always and forever."

I couldn't help laughing. "I'm sure there will come a day when you regret that, but I'm going to hold you to it," I said, taking a sip of my water.

"Do you want to join the others? Or should we stay here," Lia asked, motioning to the table. I glanced over and caught Finn's gaze. He stared back, unphased, and shame pooled in my chest, causing it to ache.

"Let's join them," I said, steeling myself for whatever Finn might say when we talked again.

There were no more empty chairs at the table, and none to be seen elsewhere either. Lia walked over to Jami, sweeping his long hair over his shoulder.

"Mind if I share?" she asked, and before he could flounder a response, she plopped into his lap. I stifled a laugh as the look of shock on his face turned quickly to a grin and he placed his arm around Lia.

I felt envious of Lia's carefree spirit. I'd been like that once, but it had been so long, it was nearly impossible to remember how to be that way again.

Lia shot Bree a cold glare, obviously still upset from their altercation, and Bree sighed.

"I'm heading back to the room, you can take my seat, Viv," Bree said, stifling a yawn. I took Bree's seat beside Finn, avoiding looking at him for as long as I could.

"I don't bite, Viv," he said, repeating my own words back to me that I'd said only a few days ago, though it felt like weeks. A smile tugged at my lips, while anxiety gnawed at my gut.

Say it, Viv, I chided myself. *It's fine, you can have fun.* Taking a deep breath, I spoke the words, "I might not mind if you did." A tingling sensation rushed through me, chasing away the anxiety and replacing it with excitement. They almost felt the same, but now I smiled freely and found Finn's gaze without fear.

He grinned back at me, and though there was surprise in his eyes, he didn't say anything about my change in countenance.

"I still don't trust you," I added for good measure.

"The feeling is mutual," he remarked, still grinning.

"Good." I turned my head to hide my smile.

"Good."

We sat in a content silence, until a scream ripped through the peace.

"Bree!" Lia jumped up and sprinted toward the room. The rest of us were on her heels. I pushed past everyone to Lia's side.

As we reached the room, the door remained open, but the lights were off and all that could be heard was shallow breathing broken up by small gasps.

Not Bree, not Bree, I thought repeatedly. All the women who had followed us out of Thalassia were like sisters to me, but Bree was different. Bree and I had been romantically involved when we were younger, and though we had decided we were better off friends, we'd always had a much stronger bond because of that.

Lia flicked on the lights, and I stared around the room in horror. Cole remained on the bed, but he'd shifted back into his human form before... I gulped, nausea pushing bile to my throat as I looked away from Cole's gutted form.

Finn, Jami, and Marley pushed past us, cries of outrage coming from them. I ignored them as I caught sight of Bree out of the corner of my eye, Lia crouched beside her, a hand pressed to Bree's abdomen.

I whirled to Bree and dropped down on her other side. She barely clung to life. The gasping breaths came from her. Nix and Korra watched in horror, clasping each other's hands.

"Bree," I breathed, my hands fluttering over her body as if there was some way to help her, but she'd already lost too much blood.

"It was," Bree forced out. The words sounded harsh and low. "A bat shifter. She..." Bree's eyes fluttered closed.

"No! Stay with me, Bree," I cried, cupping Bree's cheek in my hand. Lia smoothed Bree's hair on the other side, her eyes welling with tears.

Bree opened her eyes one more time. "A warning," Bree whispered, and I almost missed it. She looked straight at me. "Stay out of the water." And her eyes closed once more, never to reopen.

"No!" I refused to believe Bree was gone. "Bree, come back to me." I placed my forehead against Bree's. *She's still warm, how can she be dead?* I thought.

"Viv." Lia placed a hand on my shoulder. "She's gone." I leaned back, wiping tears from my eyes and heard a thump behind me. I turned to see Finn had fallen to his knees beside Cole's body.

"This is my fault," he said. "I should have known better than to think he was safe here."

"We all should have known better," Jami said. "Don't take the blame for this."

"It's not your fault," I said, my voice cracking. Finn and Jami both turned to look at me. Marley remained stoic by Cole's side, showing no signs of grief besides a slight scowl.

"I don't need..." Finn started but I cut him off.

"It's mine." Guilt wrapped around me, threatening to suffocate me as Bree's words rang in my ears. '*Stay out of the water.*' I had been the one to go into the water after the boy. I had been the one who faced the siren. I had been the one who *killed* the siren, even after hearing her warning.

"No, Viv, it's not," Lia said.

"I didn't tell you what happened after I went into the sea when that siren took the boy," I started. "I should have told you sooner, maybe they'd..." I choked back a sob. "Still be alive."

"What happened?" Lia asked.

At the same time, Finn demanded, "Tell us."

"I had the siren pinned to the bottom of the ocean, I'd already won, and she," I paused, cringing as if back in that moment. "She warned me that if I didn't let her go, the siren queen would come for me." My guilt deepened and shame joined it, burning my face.

"What does that have to do with this?" Finn growled and I flinched.

"I still killed her." I wrapped my arms around myself. "I'm s-"

Lia interrupted me, "Don't say it." She pointed at me before standing. "This isn't your doing. This is the siren queen's doing. You did the right thing killing that monster. You weren't the only one who went into the water either, Bree did. And I did." Tears brimmed in Lia's eyes.

"If I'd known she'd go after Cole, or Bree," I stopped, unable to finish as I fought to hold back my sobs.

"Lia's right. This isn't your fault," Finn's voice was hard. He stood and straightened himself once more before storming toward the door.

Jami blocked him, placing a hand on his chest to stop him. "Where are you going?" he asked.

"To find who did this," Finn answered, his chest heaving.

"You won't find them now," Jami argued. "You heard Bree, she said it was a bat shifter. They can hide almost anywhere."

Finn didn't respond, but he also didn't try to push past Jami.

I rocked on my heels as I stared at Bree. *Someone has to tell Molly,* I thought, a sob breaking free from my chest.

Arms wrapped around me from behind and I recognized Korra's arms as she held me tight. I leaned into her, letting myself fall apart. Nix settled in on the other side of me, while Lia paced before us.

"I never apologized for yelling at her..." she said. "I was still mad at her."

"You're going to drive yourself crazy," Nix said, and I could see her holding a hand out to Lia through the haze of my tears. "Bree knew you loved her."

"I'm going to kill whoever did this," Finn said. "They will suffer as Cole and Bree did. Marley, return to the others and bring Garrett back with you," he commanded. "Let them know what happened, and to be on their guard."

I lifted my head to watch as Marley ground her jaw, showing emotion for once, before nodding and turning to the window. She pushed it open and shifted into a hawk, flying out into the storm.

"Jami, help me with the body," Finn said, lifting the sheets from the bed and wrapping them around Cole. Jami started on the other side.

He had to pause, turning away with his hand to his mouth as he recollected himself.

"We need to take care of Bree, too," Lia said, gulping as her gaze fell on Bree again. I forced myself to look as well. "We should bring her back to the sea, so she can find peace." The sirens wouldn't touch an already dead body. They had no interest in eating anything unless it was alive. The churning waters from the storm were too difficult to manage, even underwater, for sirens and mermaids alike. But we'd do our best to ensure Bree and Cole were put to rest.

I placed my hand on my chest where grief had manifested as physical pain. Steeling myself as tears streamed

down my face, I strode to the bed Cole didn't occupy. I stripped the comforter from it and placed it out on the floor. Lia laid Bree down carefully, supporting her head as Bree's body slumped away from the wall. Once she was horizontal, Lia and I lifted her onto the comforter. Korra and Nix wrapped it around her as Jami and Finn had done with Cole.

"How do we get them out without alerting everyone in the inn?" Korra asked, tears rolling down her cheeks, though she stood tall, clearly trying to hold herself together.

"The window," Jami said, pointing to where it hung open, one of the panes wavering back and forth in the breeze from the raging storm. "We'll hoist them through the window, one at a time, and take them to the sea."

The sea. That felt fitting. Bree was born to the sea, and it was the chosen home for Cole.

"I'll get one of the horses from the stable to carry them," Finn suggested. "It's a bit of a walk to be carrying them ourselves the whole way."

Lia and I nodded in agreement. The beach was one street over from the inn, but we'd have to go around all the houses and businesses to get there. It would be much easier to have the horse carry the bodies while we walked alongside them. With the cover of night and the storm, no one else would be out or see us.

I caught myself wringing my hands as I fought to remain in one piece. It had been a long time since I'd lost anyone I cared about as much as Bree. I wasn't sure how the world kept turning without her in it, but somehow, it did. Time kept moving.

Finn and Jami stood outside the window, while Lia and I passed them the bodies from inside. Once we were all outside, Finn ran to the stables to grab a horse.

Thunder crashed overhead and we all jolted. Rain seeped into my clothes, bringing a deep chill that sunk into my bones, making me feel as though I'd never be warm again.

"Here he comes," Jami said, pointing toward Finn who pulled one of our horses behind him. "Cole first." He bent down to grasp Cole's shoulders while Lia held Cole's feet. When Finn stopped beside them, he took Lia's end and helped Jami hoist Cole onto the horse, followed by Bree. My heart broke at the sight of one of my best friends having to be hauled around like a sack of potatoes.

I couldn't tell if I was crying in the rain, but it didn't matter. Tears would do nothing to bring Bree back.

Finn

Night covered our procession to the sea. Three of us walked on each side of the horse. Wind buffeted us, trying to force us back, but we pressed on. The rain had thoroughly drenched us all, and I welcomed the discomfort.

I had failed my crew yet again. First the thirty men and women who had been devoured by the sirens, and now Cole.

What kind of captain couldn't keep his crew safe, let alone alive? *A cowardly captain, that's who,* I cursed myself. *My father was right. I'm not fit to be a pirate.*

I straightened my posture and lifted my head as lightning struck too close to my right. I didn't flinch; I stared ahead and thunder crashed. *I will avenge their deaths. I will prove my father wrong.*

The sea came into view, and we walked faster. Waves crashed unforgivingly against the rocks along the shore. I shuddered at the sight but didn't waver. I continued forward with the rest of the group.

As we reached what little was left of the beach in the storm, we tied the horse to a tree higher up. Nix and Korra carried Bree, while Jami and I carried Cole. Lia and Viv led us

all down the treacherous path littered with debris from the vicious winds.

"We'll need to tow them out far," Lia called over the storm, barely audible. "We can do that." She motioned between herself and the other mermaids.

"And Neros herself will reclaim them for the sea," Viv said, and I turned to her.

"I didn't know you believed in such things," I commented.

"When you are born of the sea, you believe in the sea goddess," she said matter-of-factly. Her eyes flicked to Lia before she added, "Usually, anyway."

Viv, Lia, Korra, and Nix waded into the water, fighting against the current and waves. Once they were out far enough, they shifted. Jami and I waded in after them, handing off Cole and Bree. Water churned around my legs and anxiety creeped in. My entire body went rigid as I forced myself to stay put. The mermaids towed Cole and Bree out, disappearing beneath the surface and dragging the bodies down with them.

It seemed eerie, watching them from the shore. But we had no other way to honor the dead without drawing attention and winding up in jail or some other sticky mess we didn't have time for.

Besides, the sea was where Cole would want his final resting place to be.

Jami and I retreated from the water and stood on the beach waiting for what seemed like hours, until finally, the mermaids resurfaced.

They swam to shore, shifting before reaching it, and trudged back onto land, their faces solemn.

"It is done. They can now find peace," Lia said, walking past me without looking back. Viv, Nix, and Korra all followed her, their heads hanging.

I rested my hand on Jami's shoulder. "That's it then," I said. "There's no more we can do for him." Jami tore his eyes from the sea and let me lead him back to the horse which the mermaids had left behind. I grabbed the reins and followed in their footsteps.

Back at the inn, the mermaids dried themselves with their magic and did the same for Jami and me, since we were already in our spare clothes. It left them all drained, but they had insisted.

I finished washing the clothes Jami had left to soak in the tub, hesitating when I held Bree and Cole's clothing.

I pulled them out, unsure whether we should keep them for ourselves or not. Without thinking too much about it, I shoved the clothes into the trash, not wanting to be reminded of this day anytime any of us wore the clothes.

By the time I finished and hung everything to dry, everyone else had already made the beds with new sheets, and settled in. Lia, Viv, Korra, and Nix had somehow all fit onto one bed, huddling together as they comforted one another. Jami lay alone in the other bed, facing the window.

Laying down beside Jami, my side pressed against his back. Neither of us spoke, but we didn't need to. Just as the mermaids gained solace from each other's company, so did we. So long as we had one another, we'd make it through.

I kept watch that night, unable to fully relax knowing Cole and Bree's murderer was still out there. We'd locked the window and door, but that hadn't kept the shifter out before. If the bat shifter returned, I'd be ready for them.

The storm had passed by the time morning came around, and we were able to get back on the road. We maintained a comfortable silence as we left the unnamed town that, even if I had known the name of it, I'd never want to remember.

The longer we rode in silence, the more it seemed like we'd collectively decided on making the day into a silent vigil for Cole and Bree. When we stopped for the night, camping on the beach once more, we used few words.

Come morning, things started to go back to normal, if you could call it that, in an attempt to not lose sight of our task. As much as we wanted to continue grieving the loss of our friends, the siren queen was out there and if we didn't take her down soon, more people would die. Not to mention all the trade that had been halted because of the attacks.

Jami and Lia resumed their flirting, Nix and Korra chatted animatedly about some bakery they knew was in the next town we'd come to, and Viv... Well Viv remained her ever stoic and hard to read self. She had seemed the most broken up about Bree's death, so it made sense she wouldn't be as quick to bounce back.

I rode at the back of the group, keeping an eye out for any signs of a bat following us. It would be nearly impossible to spot, with all the trees that lined the road, but I wouldn't let my guard down again.

That night, Marley and Garrett caught up with us as we settled on the beach. Garrett was also a hawk shifter, so they'd been able to make great time. If we were all able to shift into forms that could travel as fast as hawks or a lion, we'd be in Asmara already.

They landed in the sand, shifting and striding up to me.

"Captain," Garrett greeted me. "Cole was a good man."

I dipped my head in respect for my friend. "He was. But we need to focus on our main goal, which is taking out the siren queen. You're here to help ensure the rest of us make it to Asmara safely so we can do just that," I spoke with the authority I felt I no longer deserved but would fight to earn once more.

I removed Cole's sword from the side of the saddle where I'd strapped it.

"You can have Cole's weapons and his horse. Marley, your weapons are here," I said, pointing to where I'd strapped them to my saddlebag. We'd kept Cole's horse so Garrett would be able to ride with us, but we'd sold Bree's before leaving the last town. Though I'd thrown away Cole's clothes, I kept his weapons knowing Garrett would need them. Magicked weapons that could shift with shifters were far more expensive than magicked clothes, so only me and a few other of my crew were afforded that luxury. Everyone else had to carry theirs in their shifted form or be careful to remember where they'd left them.

Jami had started a fire, and everyone gathered around it, welcoming Marley back and giving a round of introductions for Garrett.

"He'll be a sorry replacement for Cole, but he'll do his best, right, Garrett?" Marley joked, her humor ill-timed, as always. I laughed though no one else did.

"He will at that," I agreed. "If you'll excuse me." I dipped my head to them, stepping away from the fire and heading for the edge of the water. I stopped before I reached it and couldn't make myself go any closer.

My blood thickened as I stared at the sea, and the sirens screams echoed in my mind as if they truly surrounded me again. In my peripheral, I noticed someone step up beside me, silencing the memory.

Turning my head to the newcomer, I blinked in surprise to find Viv there, staring out over the water. I watched her for a moment, waiting for her to speak first, but she remained quiet, her hands clasped before her.

If I wanted to talk with her, I was going to need to start the conversation, but I was wary of her response. Most of the time she was cold toward me or annoyed at my presence. Now, it seemed she had sought me out. Why else would she have come to stand beside me when there was a whole stretch of beach she could have occupied far enough away that I wouldn't try to interact with her?

Inhaling deep, I decided to take another chance. "I've always loved the sea best at night," I said. It was true, even now, when my body seemed to be repulsed by the thought of the sea, it was less so at night. I could almost imagine being back on the water, sailing over the glory of the stars reflected beneath us.

"As have I," she responded, and I bit my lip as I tried to hide my smile.

The emotions Viv could stir in me confused and enticed me. I'd never met anyone quite like her, yet she seemed so familiar every time I talked with her, like I'd known her my whole life. It made every time she pushed me away that much more frustrating. I understood why she was so distrusting of me, of people in general, because of her past that she'd yet to reveal to me, but it didn't help quell the whiplash every time I thought I'd made progress with her only to be shut down again.

"You're overthinking something," Viv sounded amused, and I thought I saw the hint of a smile tugging on her lips.

"Oh yeah?" I returned my gaze to the sea.

"Yeah. I can smell the wheels turning from here," she joked.

I laughed out loud, surprising Viv, and pulling out her real smile. The sight made the butterflies in my stomach go haywire and hope swelled in my chest.

"You're right. I'm always overthinking something. If I don't do it, though, no one in my crew will," I admitted. "They'd starve if I didn't tell them to eat, always choosing the cost of whiskey or rum over food."

"You're a better captain than most pirate captains I've met," Viv said, her eyes locking on mine. "None of them cared nearly as much about their crew as you do."

"I didn't become a pirate solely for the gold and jewels," I said, and Viv's brow rose in question. "Growing up, I used to watch pirates at the port near our town. I envied their camaraderie with one another, and their freedom. They were never tied down to one place, always heading for the next treasure grab, or to the next port."

"For some reason I can't imagine you as a child," Viv mused, releasing my gaze, and leaving me wanting more of her attention.

I cleared my throat. "Imagine me now, just without the beard, long hair, muscles, and probably... two feet shorter," I joked, but Viv only smiled. It had been days since I'd last heard her laugh and I yearned for it, the sound like hearing the birds finally after a long voyage over the sea.

"I'm trying, and it's not a pretty sight," she said, her shoulders shaking as she held back a laugh.

"Fair enough." I contemplated "What about you? It's been much longer since you were a child, has it not?" I'd tried to figure out how old she was before, but she'd been cryptic. I hoped she'd enlighten me now.

"It has," she agreed. "One of the few things mermaids share with sirens is our lifespan."

I pursed my lips. I'd heard that mermaids shifted forms were sirens, but they were so far from it, I wasn't sure it was true. Not only were sirens much more bloodthirsty, but sirens also had black eyes, and their scales continued all the way to their jaw line, while mermaids' scales stopped beneath their breastbone.

"So, there are more characteristics you share with them, then?" I decided to come out and ask. "Are sirens considered your shifted form?"

"We've spent our entire existence trying to separate ourselves from the sirens," Viv sighed. "But yes. As a lion is yours, a hawk Marley's, we also shift into a preexisting creature; the siren."

I didn't pretend to be surprised. It wasn't a big leap to make, and most everyone assumed it to be true anyway. Otherwise, how else would mermaids exist? A failed shifter who was supposed to have been a fish? It was possible, but unheard of and a bit ridiculous.

"It's why we've had such a hard time convincing the world we're not sirens, nor are we like them. We are more human than siren, just as you are more human than lion." She moved in place, digging her boots into the sand. "We share their long lifespan, their telekinesis underwater, the tail of course, their strength, and we can grow the talons in our mer form."

"How long *do* sirens live?" I asked. Lia had mentioned before that the siren queen's power was fading because of her age, but she hadn't mentioned how long that had taken.

"Upwards of a thousand years, if no one kills them before then. The siren queen herself is older than that, but she eats human hearts to stay young."

I reared back at that. "What?" I'd heard horror stories when I was little that sirens would steal men from their ships,

dragging them beneath the surface and eating them, but I'd never heard about the siren queen eating their *hearts.*

That seemed more disturbing to me than fully consuming the men.

"The sirens aren't allowed to eat the hearts of the bodies they drag beneath the surface. They are duty bound to bring those to the queen so she may consume any magic which remains in the hearts," Viv explained, scowling as she spoke.

"But not all humans have magic," I pointed out.

"Not all humans *wield* magic. All humans are capable of magic, to some degree, but most never bother trying to figure out how to use it."

I glanced at Jami who sat beside the fire, gazing down at Lia whose head lay in his lap while she gazed up at him. *If Jami could wield magic,* I thought, but then shook my head. There was no telling how difficult it would be to learn how to use magic or figure out how much he could wield.

"He has magic, too," Viv said. I glanced at her to see she had followed my gaze and looked at Jami now. "Lia or I could try to teach him how to utilize it."

"That's a decision for him to make." I turned back to the water. "I'll talk to him about it, though. He may be interested." I doubted it. Jami had accepted that he wasn't a shifter, though his entire family was, and he never seemed to resent that. I couldn't imagine Jami wanting anything to do with using magic after so many years of coming to terms with life without it.

"It's a bit cold," Viv remarked. "I'm going to rejoin the group." She offered me a pat on the shoulder as she walked by me, and the pressure of it lingered. It wasn't until she was by the fire that I realized she still hadn't answered my question about her age.

Lia

My eyes fluttered open the next morning, a sense of unease prickling my spine. Rolling my shoulders, I tried to shake it off, but the feeling clung to me. Everyone slept soundly in the sand around me.

I'd been plagued with dreams and nightmares about Bree. I hadn't apologized for yelling at her after she'd gone into the sea, and I'd never be able to change that. A hard knot formed in my stomach.

Scanning the beach, my eyes locked on a piece of driftwood about a hundred yards away. Staring back at me atop the log were two, unblinking, bat eyes.

"*Fuck,*" I gasped and jumped to my feet, waking several of the group. They rubbed the sleep from their eyes as I scanned everyone for blood or injuries. No one seemed harmed. When I looked back to the driftwood, the bat was gone.

"Lia?" Viv yawned and stretched her arms above her head. She scanned the beach. "What is it?"

"I, uh - nothing. It's nothing. A bad dream," I lied. There was no reason to alarm everyone. We were being

watched, but we could have guessed that after what happened to Cole and Bree.

Korra kept watch, but she was further down the beach, sitting on a rock and looking out at the ocean. She hadn't seen the bat.

"We should get going," Jami grumbled, still waking up. He shook Finn's shoulder; he'd slept through the commotion. My gaze softened on Jami for a moment before I hurried to reattach my pack to my saddle.

Only when we were back on the road did my heart rate normalize again. I kept looking over my shoulder to make sure we weren't being followed, but even though I saw nothing, I knew we were. The siren queen was watching us.

"Hey," Jami said as his horse became parallel with mine. "You seem on edge this morning."

"Yeah, bad dream," I repeated the lie, but Jami narrowed his eyes at me. I cast my eyes down to the dirt road beneath us, watching the mini dust clouds puff up with each step of the horse.

"I don't believe that. You're not one to let a dream weigh you down for long," Jami said, and I stared at him with wonder. He already felt he knew me well enough to make that assumption, and to my surprise, he wasn't wrong.

"You're right," I admitted. "I didn't want to tell anyone, but when I woke up there was a bat watching us."

"A bat?" Jami repeated and I nodded. "Could it not have been a normal bat?"

"When was the last time you saw a normal bat sitting on a log on the beach in the morning?" I asked, exasperated.

"Well, never, but I could say that about a lot of things. I've never seen a wolf chasing a sheep, but that doesn't mean it doesn't happen."

"Stop trying to make me sound crazy," I hissed, my blood heating.

Jami placed his hand on his chest. "I don't think you're crazy, Lia. I never meant to imply that, and I'm sorry it came off that way. I only wanted to help you feel better about seeing a bat."

"Not a bat, a bat *shifter. The* bat shifter. The one who killed Bree and Cole!" My voice rose and I knew everyone had heard me. Taking a deep breath, I closed my eyes and tried to calm myself, focusing on the movement of the horse beneath me and my sore muscles.

"I know, I'm sorry."

"You're only sorry because I reacted. If I hadn't, you'd continue going on about wolves and sheep and other obvious metaphors." I ground my jaw in frustration.

"It wasn't a metaphor," Jami said, and I whipped my head toward him. "Shit, right, not the point." He put one hand up in surrender.

"You're infuriating," I said, pulling on the reins to slow my horse and ride alongside Nix instead. Finn joined Jami at the front, and I was grateful I couldn't hear what they were saying. *Probably talking about how crazy I am,* I thought.

"What was that all about?" Nix asked, pulling my gaze from Finn and Jami.

"I saw the bat shifter on the beach this morning," I told her. They'd all heard me yelling about it now, anyway.

Nix, true to her less expressive nature, remained calm. "She didn't hurt any of us, though" she said.

"Right. Not yet. I think she's just watching us right now, for the siren queen." Speaking the words aloud caused dread to pool in my gut.

"That means the shifter is probably close." Nix flicked her eyes to our surroundings as she spoke, scanning the area. "That means we can find and kill her."

I hated the idea of killing others, but the bat shifter had killed our friends. If anyone deserved death, it was her. And if anyone could find the bat shifter, it was Nix.

"I'll find her," Nix confirmed my thought. "And I'll deliver her to you."

"I don't want you putting yourself at risk to find this shifter," I countered, knowing the danger if the shifter realized she was being hunted. Nix's father had been a member of my father's special guard and had trained her from when she was young. Thalassia might not have an army, but the special guard would come the closest to that. They were spies for the king who kept an eye on the different kingdoms on land. He wanted to be sure that no one ever did anything without him knowing despite the barrier between our world and theirs.

"Don't worry, Princess." Nix winked. "I'll be fine."

I cringed at the title. I hadn't told any of Finn's crew other than Jami the truth about that yet, and I hadn't planned on it. Being the princess of Thalassia meant little out of the water.

"The next time we make a stop, I'll take a walk," Nix said, lowering her voice. "We can't make it obvious if the shifter really is watching us."

"Okay. I'll make sure no one follows you." I gulped down my fear. "But if you're gone too long, I'm coming after you."

That night, I called everyone to a halt earlier than usual. The sun hadn't set. I wanted to give Nix a chance to search for the shifter with some daylight.

"We should camp under the cover of the trees tonight," I said, pointing to the skies which had clouded over. "They'll help protect us from the rain."

Our group headed into the forest and found a nice spot where the tree branches connected overhead and formed a shield from the rain. It wouldn't keep all the raindrops out, but it would help. Once we were settled, Nix stood, stretching as she did.

"I'm going to take a walk," she said, striding deeper into the forest.

"Maybe I should..." Korra started but I interrupted her.

"Korra, could you help me with the fire? I want to heat up some of this food." I picked up a few sticks and placed them where I wanted the fire.

Korra glanced once more in the direction Nix had disappeared and joined me in building a fire. Once we had it going, it was too late for Korra to go after Nix. She'd be hard pressed to find her.

I shared the food with everyone, even though a part of me wanted to deny Jami any because I was still upset with him. He could think I was crazy all he wanted; I knew I was right.

"Lia," his voice caught me off guard as he came up behind me.

"Yes?" I drew the word out, turning toward him slowly.

He reached out to take my hand and I let him, curious where he was headed with the gesture.

"You're not crazy," he started, and I pursed my lips to hide my smile. He wouldn't win me over that easily. "The bat was most likely the shifter. I'm the crazy one for thinking it wasn't, when we already know there's a bat shifter who is apparently out for our blood."

"Mhmm," I murmured, nodding my head for him to go on.

"I never want you to think that you can't trust me or talk to me about anything. You can, and I'll prove it to you if I have to," he said, smirking.

I bit my lip, considering everything I could have him do to prove that, but I wasn't the kind of woman to torture a man needlessly.

"I forgive you," I said, taking a step toward him and closing the gap between us. His breathing hitched. I smiled and trailed my tongue along my top lip, delighting in how his eyes became hooded as he watched.

As much as I wanted to act on the desire blooming in me, my worry over Nix won out and I stopped myself. I gave Jami a chaste kiss on the cheek and said, "I have plans for you for later."

Turning away from him, he grabbed my hand.

"You can't just say that and walk away," he said.

Looking at him over my shoulder I responded, "I can, and I will."

A branch snapping to my left drowned out his groan. My breathing hitched. *Nix?* I wondered, before seeing a bird flying up through the trees.

I needed something to keep me distracted while I waited for Nix's return. Jami would have been the perfect distraction, but I didn't want to use him like that.

He strode past me toward where everyone sat around the fire we'd built, brushing my arm, and raising goosebumps there. His glance back and half-grin told me it was deliberate.

Rain drops pattered against the leaves above us and a few dripped down on my upturned face, making me smile.

"Nix has been gone awhile, should we be worried?" Korra asked from where she sat on a log.

"Not yet," I said, dropping my gaze to her. It wasn't fair that we now had to fear for our lives on land as well as in the water. Bree should be here with us now, and I would do whatever it took to ensure that her death was avenged.

"I'd hazard to guess you're keeping something from us again," Finn commented.

Glancing around, I placed a finger to my lips before pointing to the trees above us. No one else said anything, so I think they got the hint. I sat down on one of the logs that had been pulled over, right beside Jami. Our thighs pressed against each other, and my entire body heated.

"I never minded the rain much on the ship," Marley said, breaking the silence. "But out here, it sucks." She lifted an arm, showing off the damp, sagging fabric of her sleeve.

"That's because you got used to being dry while we've been on land," Garrett said, poking her sleeve.

"I agree," I said. "There's something more irritating about being wet on land, versus when you're constantly wet in or on the water."

Jami lowered his mouth to my ear, talking low enough so only I heard. "Speaking of being wet."

Pursing my lips, I tried and failed to hide my grin as I stared at the fire burning low from the increasing rain.

I would be forever grateful that shifters could only smell arousal in their shifted animal forms otherwise this fireside chat would become very awkward very quickly.

A crash sounded behind me and everyone turned to look as Nix and another woman tumbled into our little clearing. They grappled with one another, stirring up the leaves and dirt,

but Nix wound up on top, pinning the woman face down in the dirt, her knife against the woman's throat.

"Who is that?" Marley asked from where she sat by the fire. She seemed indifferent to the fact that Nix held a woman captive right beside her. It was a bit off-putting, but I realized Marley wasn't one to show emotions. Ever.

"Our bat shifter, that's who," Nix hissed. "I've been tailing her for hours. I saw her transform from her bat form," She pulled the woman's head back even further by her hair. Finn, Viv, Korra, and Garrett all stood by, watching intently.

"Sorry to break up the party," the woman sneered, her voice strained.

"You shut up," Nix growled, pressing her knife harder against her throat. Blood welled up beneath it, dripping down the woman's neck. "Try to transform again, and I'll cut off your wings."

"What's your name?" I asked, stepping up to interrogate the woman. Jami stayed a step behind me.

Nix pulled the woman to her knees, keeping her tight in her grasp.

"You can call me Veera," the woman said, a giggle escaping her.

"But that's not your real name," I pointed out, noting her choice of words.

Veera licked her lips. "Doesn't matter, does it? You have something to call me, that's all a name is."

I couldn't argue with that. "Fine. Veera, did the siren queen send you?"

Squirming in Nix's grasp, Veera seemed uncomfortable at the mention of the siren queen.

"Why did you kill Cole and Bree?" I tried a different question.

"I was only supposed to kill one, but he got in the way, saw me outside," Veera said with a pout. "The mermaid was my target. The mermaids need to stay out of the water."

Digging my nails into my palms I tried to keep myself from lashing out. Narrowing my eyes at Veera, I asked, "Why?" Veera squirmed again. "*Why, Veera?*" I repeated.

"Stay out of the water!" Veera screeched.

"The siren queen sent you then," I said, taking another step toward Veera.

"She must be bound not to speak of the queen at all," Viv said. I turned to her, noticing how close she and Finn stood to one another, their hands almost touching where they hung at their sides.

I shook my head. "But why kill Bree? If it was retaliation against Viv for killing that siren, or a warning for me to stay out of her way..." Lia ran a hand through her hair, brushing the dirt from it. "Unless she *did* talk with one of the sirens when she disobeyed me and went into the water."

"I won't say." Veera sang the words.

"Why Cole? We learned of your presence because you killed them!" Finn growled and stepped forward, away from Viv's side. I watched him intently.

"He was easy," Veera sneered. "I caught him alone and off guard *twice!*"

My gut clenched as I saw the regret on Finn's face. We'd left Cole alone in the room thinking he was safe inside the inn, but we'd been wrong. He died because we'd been careless.

Finn lunged toward Veera, but I stepped into his path. Jami grabbed Finn's arms and held him back so he wouldn't try to push past me.

"Kill the bitch," Finn snarled. "She won't tell us anything useful."

Veera cackled, choking halfway through as Nix continued to hold her head back at that awkward angle.

"I'll let him kill you if you don't tell us something useful about the siren queen," I said, looking down at Veera.

"If you don't kill me, *she* will!" Veera's laugh sent chills down my spine. Blood ran freely down Veera's neck as she kept pressing harder against the knife as if she meant to slit her own throat.

"Then why protect her secrets?" I asked.

"What makes you think I know any of her secrets?" Veera countered. "I'm a little birdie, just like you! A pawn."

"Kill her," I said flatly, turning to Finn. As I walked past Jami, I saw the emptiness I felt reflected in his eyes. It wasn't Veera's death I craved, it was the siren queen's. As Veera said, she was only a pawn.

Releasing Finn's arms, Jami stepped back, and I watched as Finn prowled forward.

Finn

I pulled a dagger from my bandolier. My gun would have made this death too quick, and this monster didn't deserve mercy.

Veera sneered up at me. "You should have heard him squeal when I gutted him. But you couldn't. Not even when he cried out for his captain to save him." Her eyes lit with amusement as she laughed, and I slammed my dagger down into her thigh.

Her laughter cut off as she screeched in pain.

"Maybe I'll gut you like you did him," I growled, dragging my dagger back out slowly. The hatred in her eyes only spurred my anger.

Nix seemed content to hold Veera in place while I dragged out her death, but Jami stepped up to my side.

"Finn," he said, putting a hand on my shoulder. "Now's not the time."

I blinked up at him. He'd never stopped me from carrying out my acts of violence before, but as I looked past him, to the mermaids, I realized what he meant. Lia, Viv, and Korra were all leaning on one another, not looking my way. They had already moved on from Veera.

"What happened, Captain?" Veera asked. "Lose your nerve?"

Turning back to her, I didn't hesitate as I drove my dagger straight into her heart. Her laughter died out as the light left her eyes and she slumped back against Nix who released her, dropping her to the ground.

Jami

"Well, that was anti-climactic," Marley commented. "What are we doing with the body?"

Everyone else had scattered.

Rain drops broke through the leaves above us and dripped into my hair.

"I'll bury her," Nix offered, leaning down to pick Veera up by the arms.

Marley hopped to her feet and without a word, helped Nix carry the body away. It didn't erase Veera's words which hung in the camp, souring the atmosphere, and turning my stomach. *You should have heard him squeal...* I shook my head. Veera had gutted Cole alive. Or she'd lied.

I scanned the camp, looking for Lia, but she wasn't there. Neither was Viv or Korra, so I assumed she'd gone off with them. Finn had stormed off on his own, so Garrett was the only one who remained in the camp with me.

I sat beside him, and we waited in silence until the others returned. Marley and Nix were the first ones back, and they chatted animatedly, or as animatedly as either of them could, seeing as they were both particularly stoic individuals. It seemed fitting they'd find something to bond over and that it would be

something as dark as burying a body. Since we had no shovels, they'd have to improvise, but I didn't want to think about that.

Finn returned next, curling up on his blanket and ignoring the rest of us. We followed Finn's example and tried to sleep. I wanted to stay awake until Lia returned with the others, but I wasn't sure when that would be. It was hard to fall asleep with the rain coming down harder and more drops breaking through the treetops, but I managed it for a few hours.

When I woke, Lia was curled against me, sound asleep. It was dark, and the rain had stopped, but everything was still damp. I yearned to stand and shake off the excess water, but I didn't want to disturb Lia.

Picking my head up to scan the camp, I noticed the fire had been completely doused by the rain, but someone sat beside it. I squinted, and as my eyes adjusted to the dark, I recognized Viv.

"What are you doing awake?" I asked, trying to keep my voice down so as not to wake anyone else.

"We decided we should have someone on watch, in case there's someone else following us," she explained. "I just traded off with Korra. That's probably what woke you, sorry."

"Don't be," I scoffed.

"I told you so, by the way," Viv said, amusement coloring her tone.

"What?" I asked. I wished I could see her better so I could read her body language.

"I told you Lia liked you," she clarified, and I laughed.

Lia stirred against me, a soft murmur coming from her lips. I froze, waiting for her breathing to deepen again before saying anything more to Viv.

"Now I guess we'll see how long it will last," I said. My heart clenched at the idea of her walking away from me, but if she chose that, I'd let her go.

"She's different with you," Viv commented. "She's more herself. With almost every other person she's been with, she seemed to change. Like she was absorbing their personality or something. But, so far, she hasn't done that."

"I guess that's a good thing?" I tried, unsure what Viv wanted me to say.

"I'll still have a close eye on you," Viv warned, though I could have sworn she was smiling, but the damned darkness cloaked it from me.

"Fair enough." I settled back down, putting my arm around Lia, and closed my eyes.

When I opened them again, sunlight streamed down on us through the trees. Lia stood above me with her hands on her hips.

"Are you *still* sleeping?" she chided, making me laugh. She held her hand out and helped me up. Before she could walk away, I pulled her in close, kissing her. She let out a little moan of surprise, before her arms wound around my neck, dragging me down and deepening the kiss.

"We're not waiting for you to finish whatever this is," Nix said from atop her horse. My eyes found hers and heat crept into my cheeks as I released Lia from my grip.

"No need to wait, we can catch up," Lia said, winking at me and causing the heat to turn to fire in my veins.

"We're leaving, Lia. Come on," Viv said, grabbing Lia's arm and leading her toward her horse. "We have to make up for the hours we lost yesterday."

"Right," Lia grumbled, glancing back at me with longing in her eyes. I blew her a kiss and she pretended to catch it.

Viv rolled her eyes. "You act as if you're not going to be spending every waking hour together for another week."

"You're only jealous, Viv," Lia joked. "You can have a kiss too." She stretched up and kissed Viv's cheek.

"That's what it was," Viv said, shaking her head as she smiled.

I mounted my horse, and we exited the forest. It was almost like entering another world as we stepped back out onto the road. The beach seemed so calm and peaceful, in direct contrast to our night spent among the trees. If I had to guess, I'd say we wouldn't be spending another night in a forest if it could be helped. The memory of Veera had been burned too harshly into each of our minds to return to the forest anytime soon.

Viv

The ocean roiled as we rode alongside it. Thankfully, the road inclined so we were getting further away as a cliff formed and separated us from the angry sea. A part of me thought it may somehow be the siren queen's doing, since we killed her spy, but even she couldn't control the ocean like that.

At some point, when we'd slowed down for a few minutes, Finn wound up riding beside me at the back of the group. I had no idea what to say to him after watching him kill Veera the night before. It wasn't as if none of us would have done the same, but it did make me think there was more truth to all those stories I'd been told about him.

We rode in uncomfortable silence for a while, until Lia dropped back from the front and popped our bubble. I sighed in relief as the weight lifted and my anxiety eased.

"We should come to the town of Druin by nightfall, so we can stay in an inn tonight," Lia told us, her tone cheerful, though she shot me a look of concern. She'd known I was uncomfortable and that was the only reason she'd left Jami to join us.

Guilt gnawed at my stomach, turning it, and chasing away my appetite. Lia always had to come to my rescue, and I was

growing tired of it. I'd once been as fearsome as Nix, and as carefree as Lia. In the water, I still could be, but out of the water...

The closer we came to Asmara, the worse my anxiety became. It had been a while since I'd felt so helpless, and I *hated* it.

"That sounds great," Finn commented, his shoulders relaxing in Lia's presence.

"Finn, can I talk with Lia in private for a moment?" I asked, catching him off guard. I'd been quiet for so long he must have assumed I wasn't talking to him today. He respected my wish, though, and left us.

"Is everything alright?" Lia asked.

"Not right now, but I want it to be. And I need your help," I admitted. This would hopefully be the last time I needed Lia's help in this department.

Lia's eyes lit with intrigue. "Oh?"

"I want to try this whole romance thing," I cringed as I said it, but I pushed on. "With Finn. I think."

Lia laughed giddily and nearly fell off her horse. "That's amazing, Viv! Did you want my advice?"

"Yes, but I'm not going to try anything on Finn yet. When we're in town tonight, I want to practice. On someone else." I didn't want my first swing at flirting and romance to be with Finn in case I'd lost all my skills and was horrible at it and ruined everything. If I tried it with someone else first, maybe I could work out the kinks. And maybe I could learn to drown out my inner voice by then.

"You know, I don't think you really *need* to do that," Lia said. "But I'll help you. Give me your best pick up line." She crossed her arms over her chest, giving me an appraising look as she waited.

"Uh- I- I don't know any. I don't remember any, I guess," I groaned. "I used to be so good at this." I slapped the heel of my palm to my forehead.

"Not a problem! You don't need pick up lines, you're hot," she said with a wink. "All you need is confidence."

"I have none right now," I reminded her. "That's why I came to you."

"You don't need *real* confidence. You fake it 'til you make it!" Lia grinned.

"That sounds like a load of bullshit," I said. "But I'll do my best."

A statue of Neros greeted us as we entered the spread-out town of Druin. It had a more refreshing middle of the country feel as opposed to a coastal town.

I paused beside the statue of Neros, saying a quick prayer for safe travel as we passed by it. Lia ignored it, as expected. I sighed. There was no swaying her mind when it came to the goddesses. She'd determined they'd abandoned us, and she was hell bent on saving the world herself.

When we arrived at the inn, there were plenty of rooms for us each to have our own, but we paired off in twos. We'd all have a bed to sleep on for once.

"And our own bathrooms?" Nix's voice carried out to where Lia and I stood in the hall. "This is a dream."

"We're grabbing drinks, Nix, so hurry up or get left behind!" Korra called back into the room to her. Nix was at her side in an instant.

"I'd never miss out on that," she joked, though it was a fact. "Where are we headed?"

"The innkeeper said there's a bar right next to the ocean, about a ten-minute walk from here," Lia said.

Finn walked up beside me. He stood so close I could feel his body heat and I didn't dare turn to look at him for fear he'd see my intentions in my eyes. "Ready to go," he said.

"Took you long enough," Lia commented, turning to Jami who had come up behind her. She wound her arms around his neck and his hands landed on her waist.

"Get a room," Marley called from down the hall where she walked toward us.

"Gladly," Lia said before turning back to our group. "I guess we can head out." She and Jami led the way, walking hand in hand. The rest of us followed.

Outside, Finn stayed beside me, and I wasn't sure how to be around him now that my feelings for him had shifted.

I heard an owl somewhere in the distance. Otherwise, it seemed quiet. A soft breeze permeated the trees that created a U around the inn and rustled the leaves around us. Sweat beaded at my hairline from the warm air, and I yearned for a cooler climate. As soon as we took down the siren queen, I'd be heading straight for Sylvane. I briefly wondered if Finn would want to visit his home but pushed that thought aside.

Before either of us could say anything, Marley appeared on his other side.

"Bets are placed, Cap," she said.

I furrowed my brow. "Bets?" I asked.

"On whether anyone will recognize Finn at the bar," Marley clarified. "We also threw in whether it would be another woman trying to seduce you," she chuckled.

I tried to fake a laugh, but it came out too soft and high pitched. Neither of them said anything, but Finn turned his head slightly in my direction, casting his gaze at me for a moment.

"Do women do that often?" I asked, trying to shift the focus back to Finn.

"Almost every time we go out. We've learned not to expect the captain home by curfew," Marley teased and poked Finn's shoulder.

"Thank you for sharing, Marley," Finn said through gritted teeth. "Now go back to the others and tell them the bet is *off*."

Marley laughed, "Yeah, I'll get right on that." She left us alone and returned to Garrett's side. They both laughed about something, and I assumed it was at Finn's expense.

"Sorry about that. Marley doesn't quite know how to keep her mouth shut," Finn said.

"It's nothing I haven't heard in stories before," I pointed out. "Being a well-known pirate comes with some perks, I guess." *Perk number one: getting any woman or man you want,* I thought.

"It's not always a good thing to be recognized. Not everyone harbors good will toward me," he said.

"I can't understand why," I drawled, fighting my grin. "Must be something to do with all those stories I've heard."

"You keep bringing up those stories as if you want to hear them firsthand," Finn mused. "If you want to hear them, all you have to do is ask." He clasped his hands behind his back, and as he did, his muscles flexed. The tie-front shirt he wore did nothing to hide them and I knew he noticed my staring.

Tearing my gaze from him, I watched the road ahead of us. The cobblestoned street was worn down enough that it wasn't as precarious to navigate as it may have once been.

"What about the man you tore in half? I'd *love* to hear all about that story," I said, cocking my head. "Or was that one an intimidation tactic?"

Finn sucked in a breath as he ran his tongue along his bottom teeth. "There was more to that story than I may have let

on," he admitted with a low laugh. "Might have been less of tearing in half, than ripping off an arm."

I stopped walking. "An arm? You ripped someone's *arm* off?" I gaped at him before doubling over and bursting out laughing.

Finn paused beside me. "I've never known someone to laugh at that story," he said. "Besides Marley, of course."

"I'm sorry," I gasped, trying to catch my breath, and straightened. "I shouldn't laugh, but it does seem a little ridiculous."

"I was drunk, and he deserved it," Finn said.

We continued walking, now far behind the others.

"I'm not intimidated by you, you know," I said after a few moments of silence. Finn raised his brow. "I've been around long enough to know that any person who claims to be the most fearsome, or powerful, or what have you, tends to have a good reason for becoming that person. Whether it's warranted or not, I don't let titles scare me away."

"Normally that would be disappointing, but," he paused as we reached the door to the bar. "I'm more interested in finding out where this will lead." Before I could respond, he opened the door and the sounds from the bar poured out.

Inside, there was a bar along the right wall, which connected to a small dance floor, and beyond that there were tables filled with townsfolk. Some people played cards at their tables, while others simply drank and talked loudly. I could barely hear myself think in the place.

Our group had waited for us inside the door.

"We'll get the drinks; you all get a table!" Lia called to us over the noise. She and Jami broke away toward the bar. I stood rooted to my spot as the rest of our group headed for one of the only empty tables in the place.

After hearing Marley talk about how women threw themselves at Finn, I decided I *definitely* needed to practice before trying to do the same. Not that I'd throw myself at him; no man deserved all of me without giving some effort in return.

I scanned the room, trying to find someone I wouldn't mind flirting with. There were plenty of men and women in the place, but Lia had instructed me to choose someone who reminded me of Finn because it would make it a more realistic trial run.

At the bar, there was a man sitting alone who caught my eye. He had shorter hair than Finn, but the same build and similar features. Not as attractive to me, but he would do.

Isn't this how we met? Humer's voice in my mind made me pause, but I wouldn't let him get to me. Not this time. If I could overcome my fear of putting myself out there, I could make sure I wouldn't keep pushing Finn away. I *needed* this to go well.

Rolling my shoulders and puffing up my chest, I strolled toward the bar. *Don't seem too eager,* Lia had warned. *Play it cool, and sexy.* That was easy for her to say, she'd snagged Jami by drinking his spit. I shuddered at that and laughed to myself, wishing I'd been there to see the look on Jami's face. That wasn't entirely true, Jami had fallen for Lia the second he laid eyes on her.

Sliding onto the stool beside the man, I flicked my gaze toward him to find he was already looking at me, a grin pulling at his lips. *Too easy,* I thought, my old self taking control as I smiled coyly at him.

Finn

I slammed my mug on the table, ale sloshing over the rim. Lia sat in Jami's lap across from me and played with his hair as she laughed at something he said.

I scanned the room once more, lingering on Viv at the bar. A smile lit her face, and jealousy that I wasn't the one causing it hit me like a wave. Lifting my mug to my lips, I chugged down the rest of my ale.

"We've got all night," Jami said, slapping his hand on the table to get my attention. I stared at him for a moment, and he stared right back, unwavering under my gaze. Jami never did back down when it came to me.

I pushed back from the table, my chair scraping across the floor and turning a few heads in my direction.

Without a word, I walked over to the bar and flagged down the bartender.

"Another ale," I yelled over the din.

While I waited, I kept my eyes trained on the bar, tracing the whorls in the wood with my pinky. Viv's laugh reached me, and my head snapped up. I'd never heard her laugh like that.

What is wrong with you? I thought, shaking my head. *She obviously has no interest in you. You've done nothing to help that, either.*

I watched Viv for a moment. She touched the man's arm and he put his hand over hers. Viv winced, but she recovered quickly. *What was that?* I wondered, tempted to go over, and ask her, but she seemed fine now.

"Here 'ya are," the bartender said, sliding a new mug filled with ale over to me. Taking it with a grateful nod to the man, I drank greedily from the mug. "I'll be taking payment up front tonight. Don't need pirates thinking they can pull one over on me," he said, and I rolled my eyes. Of course he'd recognized me.

Handing over a sack of coins, I caught his wrist as he reached for it. "This will cover us all for the night," I said. "And if you breathe a word of who we are to anyone else in here, I'll make sure it's the last word you speak."

The bartender narrowed his gaze on me, but he snatched the bag of coins.

I honestly didn't care who knew who we were, I just didn't want Marley to win her bet.

I strolled back to the table and Lia nearly bumped into me as she jumped up, not noticing me or not caring I was there.

"Come on," she said, tugging Jami's hand. "I want to dance."

I watched, half expecting Jami to refuse. He had never been one for dancing, though I'd pulled him onto the dance floor more than once in Asmara. People always assumed it would be the other way around, but I didn't mind dancing.

Lia won her battle and Jami followed her into the small crowd that had begun to form on the dance floor. I noted that

the music had changed to a more upbeat rhythm since we'd arrived.

"What took you so long?" Marley asked as I sat back down. She eyed me as if she had overheard what the bartender had said, but I knew she couldn't have.

"Nothing." I sipped my drink and leaned back in my chair.

"Hmm," Marley mused, about to argue I'm sure, but Korra interrupted.

"Marley, want to come dance with Nix and I?" she asked.

I barked a laugh and Korra and Nix both looked at me.

"I don't dance," Marley said, ignoring me. "But thanks." She raised her beer bottle to them before taking a sip.

"I told you so," Nix said to Korra, shrugging and turning away.

"Your loss," Korra said and followed Nix to the dance floor. I watched them go but my gaze snagged on two other figures who had entered the dance floor. Viv and her new friend. My grip on my mug tightened.

"Why don't you go out there and show that guy up?" Marley asked.

I whipped my head to her. "What are you talking about?"

Marley snorted. "Come on. It's obvious you like Viv, no matter what front you put on to try to scare her away."

"Even if I did, she's clearly not interested. She's with another guy." I waved my hand toward them on the dance floor.

"Fine. Do what you do best and let her slip away." Marley hopped to her feet, surprising me. "I need another beer and a smoke. Let me know if someone recognizes you while I'm

gone." She scanned the room. "I bet Garrett's already out there smoking without me," she grumbled before walking away.

I sat alone for a few minutes, sipping my ale. After I finished my mug, I decided to take Marley's advice for once. Walking over to the dance floor, I aimed for Viv and the man who now had his arms around her waist.

"Took you long enough," Jami said as I walked past him.

"You were bringing the mood down with your sulking," Lia added, twirling around in Jami's arms.

I ignored them both and approached Viv.

"Mind if I cut in?" I asked.

The man pulled Viv aside, putting an arm around her possessively and stoking the fire burning in my veins. "She's with me," he said.

I gave him a once over, and he at least had the sense to seem wary.

Viv stepped away from him. "Give me a minute," she said, patting his arm placatingly. "Wait for me at the bar." He didn't leave right away, lingering as if to warn me off, but I didn't budge.

"Fine," he snapped before leaving the dance floor. I couldn't help but grin in triumph as he left. My smile fell as Viv smacked me in the chest.

"What was that for?" I asked, rubbing the spot she'd hit.

"What are you doing?" she asked instead of answering me. Her eyes blazed with emotion, though I couldn't tell whether it was anger or something else.

"He seemed a bore, so I decided I'd save you from his sorry ass," I said, glancing down as I picked invisible lint from my shirt.

Viv closed the small gap between us, and drew my attention back to her face. "Are you jealous?" she asked, lifting

her hand to place it on my chest. The touch burned and I yearned for more.

"Not at all," I spoke low, so only she could hear. "Only looking out for your best interests."

She scrunched her nose. "You're a bad liar," she said before pushing me back and turning on her heel.

I caught her hand, and she glanced back at me. "If I said yes?" I asked.

"Jealousy doesn't suit you," she remarked, pulling her hand from mine.

A low growl rose unbidden in my throat. The urge to shift became more insistent, and I wanted more than anything to go after her, but I let her walk away.

"Captain." Garrett appeared on my left, a grim expression on his face. "There's something you need to see." He jerked his head to the door where Marley waited.

I spared one last glance at Viv and followed Garrett outside. "This better be good," I mumbled.

Lanterns lit the road outside the tavern, and a few flickered on the street leading down to the beach providing enough light to prevent tripping over the cobblestoned streets.

"Marley and I stepped out for a smoke, and, well, look out there." Garrett pointed toward the sea.

I squinted and continued walking forward. Slowly, I was able to make out a churning in the water, past a grouping of rocks.

"What in the hell is that?" I murmured.

"I'm not sure, but maybe we should check it out?" Garrett suggested.

I sighed. "Probably, but we need to tell the others. You two head down there and see if you can figure out anything. I'll grab Jami and the mermaids." A sense of giddiness that I was

going to be able to take Viv away from the stranger at the bar had me practically skipping back inside.

My gaze found the spot where Viv should have been, but it was vacant. I turned to look at the dance floor, and then the table, but she wasn't in either place. Hurrying over to Jami and Lia, who had sat back down at the table, I skidded to a stop, bracing myself on the table.

"Where's Viv?" I demanded.

"What do you..." Lia trailed off as she looked to the bar and realized Viv was gone. She straightened and whipped her head around, searching for her sister. "I'm sure she's fine," she said, but she didn't sound convinced and stood as if she was about to go looking for her.

"I saw her leave with that guy," Nix chimed in as she strode over. "Out the back door." She pointed to a door at the back of the bar. My blood boiled.

"You all need to get outside to the beach. Marley and Garrett are already out there. There's something strange in the water. Could be something to do with sirens," I told them. "I'll get Viv."

Without making sure the others followed my directions, I cut a direct line toward the back door. I threw it open when I reached it, letting it slam against the outside of the tavern.

I scanned the nearly empty alley until I found Viv, sitting on a barrel with her head in her hands, her shoulders shaking as tears rolled down her face. I was at her side in an instant.

"What did he do to you?" I growled, searching the alley for any sign of the other man.

Viv lifted her head, wiping away her tears and straightening her back. "Nothing. I'm fine. I told him to go."

"You're not fine. Tell me what happened," my voice softened, but a mix of fear and rage gripped my heart. Viv tried

to turn her head, but I held her chin with my thumb and forefinger, forcing her to look up at me. She swatted my hand away.

"Don't," she snapped. I released her and stepped back. "I told him to go, and he did. That's all."

"I'm sorry," I said. "You had me worried."

Viv stared at me, wonder in her eyes. She blinked slowly, clearing the remaining tears.

"I didn't mean to worry you," she said, and for the first time, I heard vulnerability in her voice. "I don't mean to be a burden."

"*Never.*" I kneeled before her on the cobblestones. "You are not a burden, Viv. Never let anyone tell you otherwise." I stared up into her eyes and she held my gaze.

"Okay," she whispered.

"Tell me why," I said, dropping my gaze to the stones beneath me.

"Why what?" This time she forced me to look at her by placing a single finger beneath my chin and lifting my face back to hers.

"Why him?" I cursed myself for sounding so pitiful, but there was nothing to be done about it. Viv had pushed me away, time and again, yet I kept being drawn back to her.

"I told you, I sent him away," she said.

"Before that, though, you seemed to be enjoying his company, you seemed to...like him."

"I thought it would be easier," she said on an exhale, leaning her head back to gaze up at the stars. "Easier to try again, to figure myself out, with a stranger. But all I can hear is *his* voice." She gripped her head in her hands again.

"Who?" I asked, my mind reeling at the thought of anyone ever hurting her.

"Humer," she said, curling further in on herself. "Marcus Humer."

"He hurt you?" I managed to get out as I ground my jaw.

Her non-response told me everything I needed to know.

"I'll kill him," I growled.

Viv sighed and removed her hands from her head, grabbing onto mine and giving me a weak smile.

"Thank you. He's in prison now, so nothing to worry about," she said, but the waver in her voice told me otherwise.

A high-pitched scream broke us apart and reminded me why I'd gone after her.

"Shit!" I gasped. "The beach!" I kept her hand in mine as we stood and ran down the alley to the front of the tavern.

Viv kept stride with me and asked, "What is going on?"

"Possible siren activity," I said over my shoulder. "Though, that siren scream just confirmed our suspicions."

"What?! We wasted so much time!" Viv cried out.

"Wasted? No. I feel we used our time quite productively." I stopped as we reached the beach and saw what was happening.

Lia, Jami, and the others stood on the beach as a horde of sirens taunted them from the water. Viv and I ran down the path onto the beach.

"What are they doing?" I asked as we reached everyone.

"I don't know," Jami said, his brow creased with worry. "It doesn't look like they're doing much of anything, besides attracting attention."

"Lia, what do you make of it?" I leaned forward as I spoke so I could see Lia on the other side of Jami.

"Honestly, I've no idea. If I had to guess, I'd say they are signaling someone, or something. Why else draw so much attention to themselves?"

"Well, that can't be good." I stepped forward to see the sirens better. The lighting was horrible, and if they weren't moving around so much, I might have missed them entirely.

"One of us should stay here, in case someone *does* show up to meet them," Viv suggested. "It might provide insight into whatever the queen has been searching for."

"You're right. Though, if that person is Veera, they're going to be waiting a long time," Lia sneered, and her jaw clenched. I had a similar reaction every time I thought about the bat shifter. "But no one's staying out here alone. Whoever shows up may be dangerous," Lia said. "We also can't all stay out here; it would draw too much attention to ourselves."

"I'll take first watch," Garrett offered.

"I think a mermaid should be on each watch, in case something happens, and we need to go into the water for some reason," Lia pointed out.

"I'll join him," Korra said.

"Fine. So, Garrett and Korra will be on first watch," I said, nodding to them. "I'll take second watch."

"And I'll join you," Viv said, winking at me and sending a tremor through me.

"You two should head back to the inn, so you can rest," Lia said. "We will head back to the bar in case Garrett and Korra need us."

Viv and I waited for the others to leave before heading back to the inn. Garrett and Korra found a concealed spot on the beach behind some rocks to keep watch from. The sirens hadn't acknowledged our presence when we'd all been gathered, and I doubted the sirens cared too much about us so long as we didn't enter the water.

As we walked, Viv slid her hand into mine. I glanced down to see the hint of a smile on her face and I couldn't help but smile back.

Lia

The sirens had left me on edge. I couldn't sit still in the bar and paced beside the table. Jami held his hand out to me, and I eyed it warily.

"What if they're trying to distract us from something?" I speculated. "They obviously wanted to be seen, to be heard... It could be a trap."

Jami let his hand drop to his side and leaned back in his chair. "It could be," he agreed. "But there's nothing we can do if we don't know their plan."

"Well, we haven't seen the queen since she attacked your ship." I flicked my eyes to Jami and his gaze dropped to the table. "We'll get her back for that," I promised.

Jami's eyes lifted to mine. "That's not what I'm worried about." He held his hand out to me again, but this time I took it and let him pull me in close. The warmth he radiated eased some of my worries as I took a seat in his lap.

"No?" I asked, and he shook his head.

"No. I'm worried about *you.*" He lifted his hand to cup my cheek. I leaned down and rested my forehead against his.

"You don't need to worry about me." I pressed my lips to his. His hand trailed to the back of my neck, pulling me in closer and deepening the kiss.

A small part of my brain nagged me, reminding me that I'd barely known Jami for a week, and I had always fallen hard and fast. But I kept telling that part of myself that this was different.

"Tone it down you two," Nix joked as she returned from the bar with a round of drinks. "We are in public after all."

I chuckled and pulled back from Jami. He kept his arm around me and traced lazy circles on my hip that drove me crazy. In return, I shimmied a little pretending to resettle myself in his lap. Jami's head fell back as a small groan escaped his lips. I gave him a pointed look, and he ceased the circles.

"You are vicious," he murmured in my ear.

"Don't pretend you don't like it," I rebuked, biting my lip.

Nix chatted with Marley on the other side of the table, but I couldn't focus on what they were saying.

Instead, I stood from Jami's lap, grabbed his hand, and pulled him from his seat. Surprise flashed in his eyes, and he opened his mouth to say something, but I tugged him toward the back door.

"Be right back," I called over my shoulder to the others.

As soon as we were out the door, I pushed Jami back against it and pressed myself flush to him, letting my hands rove up and down his arms and abs.

"You really want to do this? Here?" Amusement colored his tone, and he wore a cocky grin that had me biting my bottom lip.

"Take me or leave me," I said, pressing another kiss to his lips. In response, Jami wove one hand into my hair and his

other splayed across my lower back. I ground against him, my hands dropping between us and attempting to unfasten his belt, struggling with it.

"I hate this stupid thing," I said, cursing.

"Maybe it's a sign we should wait until we're back at the inn," Jami said, sounding a bit breathless. I pushed out my bottom lip in a pout. Jami pinched my chin between his thumb and forefinger and kissed my pouting lips. "You deserve so much more than sex in this alley, my mer queen." His words sent caressing shivers through me and only made me want him more.

"Not a queen," I reminded him, flicking his nose and making him laugh. "Yet."

"Let's go back inside, we need to be alert in case something happens with the sirens," Jami said. He took my hand in his and kissed it.

"Oh, I'm plenty alert," I grumbled, but let him lead me back into the bar.

Jami

I had to be insane. Certifiably, criminally, *insane.* Lia had handed herself to me on a platter, and I'd turned her down. Not outright, of course. It took me a few moments to gain some semblance of awareness and realize anyone could have seen us in that alley.

Now, Lia stood at the bar talking with Nix.

"You look like you could use a cold bath," Marley commented, a smirk on her face. "Stop looking at her like that."

"Like what?" I asked, trying to neutralize my expression.

"Like she just kicked your puppy. Or your d–"

"Don't!" I snapped. "Don't." I rubbed my hand over my face and took a swig of my ale. Marley had always been blunt with us, and normally I appreciated it, but not that night.

"Sorry, James, just calling it like I see it." She shrugged and sipped her own ale.

"You know I hate that nickname," I groaned. "It's Jamison or Jami, not James. That was my father's name." I cringed at the thought of sharing anything with my father, even a name.

"Right, sorry Jami." Marley scanned the room, and I copied her. My eyes drifted to Lia again and her smile seemed

to light up the whole room. She caught me watching and winked at me, setting my nerves ablaze all over again. The end of the night couldn't come soon enough.

When everyone agreed it was time to head back to the inn to get some sleep, I nearly leapt from my chair. The minutes had dragged by and with no word from Garrett or Korra, it seemed as if I was wasting my time in the tavern when I could be back at the inn with Lia in my arms.

As we left the tavern, the sirens seemed to have either given up or taken a break for the night, because the water was calm and quiet. We didn't inspect it closer, trusting Garrett and Korra to be keeping a close eye on the situation.

At the inn, Nix and Marley went to their respective rooms. I didn't miss the lingering stare Nix gave Marley as she passed her. Marley seemed oblivious to it.

Thankfully, the inn had plenty of rooms for us to choose from, so we didn't need to sleep on top of each other, though I planned on doing just that with Lia. Except when I stopped at my door, Lia kept going toward the room she shared with Viv.

"You missed your chance, darling," she teased.

"You really are vicious," I joked, leaning back against my door.

She lifted her shoulder and batted her eyelashes at me. "All's fair in love and war."

"Wait..." I was about to point out that she'd said the 'L' word, but she opened her door and closed it with a squeak of surprise. Her gaze locked on mine and her jaw dropped.

"What?" I asked, striding toward her. Before I reached her, she ran past me to my room and threw open the door which I'd already unlocked. "Lia," I said, following her into my room and closing the door behind me.

"Notice anyone missing from your room?" Lia jumped on the bed, landing on her knees, and spread her arms out to emphasize its emptiness. "No one to kick out so we can have the room." She wiggled her eyebrows.

I turned in a circle and it hit me. "Finn is...no. Couldn't be."

Lia nodded. "Oh yes. He is in *my* room with Viv."

"I thought she hated him," I said, trying to remember if she'd shown any signs of tolerating Finn in the last few days.

"Stupid boys," Lia chided. "Always believing the façade."

"Oh yeah?" I strode forward, placing my hands on either side of her knees on the bed, coming face to face with her. "Is that what this is?" My gaze caught on her lips as she licked them.

"What do you think?" Lia's voice came out low and sultry, drawing me in until my lips brushed hers.

"I think I'm going to take a bath while we have the option," I said, pulling back and leaving Lia wide eyed and slack jawed. I couldn't help but smile at the effect I could have on her. She toyed with me often enough, I figured it was my turn to repay the favor.

Lia perked up though, recovering quickly.

"You don't want company?" She bit her bottom lip as her eyes undressed me. I closed my eyes and ground my jaw.

"Remind me what I did to deserve you?" I said, opening my eyes and holding my hand out to her. Jumping out of bed, she took my hand and followed me into the bathroom.

"If I ever say no to that, know that I have gone completely insane and need to be thrown into the ocean," I joked, and Lia nodded eagerly.

"So long as I can yell, 'man overboard' as I push you into the water." She giggled and it undid me.

Taking her other hand in mine, I walked backwards, into the bathroom, and tugged her along with me. Once she kicked the door shut behind her, I pulled her against me, and she started a trail of kisses up my neck.

My hand rose to the back of her head, pulling her back slightly, and bringing her lips to mine, claiming them. My tongue slipped between her lips, finding hers.

Lia's hands trailed along my chest to the hem of my shirt, lifting it over my head, and throwing it aside. In doing so, she'd broken our kiss, and I looked down at her, desire burning in my gut. Helping her remove her own shirt, I let it join mine and she practically threw herself back against me. I chuckled.

I cupped her thighs as I lifted her and her legs wrapped around my waist, and she continued to kiss me through it all. Propping her against the sink, I pulled back and made my way down to her breasts which remained covered by the corset she still wore.

My lips grazed the top of her breast, and she shivered against me.

"Jami," she murmured breathlessly.

A shock went through me at the sound of my name. "Say that again," I rasped.

Her gaze met mine and I couldn't help but fall a little harder for her.

"Jami," she repeated.

I crushed my lips against hers and placed her back on her feet. She immediately began untying the corset in the back. Once it was loose enough, it dropped down and she stepped out of it, kicking it aside.

Fiddling with my belt, she cursed as she failed to remove it.

"How am I supposed to take this off?" she asked, glancing up at me. Laughing, I helped her finish taking off my pants. "That's better," she said, kissing me and removing her leggings.

My hard length pressed against her core, and she glanced down, taking in the sight of me for the first time. I held my breath as her gaze flicked back to mine.

"Are you sure you want to do this?" I asked, sounding breathless. "We can wait, if..." I trailed off and she wrapped her arms around my neck, kissing me hard.

"I can't wait," she said against my lips.

I lifted her, backing her up against the sink once more. The hard edge of the counter dug into my thighs, but I relished the feeling.

She guided my hand from her thigh, clearly as desperate as I was for me to touch her. As I circled around her opening, she moaned for more and I obliged, thrusting two fingers inside her.

"More," she gasped. "Jami." It came out almost desperate and I moved my fingers faster, and replaced them with my cock, nudging at her opening before sinking myself into her fully. A groan of satisfaction escaped me at the same time she dug her nails into my back.

Pulling out of her, I carried her away from the sink and into the bedroom. Her legs wrapped around my waist and I ached for more as I laid her down onto the bed.

Anticipation sparked in her eyes. I lowered myself over her, kissing her and burying myself inside her again. We moaned simultaneously.

I drove into her harder, faster, until she came apart and I followed shortly after.

"*Fuck,*" she moaned as I pulled out of her and laid down beside her.

"I've never heard anything more beautiful come out of your mouth," I joked, leaning over to kiss her. "You're beautiful," I said.

"I know." She grinned as I kissed her again and she sat up to straddle me, placing her hands on my chest. "What's this one?" she asked, still a bit breathless, pointing to the tattoo on my right pec. My chest was heaving as hers was.

"It's my family's crest," I answered, trailing my hands up and down her thighs. "They're eagle shifters, hence the eagle flying above the mountains." I pointed to the shadow of the eagle that had been etched onto my skin and the mountains that rose beneath it.

"These remind me of smoke," she said pointing to the dark, shaded whorls that surrounded the rest of the image.

I peered down to where she indicated and nodded in agreement.

"Is this one supposed to be Finn?" she asked, giggling as she pointed at the lion face tattooed on my left pec.

"Yes," I said, lifting my hand to brush her hair away from her face.

She trailed her finger to the scar that bisected my tattoos. It clenched beneath her touch, and my jaw ticked.

"And this?" she asked. My eyes shuttered closed, and I took a deep breath.

"My brother, Roland, did that," I said, opening my eyes. She stroked the scar, a crease forming between her brows.

"He sounds awful," she said, and I smiled.

"He is. But let's not talk about him right now. I don't want to ruin this." I stroked her cheek with my thumb and pulled her down to kiss me.

Viv

As Finn and I walked down the hall toward our rooms, we both paused at his door. When he reached for his door handle, I inhaled sharply, surprising us both and making him turn back to me.

"I-" I tried to think of something to say, but words escaped me. All I could come up with was, "Stay with me."

"Okay," he acquiesced, taking my hand in his once more. We continued to mine and Lia's room, leaving the light off as we entered. The moonlight provided enough light to see by as we moved toward the bed. I sat on the edge, removing my boots and not bothering with changing, too nervous to do much else but exist.

The bed dipped as Finn sat on the other side. His belt clinked as he removed it and it hit the floor.

I laid down with my back to Finn, holding my breath as he shifted, and his body heat enveloped me. I knew how close he was, even though I couldn't see him.

Reaching behind myself, I found his hand and picked it up, placing it around me as I shimmied to press myself against him.

After a few minutes, Finn breathed evenly in my ear, fast asleep, though I remained wide awake. Every place my body touched his felt as if it was on fire, but not in a bad way.

I almost wished I'd given myself to him. It was the first time in a long time I didn't cringe from someone else's touch, aside from my sisters'.

At some point, the door opened, making me stiffen, and a flash of light broke through the room before it closed again.

Lia... I assumed when I heard her squeak of surprise.

Finn's arm tightened around me for a second, and he rolled over, removing his arm from around me. The sudden chill that set in with his absence sent a shock through me. Turning toward him, I inched across the bed and put my arm around him, trying to steal his warmth as sleep took me.

"Vivianne," a familiar voice woke me. "Tell me if this hurts." Excruciating pain radiated from my core where I could have sworn a knife had been shoved into me.

I screamed in agony, writhing on the metal table.

"I guess that answers that question," Humer commented amid the scratch of his pen scribbling in that accursed notebook.

I forced my eyes open and squinted against the giant light that had been positioned above me.

Humer smiled down at me. "The pain wasn't enough to make you pass out this time." He wrote that down in his notebook too.

I let out a hiss-like sound, trying to convey how I felt about that, unable to speak through the pain.

"None of that, dear." Humer tapped whatever he had placed in my stomach.

A scream ripped out of me despite my resolve not to give the doctor what he wanted, and darkness crept in around my vision, dragging me back to unconsciousness.

"Viv..." another familiar voice found me as I came back to reality. "Vivianne, look at me."

My eyes fluttered open to find Finn hovering over me, one of his hands caressing my cheek and the other propping himself up. The moonlight coming in through the window created a halo around him.

"Sorry," I murmured. "Was I talking in my sleep again?"

"You were screaming," he said, worry creasing his brows and tainting his voice. I hated when anyone worried about me.

It's been twenty years, my Vivianne, and you're still dreaming of me, Humer's voice floated through my mind.

"Sorry," I repeated, trying to ignore the voice.

"Don't apologize." Finn swept my hair out of my face, and I cringed, realizing my forehead was slick with sweat. "I'm sorry," Finn said, pulling his hand back and falling onto his side so he no longer hovered over me.

"No, it's not you," I laughed softly, reaching out to cup his cheek in my hand. The stubble of his beard scratched my palm, tickling it. His hand covered mine, and he stroked the back of my hand with his thumb.

"It's time for our watch on the beach," he said, and I groaned.

"Can it wait a few more minutes?" I pleaded with him, and he caved instantly.

"A few more minutes," he confirmed. Taking my hand from his cheek, he kissed the back of it and pulled me close, wrapping his arms around me and I nestled into him.

I splayed my hands over his chest, loosening the ties of his shirt slightly and pushing it open as I leaned back to inspect the tattoos inked there. I'd seen them briefly when he'd been naked after shifting on the beach, but I hadn't truly taken them in.

As I traced one of the lines, he shivered under my touch.

"An eagle?" I asked, wondering about its significance.

"Jami's family are all eagle shifters, sometimes we would joke that he was just a late bloomer. So, when he got his lion tattoo, I got an eagle, in case we were right," Finn explained, his chest rumbling with laughter. "We were also piss drunk at the time."

"Why doesn't that surprise me?" I moved my fingers from his left pec to the right, where the skin was uninked. "Are you going to get anything here?"

"Maybe someday. I don't have any plans to right now."

I liked this comfortable conversation. It helped keep my nerves at ease while I pushed my boundaries.

"Do you have any other tattoos?" I asked, and he bit his lip trying to hide his grin, but I caught it. "What?"

"A few," he drawled. "One on my back, one on my arm, and two in more...intimate places." He pushed his tongue into his cheek, unable to hide his amusement any longer.

"Hmm," I mused, removing my hands from his chest, and letting one drift to the hem of his shirt. "Can I see some of them?" I wasn't sure I was ready to commit to seeing *all* of them yet.

"Yes," he said, his voice raw. He waited as I grasped the hem of his shirt and slowly, carefully, lifted it. He sat up so I could remove the shirt entirely and gazed down at me. My breath quickened. I sat up, too, and he turned so I could see the tattoo on the back of his bicep.

"A compass? Doesn't that seem a bit...on the nose?" I teased.

"I was drunk for all of these, so blame the whiskey, or the rum," Finn laughed and turned fully so I could see his back.

"Oh," I gasped. On his back he had a massive helm tattooed with tentacles wrapping around it. A hawk flew over the helm. "They're all beautifully done," I said. "Is this supposed to be Marley?" I grazed my fingers over the hawk, goosebumps rising in their wake.

"Yes. She's been a part of my crew since day one. Her and...and Cole." A ragged breath escaped him, and I wrapped my arms around him, resting my head against the back of his shoulder.

A light knock on the door broke us apart. Finn hurried to the door, opening it a crack. Light poured in from the hall and I held my hand up to shield my eyes from it.

Korra's voice came into the room. "Oh," she said, gasping a little as she realized who had answered the door. "Uh, well, if you are Viv are ready to head out for watch..." She trailed off.

"Right. We'll head out there now," Finn said.

I wrapped my arms around my knees and pulled my legs against my chest as Finn locked the door and sat on the edge of the bed.

"I hope you weren't intending to hide this from anyone," he said, smirking.

"Not particularly," I countered, crawling across the bed to him. My arms wound around him once more and I kissed where his neck met his shoulder. "I already told Lia my intentions."

"You did?" he asked, sounding surprised.

I laughed. “Mmm...” I murmured against his skin, and he leaned into my embrace. “We should go,” I said half-heartedly, pulling away from him and grabbing his shirt to hand to him.

He took it and pulled it on, not bothering to lace the top, leaving his tattoo partially revealed and making my mind wander to his other *hidden* tattoos.

“If you keep looking at me like that I don’t know if we’ll make it out of this room,” he said, grinning.

Flopping back onto the bed with my arms over my head, I sighed. His gaze fell to where my corset rode up slightly and revealed some of my scars. Before I could cover them again, he leaned down, using one hand to prop himself over me while trailing his thumb over one of the longer scars.

My entire body seemed to alight with electricity from his touch and a gasp escaped me.

“The man who hurt you,” he started.

I didn’t let him finish. Sitting up, I pushed his hand away and strode to the door, grabbing my boots and heading into the hall.

“Viv,” he called after me.

I kept moving, pulling on my boots as I went, and nearly fell on my face. My dangling laces threatened to trip me up again as I walked with purpose toward the beach. Finn caught up to me easily but didn’t attempt to speak with me again.

Tension rippled between us, and my chest burned with regret and anger. I wanted to be open with Finn. I wanted him close, and I wanted to be comfortable with him touching every part of me, even my scars. But for some reason, my body had decided to run before I could make the decision for myself.

The moon shone high in the sky over the ocean, lighting it up thoroughly. It wasn't quite full yet, but I could tell the full moon was only a day or two away.

There was no sign of the sirens anymore, but that didn't mean they wouldn't return. Plopping down onto a rock high up on the beach where the tide wouldn't reach us as it came in, I placed my hands on my knees and stared out at the water.

Finn sat a little way away from me, buckling his belt that he must have grabbed on his way out of the room.

He rested his elbows on his thighs and dangled his hands between his knees as he stared at the water.

That's right, Vivianne, push him away, Humer said.

Wrapping my arms around myself, I squeezed my middle and breathed deeply.

Finn's voice surprised me. "I shouldn't have overstepped like that."

I peeked at him out of the corner of my eye. He still looked straight ahead.

"It won't happen again," he added.

A knot formed in my chest as I bit the inside of my cheek.

"He held me captive for two years," I said, a weight lifting from me as the words left my mouth. "Marcus Humer," I clarified, though Finn didn't ask.

His head turned toward me, but I couldn't meet his gaze.

"I wasn't the only one, but I was there the longest," I continued. "The scars are from his experiments. I was never told what he was doing them for, but I assumed it had something to do with shifters' fertility, or something of the like."

"Viv," his voice came out raw. He moved from his rock to kneel in front of me. "Not everyone could endure what you have and come out on the other side as strong as you."

Caught off-guard by his response, I laughed. Normally people would say '*sorry,*' or nothing at all. Somehow, his response was just what I needed.

I bridged the gap between us and took his hand in mine.

"I understand if you want to pretend this whole night never happened," I said, the words nearly lodging in my throat. I prayed that he didn't say yes, but I wouldn't blame him.

"As you know from all those stories you've heard of me, I've been with many women in my time," he started, and I scrunched my nose. Laughing he continued, "I promise this is going somewhere. I've never been one to open myself up too much because none of the women I've ever been with have reciprocated."

"Oh, goddess," I groaned, taking my hand from his and covering my face. "And I've just bared my soul to you. You probably want to run for the hills."

"All you've done is made me realize what was wrong with all those other women. None of them were *you.* I am enthralled by you, Vivianne," he said, reaching out and cupping my cheek in his rough hand. "Absolutely captivated by you."

"Oh," I gasped. Taking both his hands in mine, we stood together. I wrapped my arms around him and as I pressed myself against him, I noticed a dark form washing up on the shore further down the beach. I couldn't make out what it was with only the moonlight to see by. "There's something down by the water," I said.

Finn pulled back, looking toward where the water pulled back and crashed over the unmoving form. I took a step,

tripping on my still untied laces and Finn's arm shot out, catching me. Kneeling, he laced up my boots.

"You don't have to do that," I said, heat rushing to my cheeks.

He peered up at me from beneath his lashes.

"I'll happily spend my days kneeling for you, performing whatever task you desire," he drawled, winking at me.

The heat moved to more intimate parts of me, and I wished more than anything we'd been able to stay in bed a while longer.

After tying my boots, we investigated what turned out to be a dead siren washed up on the beach.

The dull, tangled, black hair clued us in first as we closed in on the figure. The empty eye sockets and gaping hole where her heart should have been only fueled the horrific sight. Sirens could live without their hearts, so that may not have killed her, but the claw and teeth marks all over the corpse indicated more trauma and that it had clearly not been a fair fight. I pressed the back of my hand to my mouth as I tried to hold down the rising bile.

Carved into what was left of the siren's scaled abdomen were the words, *stay out of the water.*

"Shit," Finn breathed. "That's brutal."

Turning away because I couldn't stand the sight anymore, I said, "Why the repeated message? We haven't been in the water since..." *Bree,* I finished silently.

"I've been thinking about that," Finn said. "Veera only said that the mermaids need to stay out of the water. She said nothing about us."

My eyes flicked back to Finn. "Because maybe Lia is right, and the siren queen was after one of your crew."

"We should tell the others," he said.

The sun began to rise after we fetched the rest of our group, we all stood on the beach looking to where the sirens had been the night before and trying not to look too long at the mutilated siren.

"They wanted us to find her," Lia mused, hands on her hips as she stood ankle deep in the water. I stood beside her.

"But why the same message?" Nix asked. She was further out in the water in her mer form. Her scales stopped beneath her breastbone, and she wore a simple, thin bandeau to cover herself. After inspecting where the sirens had been, Nix had found no remaining sign of them.

"I guess we won't find out now," Lia sighed.

"You said Bree may have talked with a siren, maybe this is the one," Finn suggested, and Lia turned to look at him.

"Perhaps." She dropped her shoulders in defeat and waded out of the water. I followed, and Nix shifted back into her human form to do the same. "We should be going. Dwelling on what this means is only wasting time. If this source of power truly exists, we need to defeat the queen before she finds it."

Nix used her magic to remove the water from her clothes which had shifted with her. "Or find it before her," she said.

No one responded. Instead, we all made our way to the horses. I brushed against Finn's arm and he caught my hand, kissing it before we mounted our horses.

Lia insisted on riding at the back with me so she could tell Nix, Korra, and I all about her night with Jami.

"He's definitely the second biggest I've been with. It's hard to beat a dragon," Lia was saying as I pretended to listen. I truly had no interest in Jami's size, or skill, but I knew now. And

boy did I wish I didn't. It was hard to meet his gaze knowing what I did. Lia had spared no detail.

"Are you planning on sharing, Lia? Because otherwise I don't think I can hear much more of this without going back there and finding out for myself how accurate you're being," Korra chimed in and I gave her a grateful look.

Lia sighed, "Been there, done that. Sharing is not on the table this time," she said, pointing a warning finger at Korra. "Claws off." Korra fluttered her eyelashes at Lia but said nothing more on the subject.

"But all this talk reminds me..." Lia reached into her saddle bag, digging around until she had a small bottle clutched in her hand.

"A contraceptive tonic? But Jami's not a mermaid, there's really no risk," Korra pointed out.

"He's human though, it's not uncommon for shifters to be able to procreate with humans. I'm not taking any chances." Lia tipped the contents of the bottle into her mouth, swallowing it as her face pinched and she nearly gagged. "Why can't they make them taste better?" she complained.

My hands covered my stomach without me realizing and Lia's brows shot up.

"I didn't even think, Viv," she said, reaching out to take my hand.

"You don't need to walk on eggshells around me, Lia. I don't even know if I ever wanted children. And, besides, who knows if I'll even be with a mermaid? I certainly won't need to worry about children if I end up with a non-mer." Despite my words, a lump formed in my throat. My decision on whether I wanted to bear children had been taken from me by Humer.

"If you wound up with a non-mer shifter, you could always adopt," Korra pointed out. "Or, you know, in general.

It's an option," she added, realizing her mistake. It was my *only* option. Shifters couldn't procreate with different shifter species, but they had figured out ways to have children so that people could have a family with whomever they wanted.

"None of it really matters right now, so we don't need to talk about it. I don't even have someone I'd want to have children with presently," I pointed out, though Finn's face floated through my mind.

"Do you think Marley has any attachments?" Nix asked, changing the subject. I mouthed '*thank you*' to her and she gave me a quick nod in recognition.

Nix's eyes drifted toward the front of the group where Marley rode with Garrett. When Marley caught her looking, she gave Nix a two-finger salute and a wink.

Nix whipped her head back towards us and panic whispered, "Okay, what do we think that means?" Korra laughed while both Lia and I tried our hardest to hide our grins but failed. "Come on, guys. You know I don't do this often."

"What has it been, like a hundred years?" Lia teased her.

"Not quite, but it feels like that." Nix tucked her black hair behind her ear. She'd had it tied back into a tight bun, but some of it had escaped as we rode.

"Oh, sweetie," Korra said, pouting as she gave Nix a sympathetic look. "You need to get out more."

"It's hard when I'm surrounded by you lot. You garner all the attention, so I never have to worry about things like this," Nix said. "But Marley is different. I want to...try. Is that weird?"

"Not at all!" Lia and Korra said in unison.

"You deserve to be happy, Nix. I say go for it," Lia said.

"Maybe we can relearn all this together," I added, a nervous lump forming in my throat. "It's been a while for me too."

"Who are you trying to relearn for?" Korra asked, wiggling her eyebrows at me. She'd seen Finn in my room and knew perfectly well the answer to that question.

"Hush, Korra. Let Viv keep her secret," Lia chided, but she jerked her head back toward Finn.

"You all are awful," I groaned.

"First lesson, ladies," Korra put on her best proper voice. "Never show fear. They will eat you alive." She and Lia broke out into a fit of laughter. It took me and Nix both a moment to realize the double entendre. Nix joined in their laughter, while I stifled my own, slapping a hand over my mouth.

"So, we *should* show fear then?" Nix clarified, as Lia and Korra attempted to stop laughing. Korra waved her hand in front of her, shaking her head.

"No, no," she gasped out, finally getting her laughter under control. "Sorry. No. Don't show fear, only confidence. Confidence is sexy."

"Noted," Nix said, bobbing her head forward.

"What's got you ladies all in a fit back here?" Finn's sudden appearance made us all jump. We'd been so engrossed in our conversation, we hadn't noticed him drop back toward us. His horse moved beside mine.

Korra, Nix, and Lia, all gave me a pointed look, as if to say *now's your chance.* If they only knew.

"I suddenly have the need to not be here," Korra said, very obviously, as she pulled on her horse's reins and pulled ahead of our group.

Nix did the same, whispering, “No fear,” to me before going.

“I think Jami’s calling me,” Lia lied.

Finn watched them all leave, curiosity raising his eyebrows and a smirk on his lips.

“Sorry about that,” I said, clearing my throat. “They’re all weird.”

Finn laughed. “I get that. Marley, Garrett, and Jami aren’t exactly normal either.”

“But Jami and Lia seem to be getting on great,” I said, and realized how lame I sounded immediately. “I mean, like, she told me about him, and last night, and way too much information... and now I'm rambling. Sorry.” I bit my bottom lip to shut myself up.

“Don’t apologize. Never apologize for being you.” Finn’s words struck me, making me blink in surprise. I met his gaze, and butterflies took flight in my stomach making me smile. “I love your smile,” he said, and a wave of nausea obliterated the butterflies. My head bobbed and my eyelids fluttered as if I were dazed.

“What a nice smile,” Humer said, his fingers in either corner of my mouth, pulling up my lips into a forced smile. “Why don’t I see it more often, Vivianne?”

“Viv?” Finn’s voice broke through to me and I jerked in my saddle, almost falling, but I caught myself in time. “Is everything okay?”

My head shook back and forth without me willing it to. An automatic reaction. *No. Nothing is okay.*

“Fine,” I said, despite the tears against the back of my eyes threatening to spill down my cheeks. My nails dug into my

palms as I gripped the reins tighter, and the pain centered me in the present again.

"I'm fine," I repeated more firmly.

"Got it," Finn said, but he watched me carefully as if I may zone out again or fall at any second. "Where did you go?"

I paused, turning over his question and considering whether I wanted to give him the answer he wanted.

In the end, I settled on a half-truth. "A memory."

Realization showed in his face, and he said, "We don't need to talk about it anymore if it makes you uncomfortable."

"It's been twenty years. I should be able to talk about it without the scars burning when I do, right?" I itched at the leather corset I wore, wishing I'd chosen something thinner so I could get to the scars easier. Then I remembered the whole reason I'd been prompted to buy the corset was so I *couldn't* fuss with my scars as easily.

"There's no set time limit on healing," Finn said. "You can talk about it when you're ready."

I had talked about it, time and again, with Lia. It never got any easier, though, and it never took away the phantom pains.

"I don't know if I'll ever be ready," I admitted.

"That's okay too," Finn said.

I wanted to believe his intentions were good, that he truly cared whether or not I healed and I *wanted* to trust him. But wanting something had never been enough to stop the creeping doubt, or the fear that clutched me when I thought of letting someone in again.

Instead of saying something to push him away, I kept my mouth shut in hopes he'd realize the effort it was taking for me to remain beside him.

Lia dropped back, most likely assuming I needed her, though I was perfectly happy as I was, so Finn moved back to the front with Jami. I didn't bother telling Lia yet about what had happened between Finn and me. I wanted to keep it just for myself for a little while.

Finn

"You have some explaining to do," Jami said under his breath. We pulled away from Marley and Garrett who rode behind us.

"There's nothing to explain," I countered, but the smile on my face gave me away.

"I haven't seen you this happy in a long time," Jami pointed out. "Not since your first day on the ship."

"That was a good day, wasn't it?" I mused, flashing back to that day, but Jami smacked my arm.

"What was that for?" I groaned, rubbing my arm.

Jami laughed. "You're holding back."

"I'm sorry I don't feel the need to share every minute detail about my love life as you do," I teased, and Jami scowled.

"I'm sorry. I thought we cared about each other's..." he trailed off, his eyes snapping back to mine. "Love life?" he asked, and I gritted my teeth realizing my mistake. Nothing was simple verbiage with Jami who overanalyzed everything.

"Don't make this into something it's not," I warned. I'd been intimate with Viv for less than a day; I couldn't start throwing around words like *love*.

Jami sighed, "Fine. I'll drop it. For now."

"Just because you fall in love at first sight, doesn't mean I can," I said.

Jami put his hands up in surrender. "I get it," he said. "Don't go talking like that around Viv, though. It might come off the wrong way."

Viv's laughter made me glance back to where she rode with Lia and felt a tug in my chest. I wanted to go to her. I wanted to be the one to make her laugh. I wanted to hold her again and relive every moment we'd spent together in that inn.

Her eyes met mine and she smiled at me. In that moment I reconsidered my own words. Maybe I *did* love her. Was it possible to fall in love so fast?

Jami is proof of that, I thought, turning back to my best friend.

"You're right. I won't talk that way around her," I told him. "And don't tell Lia anything I said either," I warned.

Jami mimed zipping his lips and throwing away the key.

Around noontime, we came to the next town, stopping for lunch and to restock our supplies for the last few days of our trek. This town was larger than most we had passed through, and much less rundown. The statue of Lanteria's king, King Galvin, as we'd entered the town raised a bit of a red flag for me, considering I was no friend of his. I couldn't recall any pirate who had ever spoken a kind word about Galvin. The king of Asmara, on the other hand, had most of the pirate captains in his pocket, including myself. He was a good ally to have.

I'd avoided interacting with any of the townspeople, knowing that as we neared Asmara, more people would recognize me, which was often a hindrance.

We sat on the grass in the middle of a park as the sun crested in the sky, beating down on us and making sweat drip down my temples.

"I met some other shifters when I went to grab these," Marley said, holding up her cheesy biscuit. "And I asked them if they were interested in joining our army."

She took a bite of her biscuit as if that were the only information she planned on giving me, but continued talking with her mouth full.

"They said *hell no, we don't want anything to do with that siren bitch.*" Her words came out muffled, but I was used to deciphering them, since she often had no tact when it came to manners or the like. It made me chuckle.

"Well, I guess we can't assume everyone will want to help save anyone." There had been a time when I might have also said no to such a venture. Back when I first became a pirate, I cared more about chasing away the pain of losing my mother than anything else.

A young boy spoke animatedly with his mother as they strolled through the park, enjoying the day.

"I saw it, I swear! A pirate ship! It sailed by when we were saying goodbye to Pa!" he said eagerly.

The woman, who had bags under her eyes and drooping shoulders, patted the boys head and said, "I'm sure you did. You have nothing to worry about, Pa and his men know how to handle pirates. They'll return from Aneria safe and sound, as always."

They're still sending out trade ships, I thought, surprised.

I turned to Lia and asked, "Of all the ships that have been attacked by the siren queen, how many of them were pirate ships?"

Caught off guard, her nose wrinkled, and she pursed her lips, thinking. "Um, all but one I guess," she said. "Why?"

"Maybe the kings weren't too far off thinking that this war had nothing to do with them. If none of their ships are being targeted, there is no reason for them to fear the ocean," I said.

"One of the ships bore the mark of Lanteria," Lia said. "Whether it was a mistake, I don't know, but the kings should not overlook the attack of that ship. We didn't make it in time for that attack, and everything and everyone was lost." Her eyes darkened and she stared down at the ground.

"When we reach Asmara, I will reach out to King Danforth. Maybe he didn't listen to you, but I will make sure he listens this time," I promised.

"What?" Viv asked, chiming in for the first time. We hadn't spoken since that morning, and I worried she'd let herself fall back into her old ways of pushing me away.

Before I could say anything, Marley spoke up. "There's a reason Asmara's port is one of the only ones left that accepts pirates wholeheartedly."

"I know," Viv said. "I just didn't peg Captain Finn as a pirate who would work for *anyone*, let alone a king." Her eyes twinkled with mischief as she smirked, and relief filled me that she hadn't closed herself off again.

"Our old captain, Jorge, had a lot of debts he couldn't repay. He used me and my particular skill set to take care of those debts. King Danforth had only been one of many." I hadn't minded it at the time, in fact I enjoyed a lot of the violence I had been instructed to dole out. "As it turns out, King Danforth isn't the worst man in the world to work for."

"Well, thank you, but we won't get our hopes up," Lia said.

I shrugged. It wasn't wrong for her to doubt the king. He may be a better man than most, but that didn't mean he wasn't

above letting other people suffer for the sake of his own kingdom.

We finished eating and continued on our way. As soon as we cleared the town and were back along the cliffside, Jami and I spotted a ship.

At first, we didn't notice anything odd. It was far out enough that we couldn't make out anyone on the ship, but close enough that we could see the pirate flag. *This must be the pirate ship that boy saw,* I realized.

"Should we risk going out there to warn them?" Nix called back to Lia, who remained quiet for a minute.

"Marley can do it," I said, waving her down from where she flew above us.

We all watched as she flew out to the ship, waiting to see that she made it safely. Some pirates were wary of approaching wildlife considering all the shifters who were among crews. Mine was the only crew made up almost entirely of shifters, but I knew of a few others who employed them as well.

Almost as soon as she reached the ship, sirens leapt out of the water, arcing over the ship and dragging crew members over the edge with them. The way their tails created a rainbow-like spray behind them from their power was horrifically beautiful to watch.

I couldn't see Marley clearly, because she was too far out.

Lia dismounted and all the mermaids followed her lead, leaving their horses untied as they ran for the cliff.

"No!" Jami cried as if it were a knee-jerk reaction. He cleared his throat and continued, "I mean, it's not safe."

Lia clipped a belt with a sheathed dagger around her waist. "We can't wait!" she said, backing up and making a running dive into the depths down below.

Jami hopped off his horse, running to the edge of the cliff, mouth agape as he stared down after her. Before she reemerged, her sisters followed her over, including Viv.

"Viv, no!" I yelled too late. She'd already made the dive. I joined Jami, staring down into the water below where rocks jutted out at sharp angles. None of the mermaids reemerged.

"I'm sure they're fine," Garrett said. "I'll fly out there, find Marley, and report back." He shifted and swooped down toward the water, banking as he reached it and gliding out over it.

"I feel useless," Jami groaned. "What are we supposed to do from here?"

I scanned the water and, to our right, noticed a small beach at the bottom of the cliff and pointed to it.

"We can go down there and help if they bring any injured crew back from the ship," I said. "Come on." I led the way toward the beach and climbed down the cliffside.

Rocks and roots offered hand and footholds as we descended, but the cliffside was almost too soft. It crumbled beneath our hands and had us slipping a few times. Thankfully, it wasn't too far down if we fell.

As we reached the beach, we saw Marley and Garrett circling above the ship. We couldn't make out if the mermaids were among the sirens, though.

"I hate this," Jami said, standing knee deep in the water. "What good are we in this war when we can't take part in the fighting?"

"Next time I'll be sure to have a boat," I snapped, and Jami whirled on me. We were both on edge, and it didn't help that neither of us ever held back with each other.

"They are outnumbered!" Jami yelled. "They could be hurt, or-" He released a ragged breath.

"This isn't the first time they've done this," I reminded him, though worry twisted my insides.

"They had more mermaids with them last time," Jami said. We both turned our gazes back to the ship as shrieks filled the air and waited.

The longer I stood near the water, the more my nerves itched, yearning to flee. I forced myself to stay next to Jami. The sirens' song was too far to affect us. The mermaids hadn't resurfaced, but we had to assume they were fighting the sirens.

"What's that?" Jami asked, pointing to where a rowboat was lowering beside the ship. "What are they doing? The sirens will tear that thing apart."

"It looks like there might be people in it," I said, squinting to try to see better, but it was too far to tell.

As I stared at the rowboat, a shadow appeared beside it, flinging itself at one of the figures in the boat and pulling them overboard.

I found myself standing ankle deep in the water, having waded out trying to get a better look, and nausea washed over me, making me back out quickly.

"Fuck, I can't go out there," I said glancing at Jami.

"Well, I can't either," he said, scowling as the water lapped closer to us.

I groaned, clasping my hands behind my neck. "What kind of pirates are afraid of the ocean?"

Lia

The sirens outnumber us five to one but were too focused on attacking the ship when we came upon them. There were not as many attacking this ship as there had been when they attacked Finn's ship, which surprised me. The siren queen seemed to be absent.

I pulled a siren back by the tail, whipping her through the water and willed my claws to extend out through the tips of my fingers. The siren flipped around and bit into my tail fin.

Releasing the siren, I aimed for the heart with my nails. The siren did the same, and we collided, each grabbing the other's wrist to keep from being impaled. We were matched in strength, and any time I gained an inch, I lost it a few seconds later.

"Give up, little fish," the siren hissed, her voice clear and undiluted by the water around us. That was one power of the sirens that mermaids did not inherit. We could only communicate with telepathy, or else attempt to decipher a conversation through the barrier of the water.

I bared my teeth, and the siren bared her much longer, pointier set.

Lia, I need your help over here, Viv's voice popped into my head, giving me a renewed sense of purpose. Driving my clawed nails harder toward the siren's chest, I forced the siren to focus all her attention on pushing back. While she was distracted, I released my grip on the siren's wrist and dug my nails into the siren's throat, ripping it out.

Her nostrils flared, and eyes widened before I shoved her away and took off in the direction I'd last seen Viv.

Where are you? I reached out to her.

Front of the ship. Viv responded almost immediately. I veered in that direction. Manipulating the water around me, I propelled myself even faster. Dodging sirens, I noticed Viv beside a rowboat. As I was about to surface beside Viv, something yanked me backward.

"Argh!" I cried out. It came out garbled, and water rushed into my mouth.

"Not so fast," the siren who had grabbed me said.

I focused on regaining my bearings as the siren released me and rose before me, eyes blazing and preparing to lunge.

Even though it cost me precious seconds, I reached down to unsheathe my dagger. The siren's claws sunk into my shoulder as I dodged and brought my dagger out and around to the back of the siren. On the second strike, the siren's claws found their mark in my chest, but so had my dagger. The light left the siren's eyes as I ripped my dagger from the base of their skull.

Blood colored the water surrounding us, oozing from my wounds, and blending with the siren's blood.

Pushing for the surface, I broke through beside Viv.

"Sorry, I ran into trouble," I gasped. Turning to the rowboat, my eyes widened, and I sputtered, "What the fuck?"

Three children, none more than six years old, stared at me. One girl and two boys, each with sea green eyes and sandy blonde hair.

"Yeah. My thoughts exactly. We don't usually come across *children* on pirate ships," Viv said. "They're spawns of the captain supposedly."

"Don't call them spawns, Viv," I chided, but I couldn't help but laugh.

"What's a spawn?" the girl asked.

"Nothing," I said quickly. "Why are they down here?" I returned to my conversation with Viv.

"The first mate was trying to escape with them, but he... Well, a siren got to him before he could get away." She cast her eyes to where he must have been dragged under. "I was too far out to get to him in time. I figured I should stay with them."

"How do you know he was the first mate?" I asked, though that probably wasn't the most pressing issue.

"The captain saw me down here and told me what happened and requested I help them. That's when I reached out to you," Viv explained.

"I don't think the siren queen is here, so if the pirates lay low for a bit and block out the sirens' song, the sirens will likely give up and leave them alone," I said, glancing at the children. "These three would probably be better off on land."

"Well, we can't stay here like this for long, a siren is bound to spot us any second, if they haven't already," Viv pointed out.

"Right. Let's move then. We'll let the captain worry about retrieving them later." I took hold of the front of the rowboat, towing it toward the small beach where Finn and Jami stood. "Keep an eye out underneath for any sirens," I told Viv.

"Where are we going?" the girl asked. Both boys remained silent with rounded eyes. They stared at me as if I were from another world.

"I'm helping keep you safe," I said. Viv had disappeared under the water, and I envied her. It wasn't that I didn't like children, I just didn't understand how their brains worked and they freaked me out a little bit.

"Why?" the girl asked, and I groaned inwardly. *So it begins,* I thought.

Instead of answering, I asked her, "What's your name?"

"Tabby," she answered enthusiastically.

"And what about you two?" I glanced back at the boys who both dropped their mouths open and seemed terrified that I'd spoken to them.

"They're Atty and Leo," Tabby answered. "They're twins. I'm the oldest."

"You're a good big sister," I said.

Tabby smiled. Something slammed into the bottom of the rowboat, jolting me forward and sending all three children into the water. In a flash, I righted the boat, preparing to scoop all three of them back inside, but only Leo resurfaced.

I grabbed him, placed him back in the rowboat, and dove underwater.

Viv fought with a siren far below me and Atty sank deeper into the water. Tabby was nowhere to be seen. Instead of panicking, I aimed straight for Atty, swimming as fast as I could and reaching him in seconds. Grabbing him under his arms, I heaved him up through the water, cradling him against me as I burst through the surface and hoisted him back into the rowboat. He hadn't been under too long and immediately started coughing up water.

"Stay low," I told the boys, unsure if they would listen, but unable to worry about that. Diving back under, I scanned the water for Tabby again. Viv had dispatched the siren she'd been fighting, but she wore a ring of scratches around her neck. They'd heal quickly, as my wounds would, but that didn't mean they might not scar. I couldn't think about that.

Tabby is missing, I reached out to Viv. *Get the boys to shore, I'll find Tabby and meet you there.*

Viv swam past me to the surface. In the distance, sirens retreated. None of them seemed to be dragging a five-year-old girl with them.

Do either of you see a little girl where you are? I reached out to Korra and Nix.

Not here. The sirens are retreating. Nix and I are headed back to shore and the ship is heading to port, Korra responded.

Damn it, I thought. *Where is she?* Taking a chance, I dove down toward the seafloor. As I neared it, a cloud of sand built up, obscuring my vision. I took my dagger out and continued into the cloud.

"Pretty little girl will make a nice snack for my queen," a siren sang. With an extra burst of speed, I reached the siren about to bury her teeth in Tabby's leg. I tackled the siren and drove my dagger into her chest.

The siren fought back longer than a human would be able to with a dagger in their chest, but when I tore my dagger out, she screeched, rearing back. I didn't have time to finish her off.

Grabbing Tabby, I shot toward the surface, breaking through it in record time.

"Tabby!" I cried out, pulling the girl above the water and slapping her cheeks in sheer panic mode. Tabby's eyes

remained shut, her lips blue, and her chest did not rise. As I swam to shore, I used my magic to attempt to draw the water from Tabby's lungs. Even as water dribbled out of Tabby's mouth, she didn't breathe.

Clutching Tabby close and swimming as fast as possible while also keeping her head above water, I made it back to shore. Garrett and Marley flew overhead and landed on the beach as I reached it, shifting back into their human forms.

"Jami, Finn!" I cried over the waves. "Take her! She's not breathing!" I shifted, carrying Tabby up to Finn who took Tabby from my arms and brought her onto the beach. He began doing chest compressions, but I turned back to the water to ensure the sirens had truly retreated. Viv stood on the beach to my right, rowboat beside her, and the two boys huddled together. When they saw their sister lying on the beach beside Finn, they ran to her.

I stared out over the water. The ship was moving toward the next port, which would be in Asmara.

"Lia," Jami said, stepping up beside me and taking my hand. "You're hurt." His hand found the ring of claw marks from the siren who had tried to rip out my heart.

"It will heal," I said, brushing him off.

"Faster in your shifted form," he reminded me. They'd already healed enough that blood no longer leaked from them, or the bite mark on my leg.

"I should inform the captain that his children are safe," I said, but I turned back to glance at Finn who was still attempting to bring Tabby back to life. Viv had joined him and worked in unison with him, taking more water from her lungs.

I watched, my heart racing, and ever so slowly, Tabby's eyes opened. Relief washed over me. Collapsing against Jami, I

buried my head in his chest. His arms wrapped around me, holding me tightly.

A splash sounded behind me in the water, and I turned to find that Nix and Korra had arrived. They shifted back to their human forms and joined the rest of us on the beach.

"We warned the captain to stay as close to shore as possible. I don't think the sirens have given up, only gone to get reinforcements," Korra said, her eyes wary as she stared at the ship now sailing away.

"Why do you think that?" Jami asked, lowering one of his arms to my waist as I turned in his arms to face Korra.

"We overheard them saying that what they were looking for is on that ship. And they didn't get it. There's no way the siren queen will let that go. I wouldn't be surprised if she shows up herself next." Fear sparked in Korra's eyes as she mentioned the siren queen. It was an appropriate response, I thought. The queen was horrifying.

"Then we need to find whatever it is they have on that ship that she wants..." I mused. "I'll go out there and request to board the ship. I can say I need to talk to the captain about his children." My eyes flicked back to Tabby and the boys who were huddled together, hugging.

"I'll go with you," Nix said. "You may need back up."

"I'll come too," Jami chimed in. "Now that we have the rowboat, I can be of some use."

I heard the regret and the frustration in Jami's voice at being left behind and didn't have it in me to deny him this opportunity, even if I thought it would be more effective for only myself and Nix to go. I wouldn't admit to myself that I didn't *want* to leave Jami behind again for my own selfish needs. I liked having him close so I could keep an eye on him. After

what happened to Cole, there was no telling what the siren queen would have planned for us next.

"Before anyone does anything," Marley said, putting a hand in the air. "There's something you need to know, Cap."

Finn turned to her and wiped sweat from his brow. "What is it?" he asked, sounding breathless.

"That's not just any pirate ship out there," she said.

"It's Captain Brom's ship," Garrett finished, and Marley shot him a glare as if he'd stolen her thunder.

"What does that mean?" I asked, looking from Garrett to Finn.

Finn's jaw tightened and he closed his eyes.

"Can I say it?" Marley asked, sounding excited. I'd never heard her excited about anything but apparently this was something that brought it out of her.

"Doesn't make a difference, I guess," Finn grumbled.

"Captain Brom is Finn's father," Marley said, practically bouncing on her feet. "And they hate each other."

"Are you getting excited over drama?" Nix asked as she rejoined the group. She brushed her wet hair from her forehead. "Seems unlike you."

"It's not the drama that excites her," Jami said, his voice making his chest rumble against my back. "It's seeing Finn on edge."

"Not much gets to the captain. You can't blame me for finding entertainment in the moments when he goes off the handle," Marley said, shrugging.

"Um, are we going home?" Tabby's voice made several of us jump. I'd forgotten about the children, and apparently, I wasn't the only one.

"Not yet," I told her. "The water isn't safe right now."

"Are these Brom's children?" Finn asked, wincing.

"Yes," I answered, realizing what that meant for him.

Marley laughed and pointed to Finn. "You're a big brother!"

"Stop it!" he growled. "This isn't funny. We need to figure out what he has that the siren queen wants."

"Who is going to stay with the kids?" Marley asked.

"*You,"* Finn sneered. "And Garrett."

That wiped the smile from Marley's face and turned it into a scowl.

"Korra will be with you too," I added.

"Let's get this over with," Finn said.

Finn

Nix and Lia pulled the rowboat while Jami and I sat inside. Viv swam alongside us. The oars must have been lost when it had tipped earlier, so we couldn't even help row. I was useless once more.

I twisted my hands in my lap, fighting the nausea that welled up as we moved through the water. Closing my eyes, I tried to pretend I was anywhere but back in the ocean, but nothing worked. My heart raced and I worried it may actually give out on me.

Even though being on the water made my skin crawl, the thought of seeing my father again for the first time in years had me considering jumping overboard and letting the ocean swallow me whole.

We came up beside the ship and the pirates lowered a rope for us. Lia, Viv, and Nix shifted in the water, and Jami and I helped them into the rowboat so they could climb up first.

"I'll go first, just in case," Nix said and climbed. Lia, Viv, and Jami followed, and I brought up the rear.

When my boots hit the deck, a sense of belonging washed over me and some of the unease from before fell away. As I straightened, I noticed a circle of pirates had surrounded us

and I gripped the holster for my pistol. My father wasn't among these men.

"Where are the kids?" a man stepped forward who reminded me of Cole, though this man was missing a tooth and had darker skin. He had a similar beard, hair, and burliness to Cole. I gulped past the lump of grief that built in my throat.

"They're safe, on land," Lia said, stepping forward.

"Why didn't you bring them with you?" the man growled, suspicion darkening his eyes.

"Because, as you just saw, the water isn't safe," Lia pointed out. "Tabby almost *died* because of your stupid decision to send them into a rowboat surrounded by bloodthirsty sirens."

The man sneered and closed the distance between himself and Lia, hand gripping the pommel of his sword. Jami placed himself between the pirate and Lia.

"Stand back," he growled, leering into the man's eyes. Jami stood only a few inches taller than him, but his presence seemed more domineering as he stared down at the man. "She told you the children are safe, and they will be returned to you once you make port. The sea isn't safe for anyone right now."

"Who do you think you are?"

"Jamison Dawes, first mate of the ship *Leona,"* he said, and I waited for reaction from the ship name alone. A few of the pirates around us whispered to each other, and the man appraised Jami with a new regard. His eyes flicked to me and recognition sparked in them

"Captain Finn," he said. "I heard *Leona* went down on the southern coast of Lanteria."

I nodded in confirmation and stepped forward. "You heard right." My words were more confident than I felt. If I

showed any sort of weakness, my father would jump on it and exploit it.

Jami stepped back, letting me take his place now that Lia was no longer in harm's way.

"I'm Callum. Our captain is..."

The sound of heavy boots descending stairs interrupted him. I turned to find my father, an even larger man than Callum, donning a black tricorn hat that reminded me of my own I'd lost in the attack. His long, scraggly, brown hair matched the shade of mine, but I hadn't inherited his green eyes like his other children.

"Brom," he finished Callum's introduction. "I heard my children are safe ashore?" His crew cleared a path for him as he approached us. Nix had somehow slipped away unnoticed, and I couldn't spot her.

Brom didn't notice me right away, but when he did, his entire countenance shifted. Frown lines creased his forehead and deepened between his brows. He bared his teeth as if he were about to snarl. I stood tall and stared right back at him.

"You," he hissed. "What are you doing on my ship?" His men closed in around him, readying to fight if their captain gave the command.

I tilted my head slightly, looking Brom up and down before saying, "Saving it, apparently."

"Like you couldn't save your own?" Brom spit to the side of my feet. "You should have gone down with your ship. At least then you'd be out of my hair."

"I didn't have much of a choice. These lovely mermaids pulled me from the ship as it went down," I explained, but my entire body tensed under Brom's scrutiny.

"I advise you and your men head to the next port as quickly as possible," Lia interrupted, taking Brom's attention

away from me momentarily and allowing me a few seconds to breathe. "The sirens will return and there will be more of them," she warned. "We'll keep your children safe until you arrive at the Asmara port, and we'll meet you there. You can send along some of your men if you don't trust us. But I am not sending them back out here knowing the sirens could come back any time."

"I appreciate your concern, miss, but that's not your call to make. They are *my* children." Brom narrowed his eyes at her and then looked around. "Weren't there more of you?"

Lia turned her head to me and then to the other side where Nix should have been. "Nix is shy," she said, the corner of her lip twitching. I held in my laugh. "That's nothing to be worried about. What you should be worrying about is that the siren queen thinks there is something on your ship that she desires."

"On my ship?" Brom folded his arms over his chest. "Like what?"

"That's just it, I have no idea. She's been searching for something, and I can't imagine it would wind up here without you knowing it. It's something of great power." Lia scanned the deck as if there would be a glowing orb that would lead her to whatever it was she was looking for, but no such luck.

"We have plenty of treasures on this ship but nothing that emanates any sort of power. I assume it's something of magical origins?"

"I assume, so, yes. But we truly have no idea. The queen has been searching for it for weeks, looking to use it to take over the sea," Lia explained.

I couldn't help thinking that Lia had to have an awful lot of trust in Brom to tell him all this information. He could easily

turn around and try to find the item for himself to use for his own personal gains.

"If the sirens attacked the *Leona,* that means she also thought it was on *their* ship. Does it not?" Brom pointed out, quirking a brow and eying me.

"We're not entirely sure of her motives for that yet, but she showed up herself to that attack. I imagine she thought they had something she wanted." Lia flicked her gaze to Jami.

We hadn't talked much more about who may have been on the *Leona* that stemmed the queen's suspicion after I'd told Lia that Jami and Marley knew nothing. I'd never been able to ask Cole, but I imagined the siren queen would have put him on her *do not kill* list for Veera if that had been the case. Anger burned in my veins as I thought of what she had done to Cole.

"I found something," Nix said as she reappeared, squeezing past the circle of pirates. Many of them turned to her with bewildered expressions on their faces, I was one of them.

"What do you mean?" Brom snapped, heading straight for Nix who easily sidestepped him and continued toward Lia.

"You probably didn't know about it," Nix said, glancing back at Brom. "I found it in the first mate's cabin." She waved a piece of parchment, and I realized it was a map.

"Let me see that," Brom snapped, but I grabbed the parchment first.

Looking it over, I didn't notice anything too unique about the map, other than a stamp in the corner that looked oddly similar to Jami's family crest. Otherwise, there was a single island on the map with no distinct markers and an X that looked like it might be inside a cave.

"This is..." I started, and Nix moved to stand beside me.

"Jami's? Yes. I recognized the crest from his tattoo Lia told me about," she said. "If this is really what the queen is

looking for, then it makes sense why she'd attack the *Leona,* knowing he was on it."

Jami grabbed the map from me, scanning it.

"Who was your first mate?" he asked.

"Doesn't much matter now, does it? He was eaten by the sirens," one of the crew chimed in and Brom gave him a scathing glare that had him shrinking back in among the others.

"This is all madness. That map was found on *my* ship, and so it belongs to me. I'll be taking it now." Brom held one hand out, while the other fell to his pistol at his side. His voice lowered to a growl. "And then you'll all be on your way."

"May I remind you, we have your children," Nix said, and Lia jerked her head toward her.

"We're not holding them as *hostages,"* Lia hissed.

"We're not *not* holding them as hostages." Nix shrugged. "I think it's a fair trade. Your children, for this map. What do you need it for anyway?"

Jami stared at the parchment and I peered over his shoulder. If the map belonged to his family, it was possible he'd seen it before.

"What was your first mate's name, Captain?" he asked again. Tension built around us.

"Roland Dawes," Brom sneered and Jami cursed. "Oh yes, I know exactly who he is to you."

"Your brother?" Lia asked.

I watched Jami carefully, trying to gauge his reaction. He'd hated his brothers growing up.

Jami nodded. "One of them. He and Charles always had to best me in everything. I guess Roland never gave that up," he scoffed. "This belongs to my family, and now that Roland is..."

I saw the wince before he recollected himself.

"Think of the children," Nix said in a mocking voice, reminding the captain once again who truly held the cards.

"You'd let these heathens use your siblings in this way?" Brom asked me.

"I don't have siblings," I said. "You disowned me, so as far as I'm concerned, we're unrelated."

Brom grunted in disapproval but backed away from them. "You are lucky you saved my children, or else this conversation would be going an entirely different direction," he said, the threat clear in his tone.

"You are lucky we saved your children. If Viv hadn't seen the siren pulling Roland under, we may have never known they were there," Lia said, her own voice laced with venom as well. "The sea will never be safe again if we don't take this map and defeat the siren queen. If she gets her hands on whatever this map leads to, assuming this is what she was after, then the entire world will be at stake. She'll take command of all the oceans, not just this one."

"And what do you want us to do about it?" Brom asked.

"We will ensure your children make it safely to Asmara, and we will help you when the siren queen returns for that map. In return, you will help us when we make a final stand against the queen." Lia stood tall as Brom attempted to puff himself up to make her cower.

"If you're keeping my children with you, I want collateral," Brom said.

"No," I snapped.

Brom grinned as he looked at me. "Oh? You don't want to spend some time with dear old pa? Would you rather me keep Jami here?"

"I'll stay," Jami said before I could respond.

Lia and I both shot glares his way, but I spoke up first.

"You're not staying on this ship. I'll stay," I said.

"Perfect," Brom drawled. "Now, the rest of you get off my ship or I'll throw you all in the brig."

My gaze flicked to Viv, and I immediately realized my mistake. Brom didn't miss the glance and he smiled at Viv as if noticing her for the first time.

"She can stay, too," he said, strolling toward her. Viv stood her ground, appearing unaffected by Brom's attention.

Brom reached out as if he was going to grab Viv's arm, but I moved between them, a fire lighting inside me. "Don't fucking touch her," I growled, my entire body shaking as it threatened to shift.

Brom rolled his shoulders and cocked his head to peer around me. "So he *does* have a weak spot." He lifted his hand and lazily drew an X through the air, marking Viv. Viv stiffened under his gaze, but remained rooted to her spot, a mask of indifference on her face.

A growl rumbled low from my chest, and Brom chuckled. "Oh, the things I could do to you."

Viv flinched and it was enough to send me over the edge.

The shift came over me, my lion ripping out of my skin, and I knocked several people to the deck. A dozen weapons were aimed my way, but I didn't care as I stared down Brom. He had grabbed Viv, holding her in front of himself, and placed the barrel of his pistol against her temple.

"Down, kitty," he drawled.

"Let her go!" Lia cried from somewhere to my left. I'd lost track of where everyone had ended up after my shift. "I swear to Neros I'll kill you and everyone else on this ship if you hurt her."

"This is between me and my son," Brom said, not bothering to glance at Lia. "Now, Finnian, you and the girl stay. The rest of you, get off my ship," he hissed, cocking the gun.

"Lia," I heard Jami's voice behind me. "He's not bluffing."

Jami was probably right. Brom wasn't one to shy away from bloodshed, but he also wouldn't waste his leverage against me right away. Knowing that did nothing to quell my own fear, though.

"Go on," Brom said, waving the hand not holding the gun toward Lia.

Shifting back from my lion, my clothes changing with me, I looked around. Nix had already disappeared somewhere, and Jami and Lia were climbing over the side to get back to the rowboat. I could see the pain in Lia's eyes as she looked at Viv.

Brom holstered his pistol and grinned in triumph. "Callum, you go with them and make sure nothing happens to Tabby or the boys. We seem to have a vacancy now that my first mate has become fish food, someone show our guests to their room," he said, shoving Viv toward one of his men. "Try anything unseemly, and I'll throw the girl overboard."

"No-" Lia started, almost coming back over the railing.

I turned back to her. "It's alright. I'll keep her safe," I promised.

"I'll be fine," Viv called to Lia. We had no reason to believe that, though. These were pirates, and I knew better than anyone that pirates couldn't be trusted. They'd keep their word but find a way to twist the situation to their highest advantage.

"I'll see you soon," Lia said to Viv before disappearing over the side of the ship, back down to the rowboat.

Turning to the man who held Viv, I grabbed his arm, squeezing as hard as I could and making him cry out.

A few others aimed their weapons at me.

"Let go of the lady," I said, my gaze turning hazy as rage overwhelmed me. It took all my remaining willpower not to shift again. He released Viv's arm. "Touch her again and I'll tear your arm off."

He scoffed but sidled away from Viv.

"Your room is this way," he said, aiming toward the stairs beneath the quarter deck, leading the way to a door halfway down them. "This was Roland's room."

I pushed the door open, letting Viv enter first, before shutting the door behind us.

Viv

I remained silent as we entered the cabin. A bed large enough for two was the only furniture besides a desk. Close walls made me claustrophobic. My hands were clammy and trembled as I focused on my breathing. *I told you so,* Humer said in my mind. *Trust a man and wind up a captive. I thought you would have learned.*

"No," I whispered to myself.

Finn hadn't told me about his father, and I wasn't sure how to feel about that. I'd not told him about my parents either. We hadn't gotten that far yet. After our night together, my world had tipped on its side, and I wasn't sure how everything fit together anymore.

I flicked my gaze to him and returned it quickly to the room before me when I realized he was also looking at me. I had no idea what was going through his mind. He could be regretting everything we shared because now his father had someone to target to hurt him. But, if that was true, then that meant he truly cared about me.

"Are you alright?" he asked.

"No," I answered honestly. There was no reason to lie, considering there was nowhere for me to hide and fall apart alone. "Are you?"

"No," he admitted, and I nodded as if that settled something. We both waited for the other to make the first move.

"You didn't tell me your father was Captain Brom," I said, wondering if he had done that intentionally.

"No. Would it have changed anything?" Finn asked, stepping toward me.

"Probably not," I admitted.

A knock on the door made us both jump. Finn opened it, and I heard a man say, "Captain wants to talk to you."

"I won't leave Viv alone," Finn countered, and the man laughed.

"It's funny you think you have a choice. Take him, Lewis. And remember, Finn, do anything untoward and the girl gets it."

Finn grunted as Lewis grabbed him, hauling him out of the room. He glanced back at me but didn't risk fighting back.

"Touch her and you die," Finn warned before the door shut and I was alone.

Wrapping my arms around my middle, I fell to my knees, gasping as sobs wracked through me. Tears fell steadily and my breathing became so uneven, I thought I might pass out.

I climbed onto the bed, pulling the covers over myself and forcing my breathing to slow.

"In, out," I said aloud. "It's only temporary. This will pass."

Lia

Nix and I pulled Jami and Callum in the rowboat.

As we reached the shore, Nix and I shifted and walked onto the beach with Jami following behind us.

"Where are Finn and Viv?" Marley asked immediately.

"They stayed on board," Jami answered. "Finn agreed to stay as collateral in case anything happens to Tabby or the boys, but Brom wanted them both."

"What?!" Marley's alarm made me flinch. I imagined Viv putting her arm around my shoulders. Her absence was like a missing limb.

Callum went to the children, and they leaned into his embrace. If I didn't know better, I'd say he was their father.

"We didn't have much choice in the matter," Jami told Marley, his jaw clenching. "Do you think I would willingly let Finn stay on board with that man if I'd had any other choice?"

"You're right," Marley sighed. "I'm sorry. What are we supposed to do now?"

"Can we go home now?" the little girl asked, drawing our attention back to the children. "I want to go home."

Her raised chin and defiant spark made me smile.

"Not yet," I said.

Callum stepped forward. "We have to travel on land for a while to keep you safe," he told Tabby.

Korra stared at the cliff and asked, "How are we going to get the children up there?"

"Marley and I can carry them up. Together, we can lift them," Garrett said.

The rest of us climbed the cliff and untied the horses, preparing to leave. Callum would take Finn's horse, riding with Atty, while Tabby would ride with me, and Leo with Korra. We tied Viv's horse to Jami's. Marley flew overhead, keeping an eye out for an inn, knowing we needed to find one now that we had children with us.

We rode into the night, and the first inn we found was set back in the woods along the road. If Marley hadn't spotted it from her vantage point, we would have missed it entirely.

The inn only had two rooms available, so we let Callum and the kids take one while the rest of us all crammed into the other. There were two small beds in our room, so Marley took one, and Korra the other, leaving the rest of us on the floor.

Without any windows in the room, it was pitch black when we turned out the lights and everyone kept to themselves. I curled up with Jami, falling asleep easily in his arms despite my worrying about Viv. The fight with the sirens had taken all my energy and magic, and now I needed to replenish.

Traveling with children made everything take twice as long. By the time we left the inn in the morning, the sun was already high overhead. No one complained, but tensions ran high.

Callum pulled me aside before we mounted our horses. I clenched my fists, ready for whatever complaint he was going to throw at me.

"Thank you for prioritizing the children's comfort," he said, and I blinked in surprise. "I know it's not easy traveling with them, but I've been their caretaker since their mother left, and I... Just, thank you."

"Don't mention it. Anything they need, let me know and we'll make sure they are kept fed and marginally happy. Riding horses all day isn't exactly the most comfortable form of transportation." I rubbed the back of my neck and he nodded, leaving me as he helped the kids onto the horses.

Riding at the front with Jami helped me not feel Viv's absence so keenly.

This road could be monotonous most days. The same scenery always surrounded us. The ocean lay on one side, and either a forest or field on the other. My head bobbed as I drifted off a few times.

"Do you need to take a break?" Jami asked after I nearly fell off my horse.

"I think I need to stretch my legs," I said, guiding my horse to the side of the road. "You all go on ahead, I'll catch up."

"I'm not leaving you out here alone," Jami said, following me as I dismounted my horse.

"You sure?" Korra asked. "We can wait. I wouldn't mind taking a break from this accursed saddle."

Glancing around at our group, I noticed they all appeared eager at the sound of taking a break from riding.

"Let's all take a break, then," I decided. "No one stray too far. There's still the possibility we're being followed. Marley, if you don't mind keeping an eye on everyone, and Garrett, can you scout further ahead and ensure we'll reach an inn tonight?"

"Done." Marley shifted back into her hawk form. Garrett nodded and did the same.

I walked into the woods, needing a break from the sweltering heat of the sun.

Jami followed me, but I didn't slow down for him to catch up. Something tugged me onward, pulling me toward a clearing among the trees.

The clearing appeared to be empty when I reached it. It wasn't a natural clearing, though. There were felled trees and crushed undergrowth all around it. When I saw the charred earth on the other side of the clearing, I knew exactly what had caused it all – a dragon shifter.

Heat radiated from the area and I assumed I hadn't missed the shifter by too much. He or she could still be around. Though, in dragon form, they could fly a great distance in a short time. Unease created goosebumps on my limbs and had me holding my breath. Whoever had made this clearing was nearby and possibly watching me.

A twig snapped to my left and I whipped my head that way but saw nothing. The familiar scent of smoke and a hint of cinnamon took me back to my last encounter with a dragon shifter. *Khali.*

As if thinking her name summoned her, Khali stepped out from behind a tree in human form, wearing nothing but a slip. She stumbled forward, her long golden-blonde hair swinging as she did, and I noticed the fresh burns on her arms and legs.

I raced to her side, catching her as she fell. I sat down and let her rest against my side with my arm around her shoulders. Jami ran to her other side, crouching down and putting a hand on Khali's shoulder.

"Lia?" she murmured, her bright, golden eyes widening in disbelief, before she turned to Jami and laughed. "Jami? What the hell are you two doing here? *Together?*"

I glanced between the two of them, Jami seemed equally as baffled as myself.

"What happened to you?" I asked, figuring we could go back to how we all knew each other once the immediate danger had passed.

"I lost control," Khali said. Her chest heaved with the effort it took to breathe.

"Again?" I shook my head. When we first met, she was having trouble controlling when she shifted into her dragon form. Any heightened emotion could bring it on. She'd nearly shifted the night we'd slept together. Khali introduced me to Ryder that night, and we had a lot of fun together for a while.

"I've gotten better at controlling it," she said.

"How did you burn yourself?" I pointed to the burns. She twisted her arms to look at them and waved her hand toward the charred area of the clearing.

"Don't walk through fire," she joked. "Once I shift again those will heal."

"You should shift, then."

"I need to rest first," she said, her eyes fluttering closed. I was about to protest, but she'd already fallen asleep. I cursed her inwardly for her ability to fall asleep instantly, anywhere.

"So, how do you know Khali?" I asked Jami as I shimmied out from beneath her and laid her head on what remained of the grass beneath us.

"She and Finn get together anytime we're in Asmara," Jami explained.

"Huh, I don't know how I feel about that," I mused.

"About what? Finn having been with someone you know?"

"About Finn having been with someone I've been with," I clarified, smirking. Jami looked thoughtful for a moment, connecting the dots, before he laughed and shook his head.

"Why am I not surprised?" he asked.

Jami carried Khali back to the horses, and everyone reconvened so we could keep moving.

"Who is that?" Tabby asked from where she sat in front of me on my horse, pointing to Khali who had regained consciousness as she rode with Jami. I'd given her a pair of my leggings and one of Viv's tunics to wear instead of her charred nightgown.

"An old friend," I told Tabby. "Her name is Khali."

Khali had helped me rally enough help to rescue Viv from Humer. It had taken me two years to find her in his underground laboratory, and once I did, I wasn't screwing up the rescue mission.

Khali waved to Tabby.

"We can be friends too," Tabby offered. "I have a ton of stories I can tell!"

My mind leapt to her father and the possibility of her revealing his secrets. "I would love to hear those stories," I said.

We rode together, Tabby telling mundane stories with no secrets. As the sun set, we looked for a place to stay. Garrett had flown ahead to scout out an inn and promised there was a town coming up.

If I had my geography correct, there would only be one more town after this before we reached the kingdom of Asmara. I'd been worried about Viv as we neared Asmara, but now I couldn't be with her if she needed me. I could have been overreacting. She may be fine with returning to the place she'd been held captive. I wouldn't be, but Viv *had* always been stronger than me.

"It's just up around this bend!" Garrett called back to us from where he rode beside Nix. Marley circled overhead, keeping an eye out for any threats.

I noticed Korra chatting with Callum, and he seemed to be enjoying himself. Atty and Leo maintained their silence. Whether that was because they were shy or scared, I wasn't sure.

Tabby yawned, stretching her arms up and nearly smacking me in the face.

"Watch it, Tab," I warned, and she giggled, lowering her arms.

"Sorry, I'm just so bored and tired," she said.

"Well, we're almost to the next town. We can stop for the night, and you can do whatever it is you do at night. Sleep, or play with your brothers, or both." I had to imagine the boys spent some time talking at night after a whole day of being silent. But what did I know about being a kid? I hadn't been one in over two hundred years.

Jami

Flipping my lucky coin between my knuckles, I watched as Lia and Khali ordered drinks at the bar. The children were in bed, watched over by Callum and Korra. All I could think about was Finn trapped out on the ocean with his accursed father.

I jolted as Marley snatched my coin from my fingers.

"Still have this?" she asked, looking it over before flicking it back to me.

"Maybe someday it will be of use," I said. My mother had given it to me when I was nine or ten years old. I don't remember what she'd said exactly at the time, but she told me it was lucky and to never go anywhere without it. So, I hadn't. It used to have our family crest on one side, and an old symbol that looked like waves in a horseshoe on the other side. My constant fidgeting had buffed down the once raised images.

"Now that we have our drinks," Lia said as she sat down beside me and Khali sat opposite her. "Why were you out in the forest, Khali?"

"I've been trying to help the smaller towns with importing and exporting goods. The ones who haven't been able to go out on the water because of the siren attacks. I was staying the night a few houses down from here when I had a horrible

nightmare. I was able to get outside before the shift, but it took me all night to calm down. You found me shortly after I shifted back," Khali explained.

"I thought you'd gotten your shifting under control," Lia said.

"I thought so, too. Apparently, we were both wrong," Khali sighed. She ran the pad of her finger around the rim of her glass, a light hum coming from it.

"Do you want to talk about the nightmare?" Lia asked a bit more quietly, and the rest of our group at the table had the decency to look elsewhere.

Khali shook her head. "Not here. Not now."

"I'm here when and if you're ever ready," Lia said, patting her hand. "In the meantime, when we reach Asmara, I'm going to need your help recruiting other shifters."

Khali waved her hand through the air. "That shouldn't be a problem."

"We need mostly shifters who can swim, because we're fighting sirens, so this won't be as simple as last time."

Khali scoffed, "Last time was far from simple."

"Fair enough," Lia said.

"What was last time?" I asked.

"Last time was when we rescued Viv from Humer," Lia explained.

I glanced between the two of them, unsure what exactly that meant. From their somber expressions I could tell it wasn't something I should question Lia further about.

"Where is Viv?" Khali asked. "You two are hardly ever apart."

Lia cleared her throat and fisted her hands under the table. I reached out, taking one of her hands in mine, stroking my thumb along her wrist. She smiled at me.

Lia said, “She’s with Finn–”

“With Finn?” Khali interrupted. “Where?”

“They are on Brom’s ship,” I finished for Lia. Khali knew who Finn’s father was, and he’d even asked her to keep tabs on him anytime Brom went to the Asmaran port.

“Again, *what?”* Khali pressed her hands together in front of her mouth. “Brom wants Finn dead.”

My gut clenched. It wasn’t a secret that Brom hated his son, or that Finn hated him back, but I was trying my best to hope he and Viv would both make it safely to Asmara despite the vessel where they were trapped.

Lia wore a panicked expression now, too.

“But he won’t really hurt them, will he? We have his children with us. Would he risk them?” she asked.

Khali shook her head. “I don’t know. Finn somehow played a hand in Brom losing the love of his life. I didn’t find out who that was, or what Finn did to cause that, though.”

“What?” My lip curled in confusion. Finn had never taken anything from Brom, let alone the love of his life.

“Pirates are always stealing things from one another,” Khali said, shrugging. “And they hold onto grudges even after death.”

Despite my resentment, I couldn’t argue with her statement. Every pirate I’d ever known fit that description, including myself.

“We have to find a way on that ship before they reach Asmara,” Lia said, gripping the edge of the table with the hand I didn’t hold. “We need to make sure Viv is alright.”

“Marley and Garrett are taking turns flying out there. They said they haven’t seen anything to worry about,” I reminded her. “If they do, they’ll step in, despite Brom’s warnings. That’s all we can do right now.”

"Fine," Lia said, her jaw clenching. I kissed her cheek to try to ease some of that tension. She merely sighed and turned back to Khali, asking, "Do you know anything about a powerful item the siren queen may be looking for?"

Khali cocked her head and tapped her chin.

"It's funny you mention it, I actually have heard something about that," she said, and Lia jerked back.

It didn't surprise me that Khali had heard about the magical object. She had ears everywhere with all her friends and dalliances.

"What have you heard?" Lia pressed.

"Not much," she admitted. "But there has been talk of it in the port of Asmara among thieves."

"So, more people are looking for it?"

"I think so. Word has spread that it will make the siren queen powerful enough to rule the ocean, and there are an awful lot of pirates and the like who want that for themselves." Khali rolled her shoulders and cracked her neck. "I've had a few men offer me hefty sums for any information on its whereabouts."

I stiffened. Lia didn't seem phased by Khali's words, but something told me we should keep the map to ourselves. It wasn't that I didn't trust Khali, but sometimes money and power led people astray.

"Has anyone mentioned what exactly it is?" Lia asked.

"I've heard a scepter, a stone, a crown, or about twenty other possibilities," Khali laughed. "But the one I hear the most is the scepter. I overheard Brom's first mate, Roland, talking about it the last time they were in port."

Roland. His name was like a punch to the gut. A strange emptiness had opened inside me when hearing of his death, but I wouldn't call it grief. I couldn't grieve for a man who had caused me endless torment until the day I'd left home.

"Do you know anyone who would have more information on it?" Lia asked, drawing my attention back to the conversation.

Khali narrowed her eyes at Lia. "Are you trying to go after it?"

"I'll do whatever it takes to bring down the siren queen," Lia said.

"Fair enough. I've heard rumors that Humer had been searching for it before he was apprehended. He may have some information about it."

Lia winced, but said, "I'll look into visiting him."

I gave her a confused look. "Humer? The man you just told me you had to rescue Viv from? Like hell you're going to visit with him."

Lia turned her gaze from Khali to me. "I didn't ask you for your permission, did I? Besides, he's in prison, it's not like he'd be able to do anything besides talk."

I ground my jaw. The topic would come up again, and I'd be sure to say my peace then.

Khali nodded and sipped her drink. I noticed that Marley and Garrett had slipped out, most likely to go check on the captain aboard Brom's ship.

"So, you managed to snag Jami's attention, huh?" Khali asked Lia, waggling her eyebrows at me. I groaned. *Here we go.*

Khali continued, "He was a hard one to pin down. Any time he came into port, he spent most of his time at Finn's side, or on the ship. He didn't give in to just any proposition from the many women who lined up for a shot at his heart."

"I guess me saving his life from the siren queen must have made quite the impression on him," Lia said, nudging me with her elbow.

"Ah, that could have done it," Khali teased.

The air around us shifted as the tension eased from our conversation change. It didn't help me forget that we had no idea what hell Brom was putting Finn and Viv through, or that we were no closer to defeating the siren queen.

Finn

Lewis took me to Brom's office at the top of the stairs. A desk covered in parchment and stacks of books occupied the back of the room. Besides that, there was an open door that I could see a bed and bath through.

Sitting behind the desk in a worn, overstuffed, brown leather armchair, Brom stared at me with disdain and steepled his hands before him. His elbows rested on the arms of the chair.

Lewis pushed me down into the plain, wooden seat in front of the desk.

To my right, I noted a wall with different swords on display. The left wall was blank except for a portrait that looked an awful lot like the mountains of my home in Sylvane.

"Leave us, Lewis," Brom commanded.

When the door shut, Brom turned his gaze back to me. I crossed my arms over my chest and leaned back, sticking one leg out in front of me. I wouldn't let Brom know how uncomfortable I was back on a ship. He'd already found one of my weaknesses; he didn't need more ammo against me.

"Captain Finnian," Brom said my name as if it were laughable.

"Captain Bromwell," I used his full name as well. Two could play that game.

He pulled a bottle of whiskey out from beneath his desk and waved to the two glasses he'd already set out before him. Without asking if I wanted one, he poured the whiskey and handed me a glass.

"You've always been considered so *fearsome,*" Brom said, leaning toward me. "Why is that I wonder?"

"You'd do better to ask one of your own men. I'm not one to boast my own conquests." I lifted my shoulder and took a sip from my drink. It was good whiskey.

"Yet look at you now," he said, gesturing at the room. "No ship, no crew, falling in *love,"* he hissed the last word. "Like some commoner." Brom leaned back in his seat and clasped his hands over his stomach.

"You won't fucking touch her," I growled, which didn't impact Brom in the slightest.

"I'll admit, she's a pretty one, but so long as you behave yourself, I have no interest in her."

"Why am I really here?" I asked, narrowing my eyes at him and putting my glass onto the desk.

Chuckling, he tapped his fingers on the desktop. "I want back on the water, just like everybody else. But there's one big problem with that."

"The siren queen," I finished for him.

He snapped before pointing at me. "Exactly."

"You mean to bargain with her?" I asked.

"That is a fool's mission," he growled. "I want to end her reign."

"By finding the item she searches for," I guessed. "And what makes you think you can find it?"

"I have a map," he said, pressing his tongue into his cheek as he blinked slowly.

"*We* have the map," I reminded him warily.

"I have a man standing guard outside your girl's door right now," he said, as if I wasn't hyperaware of that already.

"You want to work together to find this item?" I asked, instead of continuing to argue as if I had any ground. We both knew I wouldn't cross a line with Viv in danger.

"Who said I needed you?" He cocked a brow.

"Jami's family's crest is on the map. He's likely the only one who will be able to figure out where the map leads," I said, talking out of my ass. I had no idea if it was true, but I wouldn't let Brom get his hands on that magical object.

"Fine. Say I let you join me on this venture, what will *you* bring to the table?"

"Most fearsome pirate, remember?" I said, pointing to myself. "And Lia and Viv will be useful since they're mermaids."

"The problem of the siren queen remains. She won't let us sail through her territory unchecked. If she doesn't attack us again, she'll sure as shit have someone tailing us," Brom said.

"So, we bargain with her," I mused.

Brom sighed. "I already told you that's a fool's errand."

"Tell her you found the map she was looking for on your ship, and you'll give it to her if she agrees to let you have safe passage on the seas."

"And she'll beat us to the prize," Brom argued.

"Not if her map leads her astray," I smirked. "We can have a replica created that looks almost identical to the one we have, but make sure it's an entirely different island. By the time she figures out we've tricked her, hopefully we'll have the object and can defeat her."

Brom pushed his lips out, leaning his head back as he considered my plan.

"How do we get her to come to us so we can make this deal?"

"Oh, she's already on her way," I said. "The sirens who attacked you earlier are headed to fetch her now. We can only pray we reach Asmara before they return, or else she'll have the advantage and any bargaining we might be able to do will be useless."

"Alright. We'll try your plan, and if it all goes to shit, I'll be sure to make your life as much of a living hell as mine's been since you stole the love of my life."

I gaped at him. "What are you talking about?" I asked. "I never stole anyone from you, let alone the love of your life. If anything, *you* ruined my life by abandoning my mother and me."

Brom's cheeks flushed red, and he bared his teeth at me. "You know not of what you speak," he ground out.

"Then tell me! Who did I steal from you? What was her name?"

"Leona." For the second time in a matter of minutes, I stared at him, dumbstruck.

"My mother? How did I steal her from you? You left *her*."

Brom scoffed. "I offered her the world and she turned me down to remain rooted in Sylvane with you."

"Are you blaming me for being born?"

"I'm blaming you for killing your mother," Brom clarified, though it only deepened my confusion.

"My mother died from a mystery illness," I said.

"It was no mystery. Your mother was human, as you well know, and for a human to carry a shifter baby can cause intense

internal damage for the mother. It takes more than a human body can give, since shifters wield more magic than humans."

"So, you *are* blaming me for being born." I rolled my eyes. "There's no way she could have known I'd be a shifter, considering neither of you were. It skipped you, remember?" I sneered.

He ignored that jab. "I'm blaming you for keeping her away from me. She promised she'd return to me. I told her she could bring you with her, but she didn't want to raise you on the sea."

"And so now you're going to try to take Viv from me, is that it?" I tensed as I said it, knowing there was no way I could reach her in time without the guard outside her door being tipped off first.

"No," Brom stated. "I told you. She won't be harmed so long as the both of you behave, and I meant it. But don't think that once we end the tyranny of the siren queen that I'm done with you."

"So, we have a truce then, until we kill the siren queen?" I clarified.

He twitched his nose. "Yes. A truce." He held out his hand to me and I stood to shake it. He gripped my hand tight and pulled me closer, so I leaned over his desk. "If I don't get that map, the truce is off."

Releasing me, he finished off the whiskey in his glass. "Now get out of my office, I'm sick of your face."

I turned on my heel and strode out of the room. Lewis met me outside and made sure I returned to my room.

Inside, I didn't see Viv right away because she'd pulled the covers up over her head. My heart clenched as I thought of her hiding under there as she suffered through her trauma alone.

Walking over to the bed, I started to pull the covers back.

"For the love of Terrian, you scared me," she breathed, clutching her hand to her chest.

"Terrian?" I smirked. "Again with the gods."

"Yes. They may have forsaken me a few times in the past, but I like to believe there's more to life than... well this." She turned her body to face me.

"I gave up on the gods a long time ago," I said, rolling my shoulders back. "Mind if I hide out under here with you?" I asked, nodding to the comforter.

"I won't stop you," she said, scooting over to make room for me.

Kicking off my boots and draping my belt over the desk chair, I climbed into the bed with Viv, pulling the comforter over our heads.

"What did Brom want?" she asked.

Candlelight from the room permeated the blanket enough for me to see her in the darkness. She'd placed her hands under her head and watched me as I watched her.

"A truce."

"A truce?" she asked, sounding as surprised as I was.

"A truce," I confirmed. "Until we kill the siren queen."

"Huh." She attempted to blow her bangs out of her eyes.

I laughed and reached out to help her but paused before touching her. "May I?" I asked and she nodded, biting her lip.

Brushing her hair aside, I let my hand linger against her cheek. At the same time, the ship rocked a bit more vigorously and I inhaled sharply, clenching my hand, and pulling it back. My eyes closed as I imagined sirens swarming the ship around us.

"We're on the sea, where the siren queen is," I said, my breath hitching. Viv pressed herself fully against me, draping her arms around my neck.

"We're on the sea, where I was born and grew up, and thrived," she countered. "We're on the sea where my home is, and on which you found a new home for yourself."

Viv took my hand and brought it to her lips, brushing them over my knuckles.

"Come back to me, Captain," she said, and the way my title sounded coming from her lips undid me.

I hated it when anyone else called me captain outside my crew, but if Viv wanted to, I'd let her call me solely by that title so long as she said it as she had just then.

"Call me that again," I murmured, and she gasped, a bubble of laughter coming out of her, the sound momentarily chasing my fears away.

Viv

Pushing the comforter back to get cooler air, I moved closer to Finn. "Better?" I asked, hoping he wasn't focusing on the ship's movements.

"A little," he said. "I'm in the sea, with you." His trembling seemed to have calmed. "My sea goddess."

"That would be Neros, not me," I teased, pressing my lips to his jaw. "I'm no goddess."

"To me you are." He trailed a hand down my back.

His presence made me feel a way I'd never known anyone else's to. It was comforting, but also filled me with anticipation and excitement.

Before I could rethink it, I said, "I'd like to see the rest of your tattoos."

Finn stiffened and I worried I'd said the wrong thing. I pulled my arms against myself as he propped his head up with his hand and looked down at me.

"Are you sure? If it's too much, or too soon..." he started, taking one of my hands in his and I realized he'd only been worried about me, not what I'd said.

"Please," I said, the word sounding almost desperate. Without questioning me further, he stood and started to remove

his pants. Stopping him, I placed my hands over his. "Let me." My hands shook as I unbuttoned his pants and inched them down over his thighs. *His thighs.*

I trembled at the sight of them. Something about men and women's thighs had always had my blood heating. He stepped out of his pants and my hands reached for his drawers next, pausing. He took hold of my hands once more, pulling me up from the bed and into his arms.

"Viv, we don't need to do anything you're not ready for. If you change your mind at any time, say the word, and we'll stop," Finn promised, gazing intently into my eyes.

"I trust you," I said, kissing him. "But I want you to..." I flicked my eyes down and he chuckled. It wasn't that I'd never removed a man's clothes before, but tonight, this was the part I couldn't bring myself to do. I needed his help, and I would no longer be afraid to ask for it. Even if it was for something this mundane.

"As you wish," he said, winking. I lowered myself onto the bed, watching as he finished undressing, releasing his impressive length from his drawers. I'd seen it once before, but not hard and up close.

"The tattoo," I whispered, noticing it on his groin. "It's a star. What does it mean?"

"Oh god," he leaned his head back, stifling a laugh. "Don't leave me for this one."

"Tell me," I prompted, and he dropped his chin to his chest, shaking his head slowly.

"It's supposed to be the north star, you know, the beacon of hope, guides people home," he laughed as he said it and I couldn't stop myself from laughing along.

I covered my mouth. "I love it," I said.

"No, you don't," he rebuked. "Jami dared me to get it."

"I want to see the last one."

"May I ask for something in return first?" He stepped toward the bed, running a hand up my leg. Even through my leggings, it sent shivers through me.

"That depends," I rasped, my voice becoming thick with desire.

"Do *you* have any tattoos I should know about?" His hand traveled up and down, thoroughly distracting me.

"Um, no. No tattoos." I gasped as his hand moved to my inner thigh. "But..." Cold replaced the warmth that had pooled in my gut as I thought of my scars. "You've seen my scars." I removed my shirt in one swift motion, startling Finn. I was glad I'd chosen not to wear my leather corset today, since it was so hard to remove without help.

My fingers tentatively traced the scars on my lower abdomen. Before Finn had seen them, the only ones I'd ever allowed to see my scars were my sisters. In my mer form, they were covered by scales and undetectable.

Finn removed his hand from my thigh and hovered it over my scars. "May I?" he asked, and I nodded.

His fingers traced the lines of my scars, his touch so gentle it was almost unnoticeable. Pain creased his features and anger sparked in his gaze.

I captured his hand in mine, tugging him onto the bed. Once he lay beside me, I moved to straddle him, placing his hand on my waist.

I leaned down, pressing my mouth to his, and his free hand cupped the back of my head, his thumb stroking the nape of my neck. Grinding against him, I ached to feel him inside of me. His hand roamed from my waist to my ass, squeezing it before he slipped his hand into my leggings. He moaned against my mouth as he found me already wet for him.

As his thumb traced circles around my opening, I gripped his shoulders hard, my nails digging into his skin.

"Please," the word slipped out of me, revealing my need for him. Driving two fingers into my center, he growled low in his throat at the same time I moaned his name.

Removing his fingers, he flipped me onto my back and kissed me passionately.

"You're still sure," he rasped, and I nodded eagerly. He tugged my leggings and underwear off and threw them across the room. Starting at my neck, he began a trail of kisses down to my scars. He traced one with his tongue, before easing himself between my thighs, parting them.

My back arched against the bed as he ran his tongue up my center.

"*Fuck*," I swore, moaning again as he feasted on me. My hands wound into his hair, and I came apart under his tongue. "Come here." I pulled him up, kissing him fiercely and tasting myself on his lips.

Hitching my legs over Finn's hips, I grabbed his ass and guided him to my opening. In one powerful thrust he was inside of me. I cried out, raking my nails down his back, and kissing him again.

He picked up speed, bringing me back to the edge of my climax, and sending me tumbling over it, and dragging him along with me as I clenched around him.

His moans of pleasure were swallowed by my kisses and as he pulled out of me, a supreme sense of peace washed over me. He collapsed down beside me, breathing heavily. Sweat soaked us both, but I wrapped myself back around him, hitching one leg over his and draping an arm across his chest.

"Can I see that other tattoo now?" I asked, breathless.

Finn burst out laughing but rolled over. "Here it is, sweetheart."

I spotted the tattoo on his ass and gaped at it. "A mermaid? You have a *mermaid* tattooed on your ass?"

He rolled back over, his body shaking with laughter as he took me back into his arms.

"Jami picked that one out, too. He wouldn't tell me what it was for the longest time." Finn brushed his hand over my cheek, cupping it and resting his forehead against mine. "It has a new meaning now." He kissed my nose and I grinned.

Turning in his arms, I settled my back against Finn's chest and closed my eyes.

"It seems like you and Jami might have a drinking problem." A yawn punctuated my words. "Do you miss sailing with him?"

"Not exactly," he sighed. "Ever since the attack and losing the *Leona,* the thought of sailing fills me with dread."

That explained his earlier reaction.

"That's fair, you almost *died,*" I said.

He sighed. "It's more than that, though. Even the smell of the sea makes me nauseous."

"I understand that. The smell of jasmine makes me nauseous." Even mentioning it brought a swell of nausea to my stomach.

"Jasmine?" Finn asked.

I faced him and placed my hands against his chest. "It must have been in Humer's soap or something. He always smelled like it." I flashed back to the first time I smelled it and cringed. "It drew me in when I first met him."

"You knew him before he held you captive?" Finn placed his hand over mine.

"Barely. I met him when I visited Asmara alone for the night. I just wanted to find someone to have some fun with..."

The lights of the Asmaran port could fool you into thinking it was still daytime. There was always something going on and so many people out and about. I didn't usually visit Asmara alone; Lia normally accompanied me. But that night, I just needed to get away and have some fun.

My first stop was a bar we frequented anytime we visited Asmara. It was there that I saw him for the first time - Marcus Humer. He wore his curling blonde hair tied back, and kohl around his green eyes that made them pop. He was ruggedly handsome, charming, and, best of all, interested in having a little fun.

"You light up the room," he said, draping an arm over the back of my chair as we sat at the bar. "And your laugh is contagious."

"Are you trying to butter me up?" I teased, leaning in, and fluttering my lashes at him. "Because it's working," I murmured, brushing my lips over his.

The first red flag should have been when he didn't kiss me back. He had no interest in me sexually, only in the fact that I was a shifter.

"I thought he was bringing me back to his place, but instead, he brought me to his underground lab, and I didn't leave until Lia showed up with a whole rescue squad two years later," I finished, and Finn was speechless. At least, I assumed he was since he said nothing, so I continued.

"In the beginning, I tried seducing him, hoping that if he fell for me, he'd let me go. But he truly had no interest in me in that way, so it never worked. My brain twisted and blamed

myself for trusting so easily, and then it would blame me for not being appealing enough to entice him." I stopped, hating that I still had those thoughts.

"I truly have no idea what to say, but I would do anything to make you stop hurting over that disgusting man and the horrific things he did to you," Finn said.

I couldn't help but smile. Kissing the corner of his mouth softly, I wrapped my arm around him and settled in against him.

"Thank you," I said and turned so my back was against his chest once more. His arm draped over me and I held it as I closed my eyes.

"Goodnight, Vivianne," Finn murmured against my ear and, as if my body took that as its cue, I fell asleep. My nightmares returned with a vengeance.

"Keep her down," Humer commanded. "She's awfully feisty this morning."

My legs flailed, but one person grabbed each leg and slammed it down against the table. I cried out as they clamped the shackles onto my ankles. When I tried to move again, the shackles bit into my skin, which had already been scraped raw from the shackles I wore in my room.

I couldn't see any of the faces above me. The light shone too brightly, leaving spots in my vision.

"It's time," Humer said. "She'll need to be out for this one, or else the pain may kill her," he told one of his helpers. There were a handful of helpers, though I only knew the two men who carried me in and out of the operating room. I never made their job any easier, always making them do all the work. It was the only kind of fight I had left in me at this point.

"Here," a man said, the one I had named Scar for the jagged white line bisecting his face. I didn't have much left in me to lend to originality. The other man who helped him was Glasses because he wore glasses. Maybe I'd come up with better names for them if I stayed alive a while longer.

Since I'd been captured, there had been many other shifters who came and went, none lasted more than a few weeks and I had no idea what came of them. I prayed they had made it out, but something told me that wasn't the case.

"Send her under," Humer commanded, and a mask was placed over my face. I held my breath for a moment, hoping by some grace of the gods that I'd be saved, but no one came, and my lungs began to ache.

Breathing deeply, I inhaled the gas and faded from consciousness.

I woke later in utter agony. They had finished whatever operation they had planned but were still in the process of stitching me back up. My screams echoed through the room, piercing my own ears.

I'd never felt such pain in my life and wasn't sure I'd survive it.

"Kill me," I sobbed. "Please."

No one said anything, and they made no attempts to send me back under with whatever gas they had used to knock me out the first time.

A hand clamped over my mouth as I continued to scream and I bit down hard. Glasses cursed and wrenched his hand away.

"Please," I begged, forgetting any sense of dignity or scrap of defiance. "Just kill me."

"It's done," Humer said, pushing away from the table in his rolling chair. "Take her to the pool so she can shift and heal."

Tears streamed down my cheeks, both from the pain but also from relief that he had finished his procedure.

Glasses lifted me from the table and the movement caused the pain to flare up again, making me scream out once more before I blacked out.

My eyelids fluttered open, allowing me to take in the room around me. The candlelight on the desk wavered as the ship rocked. I registered that Finn had one hand stroking my hair and the other gripping my shoulder.

"What happened?" I asked, my voice cracking. I tried sitting up, but pain radiated from my scars, making me wince.

"You were screaming," Finn said.

My nightmare came crashing back in and I squeezed my eyes shut as my hand flew to my mouth. Finn stopped stroking my hair, but he held my other hand, and I clutched it tight.

Though Scar's face was burned into my memory, I couldn't for the life of me picture Glasses, other than the exact kind of glasses he wore. Rounded rims with tinted lenses.

I tried to sit up again, and this time, there was no pain.

"What would help you right now?" he asked, brushing his thumb over my damp forehead, moving my hair aside.

"Just...hold me?" I asked, slightly embarrassed at my request, but I didn't care anymore. I needed to accept that the closer we came to Asmara, the more my trauma would be triggered. In one day, we'd be back in the kingdom where it all happened.

Finn wrapped me in his arms, and I rested my head against his bare chest.

"You're safe, Viv," he murmured, leaning forward to kiss my forehead. "I'll keep you safe," he promised.

My nightmare did not return that night; I dreamed of Finn.

Tabby held the reins for the horse as Lia chatted with Khali.

"Are you really a dragon?" Tabby asked.

"I can show you when we reach Asmara," Khali said.

Tabby's eyes became saucers as she smiled.

"When will we get there?"

"Tomorrow, hopefully," Lia said. If we didn't hit any snags, we'd reach Asmara after one last day of travel.

Of course, we didn't find an inn to stay in for our last night. So, we made a fire on the beach and did our best to ensure the children were comfortable. Callum tucked them into the blankets we'd given them and joined the rest of us by the fire.

Khali flew ahead to Asmara to get lodgings and start trying to find shifters to recruit for our army. Tabby and the boys had loved seeing her in her dragon form. It was the first time I'd heard the boys say anything.

"Only one more night," Lia said, sitting beside me and leaning her head on my shoulder as she stared into the fire. It was too hot to get close, but we'd been able to heat up some of the packaged food we'd bought at our last stop.

"One more night," I echoed.

Tears brimmed in her eyes. I wrapped my arms around her and pulled her in close to my side, resting my chin on the top of her head.

"Viv will be fine," I said, and prayed I was right.

We sat like that, even as Nix and Korra joined the cuddle session on Lia's other side. I laughed but was happy to see Lia's spirits lifting as her tears stopped.

Garrett sat on the other side of the fire with Callum, and Marley was off checking on Brom's ship.

"Want to take a walk?" I asked, standing, and holding my hand out to Lia. Korra and Nix moved away so she could stand without them holding her back.

We strolled along the waterline so she could enjoy the feel of the ocean even if she couldn't enter it.

"I miss the water," she said, staring out at it longingly. "Don't you?"

"I miss being on a ship. The water not so much," I said, pulling at my shirt as it started to feel constricting.

"I'm sure you know that sounds odd," she pointed out. "Why don't you like the water?"

"Brings up bad memories of my brothers." I craned my neck, continuing to pull on my shirt.

Lia stopped walking, moving in front of me, and placed her hand over mine to stop me from fidgeting.

"I'm sorry," I murmured.

"Don't apologize," she said, shaking her head. "I hate to see you so uncomfortable. Would it help if we move away from the water?"

"No. I need to face my fears eventually. Being near the water isn't what gets to me, it's the thought of being under it." I shuddered.

Lia tapped her cheek thoughtfully and waded ankle deep into the water. Holding her hands out to me, she smiled. I stared at her, unsure I wanted to attempt to overcome any trauma that night.

"We won't go out far, I promise," she said.

I kicked off my boots and took her hands, letting her lead me knee-deep into the water. Wading in the water didn't give me too much anxiety. As I'd told her, it was being *under* the water that triggered me. If the mermaids hadn't been there to save us from the siren queen, I'd have been lost to the sea after freezing once I'd hit the water.

"I'll dry you off after," Lia said as she sat down in the water. It reached up over her shoulders and her bright green hair floated on the surface.

"That's not what concerns me," I reminded her, sitting down in front of her. The water lapped at my neck and I itched to stand, but stayed seated with Lia's hands in mine.

"Doing okay?" she asked.

I shook my head and gulped as the water splashed against my back. Lia stroked my cheek gently with her thumb. "Say the word and we get out."

"Talk to me," I ground out. "Give me something else to think about." I closed my eyes.

"We're hours away from Asmara, where we'll get to reunite with Finn and Viv, and find other people to help us take on the siren queen," she began talking.

I shivered as she ran a hand down my chest. Opening my eyes, I stared down at Lia, placing a hand on the small of her back and making small circles with my thumb.

My trembling seemed to calm slightly. "My sea queen," I murmured.

"I'm not queen yet," she teased, pressing her lips to mine briefly.

I trailed my free hand down her back, letting it join the other one as she leaned into my strokes.

"Are you ready to try going under?" she asked, taking my hand from her back, and holding it again.

Lia slipped beneath the surface of the water. Resurfacing, she ran both hands through her hair, pushing it back out of her face. I stared, desire warring with the pit that had formed as I considered going beneath the water.

"I hate this," I said, but I took a deep breath and leaned back, closing my eyes as I submerged myself entirely.

At first, nothing happened. It wasn't as if every time I was under water I panicked. I'd taken plenty of baths in my lifetime without incident. But something about being in the cooler water of the sea reminded me of those ice-cold baths my brothers had forced me into. Squeezing Lia's hand, I forced myself to remain beneath the surface a little longer.

Stay down, Jamesy. No one cares whether you come back up, Roland's voice rang in my ears, and I jolted out of the water, standing and splashing Lia.

"I'm here," she said, pushing to her feet and wrapping her arms around my neck.

I pulled her tightly against me and relished the warmth of her body.

She looked up at me and the moonlight shone in her eyes, making her appear ethereal.

"We should get back to the others, I don't want Nix and Korra to worry," Lia said, kissing me once before leading me out of the water.

Lia

Once we were on the road in the morning, I positioned myself next to Jami, while Tabby rode with Nix. I wanted to discuss a plan with him in case anything went wrong when we met with Brom again to get back Finn and Viv. We figured Marley and Garrett could fly ahead and be our lookouts, while Nix snuck on the ship to be a backup in case things went south. Otherwise, Jami and I would be the only ones walking onto the ship.

"May I see the map?" Jami asked.

Contorting myself and reaching into my saddle, I managed to grab it without falling from my horse and handed him the protective tube I'd put it in.

When I'd first seen it, I thought it looked like any other treasure map. Not that I'd seen many, they weren't used much anymore among pirates. There was an X marking whatever the map led to, and a crude drawing of an island. There were no coordinates, or distinct markers that helped indicate where the island may be.

In the corner of the map, though, I recognized Jami's family crest: a shadow of an eagle flying above mountains and surrounded by dark whorls.

"My family came into a large sum of money out of nowhere when I was about ten years old," he said, rolling up the map once more. "I wonder if this has something to do with that."

"That was about the time Roland had pushed me out of a tree and nearly killed me," he added. "That's how I got the scar." He rubbed the scar on his chest as if it still pained him. "Finn left a nice scar on Roland for retribution, though."

"Maybe there is more on that island than treasure," I suggested. "Maybe we're right in thinking whatever the siren queen is after is also there."

"But if it's so powerful, why wouldn't whoever made this map have taken it? I can't imagine my father giving up that kind of power."

"Unless they didn't know it was there at the time," I said.

"We should give it to Korra and have her stay somewhere safe while we meet with Brom." He handed it back to me.

"I'll ask her," I consented. "Khali is meeting us at The Flight Deck Inn where we'll be staying. We should go there first so Korra won't be alone in case the siren queen decides to send another message."

I cringed as the image of Cole's disemboweled body flashed in my mind and Bree... I shook my head. It wouldn't help anything to fall into grief now.

"The inn is only a block or two from the port," I continued. "So, we'll stop there, confirm our plan with everyone, and go straight to the ship. You fill in your crew and I'll fill in my sisters. We have to make sure Callum doesn't overhear anything." I glanced back at the pirate who rode in the middle of our group with one of the boys.

As we neared the border of Asmara, we started passing more people on the road. The trees disappeared, and farms started popping up. At the official border between the kingdoms of Lanteria and Asmara, there was a large stone archway with *Welcome to Asmara* carved into the top of it. All down the sides were carvings of different animals representing most of the shifters. A few had been left out, but there were so many kinds of shifters, it would have been impossible to include them all. Asmara had been the first safe haven for all shifters following the shifter wars.

Moving forward past the official border, houses were built closer together, and there were a few shops mixed in among them. Tabby begged to stop at a bakery for sweets, but Nix shut her down despite her own sweet tooth. Laughing to myself, I made a note to never let Nix be in charge of a child again.

About an hour later, we reached The Flight Deck Inn. It was set apart from the other houses and shops, with shrubs surrounding it and a long, cobblestone driveway leading up to it. The inn was at least three times the size of any of the others we'd stayed in.

Inside, there was a large entryway where we checked in, and off to the right, I could see a dining room through the archway, and to the left, a bar. Neither were occupied.

"We have reservations for eight, under Aurelia," I told the woman behind the front desk. She scanned a book in front of her, smacking her lips as she did.

"Ah, here ya are," she said, reaching behind herself to grab four keys. "These are your room keys. Don't lose them, we don't have spares," she warned with a toothy smile.

"Thanks." I took the keys and gave one to Marley, one to Jami, and one to Korra.

Reaching into my bag, I pulled out a letter I'd written the night before to send to our sisters in Lanteria. Handing it to the innkeeper, I asked, "May I leave this with you to be sent out?"

"Yes'm," she said, taking the letter and setting it with a few other pieces of outgoing mail.

"Let's drop our stuff in our rooms and head out." I told everyone, and no one argued.

Grabbing hold of Korra's arm before she could follow everyone else, I pulled her toward me, quickly taking the map from my pack and shoving it into hers.

"Keep that safe," I whispered. "You're going to stay here while the rest of us head to the port to trade the kids for Finn and Viv. Let Nix know she's going to go ahead and hide out on Brom's ship until we arrive."

"Okay," she said, nodding.

Releasing her, we followed the rest of the group to our rooms. They were at the end of the hall on the third floor of the place. Callum and the kids waited in the hall. Callum wore a mask of indifference, but I noticed him watching our every move. He *did* offer to help with our packs, but no one had taken him up on it.

When we all reconvened in the hall, Korra remained in her room.

"Korra's not feeling well so she's going to stay behind," Nix said.

"Jami and I are the only ones who need to go to the ship, so why don't the rest of you just do your own thing?" I suggested. "Find some food, and if you can recruit anyone for our cause, all the better."

We left our horses in the stable, not needing them now that we were in the hub of Asmara. Everything was within walking distance.

"Can I walk with you?" Tabby asked as she came up beside me.

"Sure," I responded, trying to smile back at her. It was hard looking at her and not putting some blame on her, knowing that her father held my friends captive. She took my hand, reminding me how young she truly was, even though sometimes she seemed older. That must have come from growing up surrounded by pirates.

As we walked, Nix slipped into the crowd, followed by Marley and Garrett. Jami stayed by my side.

The ship came into view as we rounded another corner and entered the fray of the port. There were people everywhere, going to the street vendors along the boardwalk and meeting with friends who were coming in off ships. The Asmaran port was the place to be if you wanted to have some fun or deal in black market goods. There was little policing, which was why it was the most popular place for pirates to make port.

"I see it!" Atty cried out, and I turned to see him start running toward the ship.

"Atticus!" Tabby yelled after him. We picked up our pace to catch up with him, but he was small and wove through the crowds easier. Thankfully he made it safely to the gangplank leading up to the ship.

"They got him," Callum said, breathing a sigh of relief as one of the pirates helped Atty aboard.

We arrived at the gangplank shortly after, and Leo ran ahead to reunite with Atty.

I tensed as I dropped down onto the deck of the ship, expecting to be rushed the moment I got aboard, but nothing happened. Everyone continued about their business and no one approached me except Captain Brom.

"You upheld your end of the bargain," Brom said, nodding to his children. "And so will I." He snapped his fingers. Finn and Viv came out into the open, looking perfectly well and unharmed.

I rushed forward, wrapping my arms around Viv and squeezing her tight.

"Thank the goddesses," I murmured.

"And I thought you didn't believe in them," Viv teased before adding, "I'm alright." She squeezed me back.

"Get them out of my sight before I change my mind," Brom growled, turning on his heel.

Pulling away from Viv, I turned to Brom. "What about the siren queen? Will you help fight her?" I asked.

His eyes flashed to Finn before answering. "We'll see. We shall remain in port a while longer, as you suggested. Now go."

I didn't wait for him to change his mind and moved as fast as I could toward the gangplank, pulling Viv along with me.

Once we were all safely off the ship and moving through the crowds, I felt safe to say, "That was too easy."

"We'll worry about his plans later, right now, let's get to the inn," Finn said. He and Jami cleared a path through the people as we went, allowing me and Viv to remain side by side. I never wanted to let her out of my sight again.

Viv

Finn held the door as everyone entered the inn. Lia had her arm looped through mine and I didn't think she ever planned on letting go.

"If we can meet in one of the rooms, I need to tell you all--" Finn walked in behind us and let the door fall shut. He stopped dead in his tracks as Korra and another familiar face stood in the entryway to the dining room. I furrowed my brow, recognizing Khali from Asmara.

Apparently, Finn also knew her.

"Khali?" he said, but she was already bounding across the room as her name left his lips.

"Finn!" She wrapped her arms around his neck and a blush bloomed on his cheeks. "I've missed you," she said before kissing his cheek and pulling away.

I didn't want to make any assumptions but watching them made my heart pound.

"What a small world! You traveling with Lia and Viv like this," Khali said, turning to wave toward us. "Lia told me you were on Brom's ship, and I almost didn't believe her."

Our group headed into the bar area, and I followed, heading straight for the bartender. Lia, still attached to me, was along for the ride.

"What's going on Viv?" she asked, obviously noticing my distress.

"Nothing," I snapped. "I'll tell you later," I added when I saw her hurt expression.

Taking a seat at the end of the bar, I tried to calm myself down.

"Do you know how Khali and Finn know each other?" I asked Lia.

"Jami told me they get together anytime the pirates are in Asmara," Lia said. "Viv, what's going on?"

I put my head in my hands and tried to take deep breaths as anger pulsed through me.

"Finn and I slept together," I said. It came out muffled.

"Not to take away from your revelation, but I did assume after seeing the two of you in bed together the other night," Lia said, putting her hand on my knee.

"No, not then," I lifted my head. "Our first time was last night."

"And now Khali..." she turned her gaze to Khali and Finn who were walking toward us. Khali veered to sit with the others at a table in the middle of the room.

"Do you want me to stay?" Lia asked.

I shook my head. "No. I'm okay." She squeezed my knee before hopping off her chair and joining everyone else.

Finn took Lia's seat, sitting with one elbow propped on the bar, one on the back of the barstool, and his hands clasped before him.

"What's going through your mind?" he asked, his soft smile making me melt.

"I'm flustered," I said. "Lia tells me that you and Khali have been sleeping together."

"We used to, yes. But I told her I don't want to do that anymore," Finn said.

"You never told me about her," I continued, and his shoulders sagged.

"No, I didn't think it was worth mentioning," he said, and he seemed sincere, which only made me sorry for Khali.

"How long were you two together?" I asked.

He bit the inside of his lip as he looked thoughtful. "About six years, maybe?"

"Six years?" I gaped at him. "That's a big chunk of time."

Longer than the time we spent together; Humer's voice echoed in my mind.

"It was never serious between us," Finn said.

"Oh," I breathed, still half lost in my own thoughts. I tucked my hands beneath my legs on the chair, considering what I should do, or how I should react.

There was a time when I'd brush this kind of thing right off, never sparing it another thought. That wasn't who I was anymore, and I wasn't sure that was a bad thing.

"What's going through your mind now?" Finn asked again, cocking his head to the side.

"Too many things," I said. "It never seems to stop these days."

"Tell me what you want me to do to prove to you that I care about you, that I would never intentionally hurt you, and I'll do it. If you want me to get down on my knees and beg for your forgiveness, I'll do that, too."

He slid off the barstool and dropped to his knees before me, grinning as he did.

"That's a sight you won't see every day," Marley called from the table.

Laughter bubbled out of me.

"You're making a fool of yourself," I said. "People will start to doubt how fearsome you are."

"I'll happily give them a reminder," he said with a wink. "Now, Vivianne, will you forgive me?"

"Yes, *Captain* Finnian, I forgive you," I said, holding my hand out to him. He took it and stood, kissing me, and there was a chorus of comments from the group.

Finn and I joined the others at the table before we all moved up to Lia and Jami's room. It was meant to be for me and Lia, but it didn't take much convincing for her to swap me for Jami so I could stay with Finn.

My sisters joined me on the bed set against the left wall. Opposite us, Garrett and Marley occupied the two chairs next to the small round table beneath the room's one window. Jami and Finn stood beside them, and Khali had left to work on recruiting.

"While we were on Brom's ship, I made a deal with him," Finn started. Jami's eyes narrow as he considered Finn's words, Marley and Garrett appeared equally as suspicious, but none of them interrupted Finn. "We give him the map, and we work together to find whatever magical item the siren queen wants."

"No," Jami said immediately. "We can't trust him."

"He'll slit your throat as soon as let you anywhere near an item that powerful," Marley added. "He still thinks he's the most powerful pirate captain."

"We made a truce," Finn said. "If I don't bring him the map..." he trailed off and his eyes flicked to me. I knew exactly what Brom had threatened if Finn didn't deliver the map to him.

"So, we have no choice, then," Lia said. "We work with him."

"But how will we find the item if we can't go out in the water?" Marley asked.

"Brom is going to make a deal with the siren queen. A fabricated map that is almost identical to the one we have, for safe passage on the seas," Finn explained. "And, by the grace of your goddesses, she won't notice it's fake until it's too late."

"Seems like a lot is weighing on a game of chance," Marley mused. "I like it. This is my kind of game."

"I don't like it, but Lia's right. We don't have much choice," Jami said.

My gut twisted with guilt. I was the reason we didn't have a choice.

"There is something else I learned from Khali." Lia's arm went around me, and she rested her head on my shoulder.

"What?" I asked, figuring it was the mention of Khali that had her being so touchy.

"Humer had been looking into some magical object that may be what the siren queen is hunting for, before he was apprehended."

My body shook at the mention of him.

"Humer is in prison," I said, as if Lia didn't know, but deep down I knew where this was headed.

"I'm going to the prison to talk with him and see if he'll give me any more information," she said. "I think he'll be more willing to talk if you're with me, but I understand if you don't want to go."

I put my head in my hands, rubbing my temples as I considered what she was saying.

Since arriving in Asmara, I'd been too distracted to think much about how close we were to the man who had stolen two

years of my life and so much more. My body reacted physically to the memory, my scars aching and my stomach roiling.

But Lia needed me. The whole *sea* needed me. If we could get more information on the object of power, we could potentially find it before the siren queen and get a leg up on her.

Taking a deep breath, I gave Lia my answer, "I'll do it." I lifted my head to meet her gaze, holding it so she'd know I was unwavering, even though my mind was screaming at me how horrible of an idea it all was.

"Okay. We'll leave the day after tomorrow." Lia squeezed my shoulder.

"I'm coming with you," Finn said.

"If you do, you can't come inside with us. We can't risk you saying or doing anything that will make Humer want to keep his secrets," Lia warned.

"She's right," I added, looking up at Finn.

"Fine. I'll be right outside though." Finn turned to Jami and added, "You're coming too, right?"

"Of course," he said.

"We'll all go," Nix chimed in.

Lia shook her head. "No. Some of us need to stay here, to continue recruiting for our army, and keep an eye on the ocean. Viv, Jami, Finn, and I will go."

I closed my eyes and prayed to the goddesses I wouldn't fall apart in the face of my captor.

That night, we went out in hopes of finding shifters to join our army. It wasn't as easy as I'd hoped it would be. Being around for as long as I had, I learned to tell some of the things that differentiated a shifter from a human. Their eyes, sometimes their smell, or even how they dressed. But I was too

distracted by the thought of coming face to face with Humer again and couldn't focus on our task.

Finn and I approached a group of people at the bar we'd stopped at. There was a dance floor filled with people in the center of the room, taking up most of the area. We skirted it.

"How can you tell that other people are shifters?" I asked Finn.

"Shifters are always willing to talk about their shifted forms," he said, adding, "But, with other big cat shifters, it's almost like warning bells go off in my head when they're around. It's probably a scent thing that I can't fully pick up on in my human form. Follow my lead."

Finn strolled up to the group and inserted himself into their circle. I came up behind him but remained outside the circle.

"Did I overhear talk of a round of shots?" Finn asked and all the faces turned to him. A couple of the women raked their gazes over him hungrily and jealousy sparked in my chest.

Stop, Viv. Finn is yours; they can look all they want, but he'll be with you at the end of the night, I reminded myself, washing away the jealousy with smugness.

"Why, are you buying?" one of the men asked, widening his stance as if to claim his territory.

He's a shifter, I thought.

Finn waved down a waitress and requested a round of shots for the group. That's when he noticed me behind him and ushered me into the circle.

"We're trying to feel this place out," Finn said, leaving his arm around me, much to the dismay of a few of the women in the circle. "Figure out if it's a safe space for shifters."

"Look around, buddy," the same man said, opening his arms to the room. "We're all shifters here." A grin spread across

his face, and I turned to take in the room with the new knowledge he'd given us. Now I could see it.

"You wouldn't happen to know anything about the siren queen?" I asked, and the grin slipped from his face.

"All I know is we haven't been able to go in the water for weeks because of that bitch," he snapped.

I perked up. "Then I think I have the perfect proposition for you."

The waitress returned with the round of shots, and everyone grabbed one.

"We're looking for shifters who can fight in the water to help us take down the siren queen," I said. "If any of you are willing."

The man pursed his lips. "If it means freeing up our port again, I'll consider it."

"Me too," another of the men chimed in and a few women echoed his statement.

"Awesome. Anyone you find that wants to help too, send them to The Flight Deck Inn and ask for Khali. She'll give you all the information you need."

"To taking back our sea," Finn said, raising his shot glass. Everyone followed suit, including me, and downed our shots. I nearly gagged it back up but managed to choke it down.

"We're needed elsewhere, but find Khali when you can," Finn told the group before placing his hand on the small of my back and leading me away.

"Where are we heading now?" I asked, excited that we'd been able to find people for our army.

Without answering me, Finn took my hand and led me out to the center of the dance floor.

"You want to dance?" I asked. I had never pegged Finn for a dancing guy. I'd assumed he'd only tried to cut in the other night because he'd been jealous.

"With you, yes." He pulled me against him, and we moved out of time to the music. "Though I'm not claiming to be any good at it," he murmured in my ear.

I laughed. "I used to love dancing, but I don't do it much anymore."

"So, you should lead the way," he said, spinning me out and back in.

"Oh, just because I loved it doesn't mean I was any good at it either," I clarified. "Surprisingly enough, Nix is the only one in our group with any rhythm."

"Finnian!" A woman cried from somewhere to my right. "What are you doing here?" She ran up to us, practically shoving me from his arms, and wrapped her own around him. I caught the smell of the ocean as she arrived, and I knew right away she was a mermaid, too.

She had long, copper hair that matched the smattering of freckles across her nose and cheeks. Her green eyes sparkled under the colored lights above.

Finn hugged her back but gave me an apologetic look over her shoulder.

"Misty," Finn said as he placed his hands on her arms and moved her away from him. "It's been a long time."

"It's actually Farah," she corrected. "Misty is at the bar, though, if you're hoping for a round three. We're just missing Jami." She winked, and bile rose in my throat. I looked to the bar where there was an identical woman only with shorter hair, flirting with the bartender.

Instead of watching everything unfold as I would have before, I stepped up to Finn's side and smiled at the woman.

"Hi, I'm Viv," I said, holding my hand out to her. She stared for a second before throwing her arms around me. "Oof," I grunted from the impact.

"So nice to meet you! So sorry, I shouldn't have cut in, but when I get excited sometimes my brain stops working!" She giggled and released me from her embrace. "Come over to the bar with us, Misty will be so happy to see you!" Farah started walking away.

"I'm sorry, I should have warned you that there may be some reunions while we're out. We frequent Asmara quite a bit." Finn combed his hand through his hair, seeming uncomfortable.

I smiled at him. "Don't worry about it. I do have a question though," I paused, and he grimaced but nodded for me to go on. "Was it before or after you fucked them that you got your mermaid tattoo?" I kept my voice calm, though annoyance simmered beneath the surface.

"I told you, Jami picked that out one night when we were wasted. I barely remember getting it."

"That's not what I asked."

Finn sighed, "After."

"Okay," I said, and started walking toward where Misty and Farah waited at the bar. Finn hurried after me, catching my arm.

"What does that mean?" he asked, and I relished the uncertainty in his voice. It was his turn to be unsure in our relationship, if only for a little while.

Without answering, I sat down on the stool beside Misty and introduced myself to her as well.

"I'm Viv, Finn's arm candy for the night," I said, and Finn stiffened beside me.

"Candy indeed," Misty drawled, her gaze raking me up and down.

"Back off, Misty, she's mine," Finn said, putting his arm around me.

"You can come too, Finny boy." She grinned and took a sip from her drink as she shifted her sultry look to Finn.

"It's a tempting offer," I joked. "But I think we'll pass tonight."

"It's a standing offer," Misty said, finishing off her drink and leaving us behind for the dance floor.

"I'm going to join my sister. Have a nice night!" Farah said. Finn grabbed her arm before she could go.

"Khali is staying at The Flight Deck Inn, you should stop by and see her," he said, and Farah agreed before running to the dance floor.

"They seem nice," I commented as I watched them on the dance floor. Finn stepped in front of me, blocking my view of them.

"So, you're okay?" he asked, searching my gaze. I wrapped my legs around his waist and placed my arms over his shoulders.

"I know you have a past, and I may wish that you'd spent your entire life just waiting for me to walk into it, but that's irrational." I lifted my shoulder in a half shrug. "As long as you don't lie to me, or hide anything from me, we'll be fine."

"I think I'm falling in love with you," he said, placing his hands on my waist.

"Well, don't say it until you're sure," I warned, half teasing. Leaning down, he kissed me, and the rest of the world seemed to disappear. I could almost forget we were in a crowded bar, and most likely drawing attention with our public intimacy.

"Can we get out of here?" I asked.

"Yeah, let's go." Finn led the way out of the bar, his hand wrapped around mine.

Finn

The moon was full that night and it seemed every citizen of Asmara was out celebrating.

Viv and I strolled along the beach until we came to a long piece of driftwood and took a seat.

"You're quiet tonight," I said and Viv glanced at me. I nudged her with my shoulder, making her smile.

"Am I not always quiet?" she asked.

"Well, you weren't so quiet the other night," I said. Her cheeks immediately reddened as she laughed. "Or the following morning," I added, and she smacked my arm.

"You're ruthless, you know that?" she joked.

I ran a hand over my stubble which was turning into a beard.

I lowered my voice and said, "Anytime you need me to remind you of how *ruthless* I can be, just ask."

Viv cocked her head to the side and dropped her gaze to my pants, letting it trail back up slowly to my mouth, making my entire body heat with desire.

"And if I wanted more?" she asked, biting her lip.

"More?" I pursed my lips. "Define more." I waited patiently as she seemed to struggle with her response.

"More..." she started. "More than a hook-up. More than a fling. I want something real, something that will last."

"Those can be two very different things. Something can be real but not last, and vice versa," I pointed out.

"Do you have a lot of experience in that area, then?" she asked.

"A little," I said. "What about you?"

"Probably more than you," she said, hinting at our age gap. I knew she was much, *much* older. But it wasn't something that bothered me.

"Oh yeah?" I perked up.

"More so with relationships that aren't real, but yes. My last *real* relationship was," she paused, tears glistening in her eyes. "With Bree."

"I'm so sorry, I had no idea you two were together," I said, swallowing as a lump formed in my throat.

"We weren't together when she died. This was over a hundred years ago," Viv clarified, giving me a hint at her age. "It wasn't meant to be for us. We had very different visions of our lives. She wanted to settle down and start a family, but I wanted to travel the world. I still want that."

"I don't think I've ever had anything real, and nothing that lasted either," I chuckled. "But if that's something you want, I'd be willing to try."

Viv's breathing hitched and I placed my hand on her knee.

"Y-you're sure?" she said.

"I'm sure if you're sure," I said.

"I'm sure," she said, her voice unwavering. My grin widened. "But will you resent me for becoming a weakness for you, most fearsome pirate?"

"You are not a *weakness.* You are more than capable of handling Brom or anyone else who tries to threaten you. I have no doubt about that. But I won't let anyone get close enough to hurt you."

"Then I won't worry about it," she said, sounding breathless. My heart raced as I leaned down, pressing my lips to hers.

"Good," I murmured.

"Good," she repeated.

"Does this mean I finally get to learn how old you are?" I asked. Viv leaned her head back laughing.

"You first," she said.

"Twenty-eight," I said. Viv didn't seem surprised. "Your turn."

"Two hundred and ninety," she admitted, and I didn't flinch. It was about what I expected. "Mermaids live the same life span as sirens, which is about a thousand years. Sirens can live longer, but most mermaids don't. In human years, I'm about thirty."

"You don't look a day over twenty-nine," I teased, making us both laugh.

"What about your family? Other than your father, of course," she said,

I took a second, breathing deep and letting out a long sigh as I thought of my mother. "It was just my mom and me until I was eight years old, which is when we found Jami. He spent a lot of time with us to escape his own home life. She treated him like another son. She died on my eighteenth birthday from a sickness that had ailed her most of her life. None of the doctors could ever figure it out or slow it down."

"I'm sorry," Viv whispered.

"It's been ten years and it still feels like yesterday sometimes."

"What was her name?" she asked.

I smiled as I said, "Leona."

"You named the ship after her?" She smiled too, and I nodded. "I love that."

"What about your family?" I countered.

"Lia and my sisters are all I have left. I never knew my father; he didn't stick around once I was born. And my mother, well, she didn't care for me much. As soon as I was old enough, she pushed me off onto another family."

"That's awful," I said, running a hand down her arm and feeling goosebumps.

"It's not uncommon for mermaids to be raised by other families. The dynamics in Thalassia are much different than up here. Everyone is kind of one big family in a way. But we also don't get as attached to our own children as other humans and shifters do. I think that's the siren in us. It's not like that for all mermaids, but some, like my mother, are more indifferent to that kind of love."

"You're not that way," I stated.

Viv cocked her head and met my gaze. "What makes you think that?"

"The way you are with Lia proves you can love deeply. I see it with Nix and Korra, too, but more so with Lia."

"Well, maybe you're right," she said. "It was Korra's family who raised me, and once I was old enough to be on my own, Lia and I traveled the world together. Nix came along later, she's the youngest of us. She's only a hundred and eighty years old."

"*Only*," I mocked and smirked.

"Mmm," she murmured, scrunching her nose.

"How did all of your sisters come together?" I asked.

"Lia brought us all together. We had all been abandoned by our own families at some point, and she knew we'd connect, which we did. I brought Korra with me. She and Nix are the only ones who were raised by their actual parents," she explained. "Lia's parents were too busy for her. Her mother was terrible and treated her like trash because she was jealous of her, but they couldn't give her to another family because she's the heir."

"Wait, what?" I asked, stopping her story. She put her hand to her forehead. "Heir to what?"

"Well," Viv sighed. "She may or may not be the princess of Thalassia; heir to the throne."

"And she's just casually risking her life trying to save the world right now?" My eyes widened in disbelief.

"Yeah, I guess," she said. She trailed her hand down my chest, and I shuddered beneath her touch. The sensation sent a shock through me, making my entire body heat in anticipation.

"Are you trying to distract me from the bomb you just dropped on me?" My voice lowered, and my eyes became heavy as I gazed at her.

She wound a hand behind my neck and pulled me closer, pressing her lips to mine.

Jami

Lia and I found a couple shifters who seemed somewhat interested in joining our army, but they weren't promising. We decided to head back to the inn once the bars started to clear out.

"Do you think any of them will seek out Khali?" Lia asked as we walked arm in arm. Her head rested against my shoulder.

"I hope so," I said, trying not to let my own doubts ruin whatever hope she may cling to. "But there is always tomorrow. We haven't even made it out to the surrounding town yet."

She yawned and gripped my arm tighter. I smiled down at her.

"I know you," a low voice drawled making the hair stand on the back of my neck. A man stepped out from the cover of darkness the alley we were passing offered and sneered at me. Automatically, I pushed Lia behind me. I recognized him as another pirate, but I couldn't place him.

"You do?" I asked, placing my hand on my gun holster.

"Uh, uh, don't do that," he said, waving a finger at me.

Lia grunted behind me, and I turned to see another man with his arm around her neck and a pistol shoved into her side.

Putting my hands up away from my own weapon, I scowled.

"We have unfinished business with your *Captain."* He spit out the word like a curse. "But I think we'll send him the message through you."

"Finn will kill you," I said, but he only laughed.

Grabbing my arm, he threw me to the ground, and I didn't fight back.

"Let me go!" Lia yelled, trying to break free. The streets were mostly empty now, and we were too far from the port for anyone to hear her.

A boot connected with my ribs and pain radiated through me. I closed my eyes, taking each kick the man landed, and refused to give him the satisfaction of crying out in pain.

When a beat passed without any assault, I cracked an eye open to see Lia staring down at me with rage in her gaze. Gripping the arm of the man who held her, she bit down on it. Dropping out of his grasp, she kicked the hand that held the gun. It clattered to the ground, and she grabbed it.

"Hey!" the man who had been delivering his 'message' yelled and started for Lia.

Pointing the gun at him, she cocked it and pulled the trigger without blinking; her bullet finding its mark. I jerked in surprise, making my entire body ache. Wincing, I pushed myself to a sitting position.

The other pirate ran before Lia could turn on him.

When she turned back to me, the rage had gone from her eyes. She stared at the gun for a few seconds before dropping it and running to me.

"Are you okay?" she asked.

I opened my mouth to speak, but my gaze snagged on the body beside me. Blood pooled on the cobblestone street,

running downhill toward the port. Someone would be there shortly to investigate the gunshot and would find us.

"I'm okay," I finally said, taking Lia's hand and letting her help me to my feet. "But we need to get out of here." Nausea hit me like a wave from the pain as I became vertical.

I doubled over, which only exacerbated the pain. Lia pulled my arm over her shoulders and held me upright.

"We'll get you help when we get back to the inn," she said, struggling to walk with me weighing her down.

I forced myself to take one step after the other, despite the pain lancing through me with each movement.

After an agonizing ten minutes, we made it to the inn and to our room where Lia laid me on the bed.

"I'll only be gone a minute," she said, before the door closed.

Groaning in pain, I waited as the seconds ticked by.

The door opened again, and multiple sets of footsteps entered.

"What happened?" Finn asked.

I didn't listen as Lia told him the story.

"We need to see what other damage they may have done," Finn said. "I don't see any blood."

"I can see if there's a healer nearby," Viv offered. "Sometimes they will have them at inns like this."

"I'll check him over while you do that," Lia said.

The bed dipped under her weight, and I opened my eyes to see her kneeling beside me. Hands shaking, she reached out to lift my shirt. I flinched.

"You're safe," she said, reaching down with her free hand to cup my cheek.

I faded out for what I thought was only a few seconds, but when I came to, there was a woman hovering over me, applying a salve to my abdomen.

"Make sure he drinks this again in the morning," she said, placing a glass of orangish liquid on the side table. "It takes care of any internal damage."

"Thank you," Lia said.

My eyes fluttered shut.

When I opened my eyes, sunlight streamed into the room.

"You're awake!" Lia said, relief clear in her voice as she propped herself up beside me so that she was slightly above me.

Smiling up at her, I reached out to brush her cheek with my knuckles.

"Drink this," she said, lifting my head and holding a glass to my lips. I obeyed and chugged the liquid. "How do you feel?"

"Much better," I said. It was true, the pain was almost completely gone, despite the nasty bruises on my ribs that I could see when I glanced down at myself. There were no other visible injuries.

She trailed her fingers over the bruise on my ribs and I clenched my jaw, making her pull her hand back.

"Come here," I rasped, placing my hands on her waist and half lifting her into my lap. Laughing, she adjusted so that she was straddling me on her knees. "You saved me." I gripped her thighs and leaned forward to kiss her.

She smiled before kissing me back and parting my lips with her tongue.

A single knock was our only warning before the door opened and Finn walked in with Viv close behind him.

Lia pulled back, not bothering to move off me as they stopped in their tracks.

"Glad to see you're feeling better," Finn commented.

"Sorry to interrupt, but we brought sustenance," Viv added, stepping forward with a plate of toast and eggs. "We'll leave it for you and head out." She winked at Lia, handing her the plate while Finn placed the glass of water on the side table.

"Enjoy," Finn said before they walked out, shutting the door behind them.

"Where were we?" I asked, grinning at Lia, and rubbing my hands up and down her thighs.

"Food first," she said, holding a forkful of eggs up to my mouth.

"I can feed myself; I'm not that injured," I reminded her, but she shook her head and moved the fork closer. I sighed and ate the eggs, indulging her need to feed me, though I was hungering for something much more delectable.

"He could have killed you," she said, her voice soft. I could see the pain in her eyes as she stared down at the plate in her hands.

"But he didn't," I said, stroking my thumb across her cheek and wiping away the tear that had slipped out.

"Why did he do this to you?" she asked, outlining the bruise on my ribs before grabbing the fork again and feeding me another forkful of eggs.

After swallowing, I answered, "Because Finn and I have made too many enemies."

Leaning over me, Lia put the plate on the side table and grabbed the water. As she moved, her thighs squeezed mine, causing my body to heat in anticipation. "Here." She offered me the glass of water and I took it, drinking a big gulp before returning it to the table. My fingers trailed along the hem of her corset, and she shivered under my touch.

"Let me take care of you, now," I said, guiding her down from my lap onto the bed.

"You should probably be resting," she argued, but made no move to stop me as I tugged her leggings off.

"I'll be sure not to do too much physical labor," I countered, and she smirked, watching me as I tossed her leggings aside and positioned myself between her thighs.

Using my tongue and fingers, I feasted on her until she screamed my name. Her hand fisted in my hair, and I let her guide me before taking over again and finishing her off.

"Oh gods," she cried out. "I love you." Her proclamation caught me off guard and I paused for a second, making her gasp. Lifting my head, I made eye contact with her, relishing the flush on her cheeks and the gleam of sweat on her brow.

"I-I didn't mean," she started, sounding breathless.

"Say it again," I commanded, making her smile.

"I love you," she repeated. I propped myself up, rising above her and placing a hand on either side of her. I fought back a wince as my ribs ached, but I couldn't care less about that pain in the moment.

"I love you, too," I responded, before claiming her mouth with my own.

We tired ourselves out and slept away the afternoon. Moonlight streamed through the window when I woke again. I couldn't tell what time it was, but my stomach growled. The cold eggs and hard toast on the side table held no appeal.

I rolled over, groaning as my head pounded. I climbed out of bed. Lia lay sprawled beneath the sheets, her hair splayed around her like a halo. Leaning down, I kissed her temple, then headed for the bathroom.

When I looked in the mirror, I almost didn't recognize myself with the black eye glaring back at me, and my hair a mess. I ran the bath water and waited for it to fill, turning off the light again when it became too much for my head.

Climbing in the tub of hot water had me hissing, and then moaning in pleasure as it soothed my muscles. I scrubbed soap into my hair and dunked myself under the water. When I came up, the light was on, and Lia stood in the doorway in nothing but my shirt.

She yawned as she ran a hand through her hair and squinted in the light.

"Are you taking a bath in the dark?" she asked, her voice still rough from sleep.

"My head is killing me," I explained, and without hesitation, she flicked the light back off.

"Sorry," she mumbled. She walked over and kneeled beside the tub, resting her head on the edge. "I'm only half awake."

"You can go back to sleep, I'm fine," I told her, but she didn't move. "I promise I'll be right back to bed."

"S'okay. I can stay," she said through a yawn. Her eyes fluttered shut.

"Okay," I laughed. After I finished washing myself, I climbed out of the tub and dried off with a towel, wrapping it around my waist. Lia had fallen asleep leaning on the tub, so I lifted her into my arms and carried her back to bed.

I stayed awake the rest of the night; my headache so bad I couldn't find reprieve.

Viv

Finn and I had spent the morning in bed, dreading the trek we'd have to make to the prison to visit with Humer.

"I wish we could stay like this forever," I said. "Nowhere to be, no impending doom, and limitless room service." I traced the tattoo on Finn's chest and rested my chin on his pec. His arm tightened around me.

"As soon as this is all over, I promise to spend numerous endless days in bed like this with you. Wherever you want to go, we'll go."

"That's an awfully serious promise," I teased, peeking at him from beneath my lashes. "Don't make any promises you don't intend to keep."

"I-" he started, but he was interrupted by a knock on the door. I got up first, wrapping the sheet around me, and opened the door to find Lia and Jami there.

"A letter arrived for Finn," Lia said, holding the letter out. I took it, bringing it back into the room to him on the bed.

He opened it and read it.

"It's a response from King Danforth. He wants to meet with me tomorrow," Finn said.

It took a second for that to settle in before my heart clenched at the realization that he couldn't be in two places at once. He'd either have to meet with King Danforth or come to the prison with me and Lia.

"You have to meet with him," I said, deciding to spare Finn from the charade of going back and forth with the decision. There was no other option. We needed King Danforth's support if we were going to defeat the siren queen. Even the promise of finding the magical object she desired didn't change that. There was no telling whether it would be strong enough to do the job, despite the stories being told.

"Are you sure? I can send someone else in my place," Finn tried to argue.

"No, you can't. This is the *king.* You're going, and that's it." I clutched the sheet around me, trying not to let Finn see my trembling hands. My chest burned with anxiety. I'd been looking forward to having Finn waiting for me outside the prison to push myself through. Now, I'd have to look forward to seeing him once we returned to Asmara.

"Okay," Finn agreed. "You're right."

"I should go with you," Jami said, his gaze flicking between Lia and Finn as if he was torn with the decision. "This is a big deal, and we need the king's support. You can't take Marley in there."

I laughed at the thought of Marley going up against the king. They would be quite well matched since Marley never showed her true feelings. The royals would never guess what she had up her sleeve.

"I could go alone," Finn said.

"Or you can take Nix with you," Lia suggested. "She can be our representative since we can't be there."

"Alright, I'll take Nix," Finn agreed.

"Well, we need to get going if we want to reach the prison by tomorrow," Lia said, and my heart rate increased. "I'll fill Nix in before we go."

Lia and Jami left, closing the door behind them.

I sat back on the bed, wrapping my arms around myself as I fought the impending panic attack.

Finn leaned over, putting his head in my lap as he looked up at me. "I have faith in you," he said.

I shuddered. "You, who has faith in no gods or goddesses?"

"Exactly." He reached up, cupping my cheek in his palm. "I have more faith in you than any deity."

"Well, thank you, but I don't know that I have so much faith in myself." I dropped my hands to his hair, smoothing it out of his face.

Finn

Viv, Lia, and Jami readied their horses for their trip.

"We'll only be a two-day journey away, which Marley or Garrett could fly in a few hours if you have any news or need to get in touch with us fast," Lia said. She mounted her horse, having already said her goodbyes to everyone, and Viv followed her lead.

"I'll be anxiously awaiting your return," I told her, and she smiled, but I could tell it was forced. It didn't reach her eyes.

Korra hurried out to us from the inn.

"Before you go," she said as she stopped next to Lia. "I had a replica of the map made. It's ready for the siren queen."

"Give it to Finn. He can take it to Brom," Lia said, and Korra handed me the rolled-up map.

"I'll bring it now. And I'll let him know the real map is coming once you three return. It's the only way we can be sure he won't take it and leave without us," I said. Brom wouldn't break our truce, but that didn't mean he wouldn't conveniently leave us behind to search for the magical item on his own.

"What will stop the queen from using her siren song and taking the map from Brom?" Nix asked.

Blowing out a long breath as I tried to wrack my brain, I swore. “Well, fuck.”

“Mermaids aren’t affected by the song, but it can’t be one of us because then she’ll know we’re working with Brom,” Nix said.

Jami cleared his throat. “For some reason, I’ve never been affected by the siren song. Brom can pretend he’s taken me captive for that reason; to bargain with her on his behalf.”

“That puts you too close to her,” Lia countered. “I don’t want you anywhere near her.”

“This is our only option. There are so many ways this can go wrong, we need to be ready for everything,” Jami said, taking her hand and kissing it. “I promise, I’ll still be here when you return.”

“We’ll return as swiftly as possible,” Lia said. “I don’t want to hear about any injuries, or hitches in the plan. Everything will go *perfectly*.”

I watched as they left, waiting for them to fade out of sight. Once they did, Jami and I headed for the port.

“I’m coming,” Marley said, skipping up beside me. “I’m not letting you visit Brom without backup.”

“Lia won’t be happy if we leave this to you,” Nix said, coming up on my other side. “If there’s so much as a scratch on Jami when she returns, she’ll be showing no mercy.”

Jami’s eyes widened in surprise, and he grinned giddily.

“Don’t act like you didn’t already know she’s crazy about you,” Nix chided, but it didn’t dull Jami’s glee. “She is also just crazy,” she added, joking.

“If she wasn’t, we’d never have become sisters to begin with,” Korra chimed in, and I realized she and Garrett were behind us. “But enough about our princess.”

“Princess?” Garrett asked.

"Whoops," Korra laughed. I stared at Marley, silently asking if she'd known too, and she nodded. Somehow, she always picked up on my inner thoughts. I was half convinced she was psychic.

"What, you all knew?" Jami glared at us all. "I thought Lia only told me."

"I didn't know, but it would be weird if I did," Garrett said.

"The one and only princess and heir of Thalassia," Nix said, flourishing her arms out to either side of her as if feigning a bow.

"Viv accidentally told me," I admitted.

"Nix told me," Marley said. "It wasn't an accident though." She gave me a smug smile. She'd always enjoyed having a leg up on Jami and me, if only to torment us with the fact that she'd beaten us to a punch.

"Back to the problem at hand," I diverted the conversation. "We're not all walking onto Brom's ship. Jami, Marley, and I will meet with Brom while the rest of you do something else."

"I'll be on the ship in case you need me," Nix said.

"If you think Captain Brom won't sense you prowling around his ship, you're wrong," I warned.

"He didn't notice me last time, what makes this time any different?" she asked, her brows raising.

"He'll be expecting you once I arrive."

Nix waved her hand, "Nah. It will be fine."

"Don't say I didn't warn you."

The port was as busy as always when we arrived. We had to weave our way through the crowds. Brom's ship was exactly where it was when we'd left it.

There were two men guarding the gangplank, but they allowed me to pass without question. Brom must have told them I'd be coming with the map. He'd be disappointed he wasn't getting it just yet.

Nix had disappeared as soon as we'd neared the ship and I didn't bother to look for her. Marley stayed by my side instead of shifting. Garrett flew overhead.

Lewis approached us as soon as we set foot on the deck.

"This way," he grunted. Leading us to the captain's quarters.

Brom sat behind his desk as he had the last time I'd met with him.

"Well?" he asked. "Where is it?"

I placed the replica on his desk. "This is the replica for the siren queen. You'll get the real one when Viv and Lia return. They had an errand to run before we begin our search." I didn't trust him enough to let him know what they were really up to.

Brom pursed his lips. "How will I get the siren queen to come to me? I'm not taking my ship out of this port until she grants us safe passage."

"You'll need to leave the dock, at least. Then, I'm sure she'll arrive with her sirens in tow to claim that map. You can make it easier by offering it to her. We will send reinforcements to keep her sirens at bay while she speaks with you."

"What will stop her from using her song on me and taking the map?" he asked.

"Jami. He's unaffected by the siren song. He'll stay on your ship in case she comes before we can enact our own plan to lure her." I explained the entire plan to Brom, reminding him that Jami was only a fake captive and was expected to return to shore unharmed.

Brom agreed. He would take his ship out into the water the following day. As soon as Lia and Viv returned, we could leave.

When we got back to the inn, I figured we should fill Khali in on the plan so she could rally whatever troops we'd already gathered and have them ready for the following day. We needed to present a big enough threat to the siren queen that she wouldn't think she could easily take down Brom's ship and consider the deal with him the better option.

When I knocked on her door, a man answered, half dressed.

"Who is it, Torik?" Khali called from inside.

"Finn," I said before the man could ask.

"Let him in. There's nothing he hasn't seen before."

I laughed at the aggrieved expression on the man's face and pushed past him into the room. Khali lay on the bed covered by the sheet.

"We're going to need whatever shifters you've gathered for our army so far to be on the beach tomorrow," I told her.

She sat up. "Tomorrow?" she asked, gaping at me.

"I think so, but I guess that depends on whether the siren queen shows up or not. We don't expect to take her out, only present a big enough threat that she'll make a deal with Brom."

"Hmm," she mused. "I'll see what I can do. And, just so you know, I'm happy for you," she said, clearing her throat as if the words had almost stuck there.

"Thank you. I truly am sorry that I wasn't clearer with you about everything." I rubbed the back of my neck.

"I'm over it," she said, waving to Torik who still seemed miffed that I was in the room.

"Clearly," I laughed. "I'll leave you two to whatever you were doing, and we can talk more about the plan later." Giving them a salute, I backed out of the room and headed back to mine.

Lia

Viv and I made it to the prison without issue the next day. It was in a secluded area, surrounded by water on three sides, with only one road in and out. We kept moving down the road past the prison toward the inn which was about twenty minutes away.

Once we were settled in our room, Viv burst out crying. I stared at her at first, unsure what was going on, before I snapped back to myself and realized I needed to do something.

"What's happening?" I asked as I sat down beside her on the bed and put my arm around her shoulders. "What's wrong?"

She sobbed while simultaneously wiping at the tears streaming down her face.

"I-I'm s-s-sorry," she gasped out.

"What did I say about apologizing?" I squeezed her and kissed her temple. "You never need to apologize to me."

She hiccupped as the sobs subsided.

"He's so close," she spoke in a hushed voice as if talking any louder about Humer would summon him. "I didn't think it would affect me so much."

"But you held yourself together until now, which is a feat on its own! You are so much stronger than you think," I said. "I'm so proud of you for being here." I leaned my head on her shoulder.

"Can we wait a little bit before we go to the prison?" she asked. "I know you don't want to waste any more time, but I think I need some time to accept we're really here, and he's really in there."

"Of course. Take a few hours. I'm going to take a walk." I stood, stretching before heading for the door. "Do you need me to get you anything?"

"I'm alright. I'm going to take a nap."

Leaving Viv behind in the room, I headed downstairs. This inn wasn't nearly as big as The Flight Deck Inn, but it did have two stories, so it was bigger than most we'd stayed in. I figured it had to be since it was the only one for visitors to the prison to stay in for miles around.

The woman behind the front desk smiled at me as I entered the room. Much like The Flight Deck Inn, there was a bar to the left of the front desk, and a dining room to the right. There were a few people in the dining room, but no one at the bar.

"My sister and I plan on visiting the prison and I was wondering if you have any information on that process?" I asked the woman and she sighed heavily.

"I know too much about that process, unfortunately," she said. "Depending on who you're visiting, you'll need to be on their visitor list, or you may need documentation from the king if they are in high security."

I figured as much. I'd had Khali get me some fake documentation, but if they looked closely, they'd know.

"I have documentation," I said. "How many checkpoints are there?"

"Well, they'll ask to see your documentation at the front gate. Then, they'll bring you inside where the main guards will take your documentation and admit you into the prison. From there, someone will take you to the cell of whomever you are visiting. There's no visiting room for people who you need documentation to visit. They are kept in their cells as much as possible."

"Huh," I breathed. "Okay, thank you."

"If you have any other questions, feel free to ask."

I returned to the room to find Viv fast asleep. Curling up beside her, she stirred, waking up.

"Viv?" I asked.

"Hmm," she groaned. "I'm awake."

"How you doin'?" I rolled to face her.

"Not great, but I'm ready whenever you are," she said, and I heard the anxious strain in her voice.

"If you change your mind, I can go in alone. You don't have to go through with this if it's too much," I reminded her, reaching out to stroke her hair. It had grown longer on the sides and was due for a shave, while on the top she preferred longer anyway, so it could wait.

"No, I want to do it." She reached up to where I played with her hair and groaned. "I wish we had a razor so we could fix this before we go. Is it weird to want to look my best for my tormentor?" She forced a laugh, but from the falseness of it, I knew she was serious.

"No. He should see you at your best to know he didn't break you. You're out here living your best life while he's in there, rotting away."

"That would be nice..." she trailed off.

"I'll find a razor," I said a bit too enthusiastically for the situation, but I was eager to help Viv.

I hurried out of the room and down to the front desk, where the woman sat, reading a book now. When I asked her for a razor, she produced one almost immediately, which had me wondering how often they needed razors around here, but I didn't stick around to ask.

As I glanced to either side, I noticed the dining room was bustling with activity. The bar had also filled up. I had no idea where all the people came from. There must have been a town nearby. Unless they'd all just been in their rooms when we'd arrived earlier.

I grabbed a plate of assorted food for Viv and I and headed back to the room.

"I come bearing food!" I announced as I waltzed into the room and Viv grinned. It made my heart sing to see her smiling despite the situation we were in.

"Thank the gods, I'm starving." She took the plate from me and grabbed a scone before setting the plate on the side table.

"And I have a razor!" I flourished it before me like a sword and Viv laughed. "Time for a haircut."

We moved to the bathroom and Viv sat in the tub while I shaved the sides of her head. She sat with her chin resting on her knees which she had pulled up to her chest.

"Do you want me to cut any off the top?" I asked. The longer part reached just past her ears.

"No, I like it right now. By next week it will probably start bothering me, but I'll deal with it." Standing in the tub, she brushed as much hair as she could off herself, then we scooped up the excess hair into the trash.

"I feel a little better," she said.

"Good." I hugged her, feeling the tickle of a stray hair on my nose.

Finn

King Danforth sent a horse drawn carriage for me. Nix rode with me, looking out the window every few seconds as if it unnerved her to be inside the carriage.

"How do we know if anyone is following us?" she asked, craning her neck to try and see behind the carriage out the window.

"We don't. That's for the driver to worry about," I told her.

"Huh. I don't like it," she said, huffing as she sat back against the seat. "Do you think we'll make it back in time to help fight the sirens?"

"I told Brom not to leave port until we return, so as long as he listens, then yes."

Nix bobbed her head slowly. "Good."

It took about an hour in the carriage to reach King Danforth's castle. The cobblestone drive leading up to the gates was flecked with bits of gold. The gates themselves were pure gold, tipped with little figures that looked like all different animals representing the shifters.

The gates swung open as we approached and beyond lay the castle grounds. Apple trees lined the road, and bright green

grass covered the ground. Flower gardens had been planted in circles all around, but only a few could be seen from our carriage. The castle itself towered over the entire scene, casting a shadow as the sun rose behind it. The bottom half looked as if it had been dipped in gold, while the rest was a pearlescent white that shone everywhere the sun hit it.

Our carriage came to a stop before two grand doors made of red-tinted wood and adorned with wrought iron.

"Captain Finnian," the footman said as he opened the carriage door and waved us out. "You shall be escorted by Damien."

The man who I assumed was Damien didn't look a day over fifteen. His short, floppy, brown hair kept swooping in front of his eyes no matter how hard he tried to push it back.

He led us into the castle, down a hall with a lush, burgundy carpet, and abstract art lining the walls.

"Those are all done by local artists," Damien said when he noticed me studying the art. "The king likes to support his people in all ways."

"How big of him," Nix commented. There was a touch of sarcasm in her voice, but Damien clearly didn't pick up on it as he smiled at her comment.

"Yes. He is a great king," Damien said. "Right this way." He veered to the right through a giant opening in the wall, and into a large chamber filled with rows of benches. At the end of the room, King Danforth sat on his throne with his queen, Carine, beside him.

"Welcome, Captain Finnian, and Nix of Thalassia," King Danforth greeted us. As Damien stopped, we all bowed.

"Thank you for agreeing to speak with me," I said, keeping my head low.

"I was quite interested to hear that you were working with the mermaids," King Danforth said, and I raised my head to meet his gaze. "Princess Aurelia did come to me with a request, though I denied it." Nix stiffened beside me but had the sense not to speak.

"I know, but things have changed since then," I said. "We've discovered the siren queen's true motivations now."

"Oh?" King Danforth leaned forward in his throne, intrigued.

"It is said there is a magical object that can give a single person the power to control the entire ocean," I explained. "She is searching for it so she can continue her reign for as long as possible."

"And how do you intend to stop her?" King Danforth asked.

"We intend to find the object first and use it against her. But we will need your assistance to fight off the rest of the sirens in case the object doesn't exist or doesn't work."

"If you do find this object, what will you do with it once you've defeated the siren queen?" King Danforth asked.

"Destroy it," Nix answered. "No one should have the power to control the entire ocean. The ocean belongs to everyone."

King Danforth clucked his tongue. "Hmm. Seems an awful waste. What happens if another siren queen comes to power who is just as bad, if not worse, than the current one? Might we need that object of power again?"

I ground my jaw as I realized what he was trying to do. No matter how *good* or *well-intentioned* a king may seem, they were all the same. They sought power to put themselves above everyone else, even the other kings.

"We will determine what to do with the object if we find it. But I think everyone who has a stake in it should be present to make that decision. All the kings and queens, from all the kingdoms," I diverted. It wasn't something we could worry about now. We needed to focus on the current threat we faced.

"Find that magical object, and I will agree to help you. Otherwise, I don't foresee an outcome that will benefit my kingdom," King Danforth said, making my heart drop.

"You only want us to find that object so *you* can have it," Nix hissed. "You sit on your throne pretending to be a king for the people, for the shifters, and yet when we need your help, you hide away in your castle like a coward." Turning on her heel, she strode from the throne room.

"Let her go," King Danforth called to his guards. "She will soon see the error of her thinking when she comes to realize this is a losing battle."

Clenching my hands at my sides, I took a deep breath, steadying myself. "Please reconsider," I said. "The siren queen is a threat to us all, whether you believe that now, or not."

King Danforth's attention was still on the door Nix had left through and he appeared bored. I had lost him.

"As I said, I shall reconsider if you find this magical object. Otherwise, we're done here," he said, waving his hand to me.

"After everything I have done for you," I began but he pinned his gaze on me, and I saw the fire burning there.

"Do not mistake my leniency of your piracy for comradery, or kindness. There are no debts to be paid, nor favors to be had." He narrowed his eyes. "I would tread carefully if I were you."

Dipping my head to him, I forced myself to say, “Thank you again for your time.” I wanted to storm out as Nix had, but I refrained. “I’ll send word as soon as we have the object.”

“I’m glad one of you remains optimistic.” King Danforth grinned.

Viv

Lia and I ate before heading out. During the entire ride to the prison, my stomach churned with anxiety. I kept thinking I would throw up, but then it would pass.

I may have been overstimulated and imagining things, but I kept thinking I saw someone in the woods along the road, but there was never anything there when I looked again.

We reached the prison which sat on a cliff with an inlet from the ocean behind it. We were far from the ocean itself, but even being near this small piece of it helped ease my mind. Though my brain screamed at me to run the other way, I ignored it and we pressed on.

A stone wall surrounded the entire place with a gate set into the front of it. Two guards sat on either side of the gate, tossing something back and forth between them. When they saw us approaching, they stood to face us.

"What business brings you here?" one of them asked. He had cropped, white-blond hair, and I could see a star tattooed on the side of his head.

"We are here to visit Marcus Humer," Lia said, dismounting from her horse to be level with the guards.

"Do you have the proper documentation?" he asked.

"Yes. I have it right here." Lia turned back to her horse and dug around in her saddle bag, pulling out a handful of papers. My heart pounded as I waited, staring up at the prison.

You're so close, my Vivianne, Humer's voice echoed in my mind, and goosebumps covered my entire body.

"I'll take those," the guard said, holding out his hand to Lia. She didn't hesitate before handing over the false documentation.

The guard inspected it only a moment before he nodded and waved to whoever operated the gates. A large click sounded, and the gates ground open.

The other guard, who wore glasses and fidgeted with the gun at his side remained silent. I narrowed my eyes at him and was hit with a wave of familiarity. *The round rimmed glasses, tinted lenses.* His hair was different now, the blonde waves cropped close to his head, but without a doubt, I knew it was him. One of Humer's henchmen. I stopped breathing as he locked eyes with me and I knew he recognized me, too.

Turning away from me, Glasses walked with the other guard through the gate and Lia followed, pulling on my hand to make me move with her. Soon we were inside the gates with them slamming shut behind us. There was no turning back.

"Lia," I whispered to her, and she shot me a glance but kept moving. "I know that guard. The one with the glasses." That made her pause, but we couldn't stop because the guards kept moving.

"What do you mean?" she asked.

"He worked with Humer. He was one of the men who helped hold me down or carry me from room to room." I shuddered as I recalled the memory.

"What the fuck?" Lia said a little too loudly and the guards turned back to look at her. "Sorry, stubbed my toe," she

said which appeased the one with the star tattoo, but Glasses narrowed his eyes and his hands twitched at his sides.

"What's he doing guarding the prison?" Lia asked, much quieter this time. "Maybe this can work in our favor. Maybe he's trying to turn a new leaf and we can threaten him with exposure if he doesn't help us!" The more excited she became, the more horrified I felt.

"What if he's planning to break Humer out?" I asked, my eyes rounding and mouth drying at the thought. I wanted more than anything to turn and run.

"By himself? It's a maximum-security prison, Viv. I don't think he could single handedly take on every guard in this place to break out Humer." She tried to convince me, but my breathing only became more rapid.

"What if there are more of them? What if he's *not* alone?" I suggested.

Before she could answer, we'd reached the front door to the prison, which was a large, metal, armored door that reached up to about three times our height. When it swung open, musty air wafted out to us and only dim light could be seen within.

The next set of guards sat in a small office that had windows on all sides so they could look out into the prison, even though this area was just hallways leading off in different directions.

We were led into the office so the new guards could inspect our paperwork and I wound up standing beside Glasses at the back of the room. My heart beat so hard in my chest I wondered if he could hear it. He stood stock still, his hands clenched at his sides, and it seemed as if he was holding his breath.

The two guards in the office wore nametags, one read *Kellin* and the other *Rodero.* Rodero studied our

documentation intently. It made me wonder how many people cared enough to try and sneak in here. Of course, that's exactly what Lia and I were doing.

"Huh," Rodero said as he pointed to one of the pages. Relief at the thought that we wouldn't be allowed in to see Humer hit me. Soon after, realization that we *needed* to talk to him spurred me into action.

Panicking, I turned to Glasses and nudged him with my arm.

"Help us or I'll out you," I threatened under my breath, knowing it was a long shot. There was the possibility these men knew exactly who he was and didn't care. There was also the possibility that if I tried to tell them who he was, they wouldn't believe me. Why should they?

Glasses remained rigid, and I assumed he'd ignored me. But a few seconds passed, and he stepped forward.

"All set?" he asked. "I can take them myself; you don't need to interrupt your own work."

Rodero lifted his gaze to Glasses and cocked his head to the side. "What a small offering," he commented, and Glasses groaned, it was so quiet I'm sure I was the only one who heard.

"I'll take up the meals," Glasses offered, but Rodero continued to stare, expecting more. "And clean out the chamber pots." Glasses shot me a glare and I quickly found anywhere else to look, holding in a laugh. He deserved it and so much worse for what he'd helped Humer do to me and all those other shifters.

"All set," Rodero said, slamming the paperwork down onto the desk. "Take them up, Manes."

Manes, I thought. *Huh, so he has a real name.* Lia latched onto my arm as we followed Manes out of the office. He led us down the hallway to the right of the office, there were

doors lining the hall and I wondered what they all led to. How many more monsters filled the rooms of this prison?

Once we were well out of earshot of the office, Manes turned to us, a fire blazing in his eyes.

"Why are you here?" he snapped, his jaw ticking. I winced and cursed myself for reacting so visibly.

"To visit Humer, just like we said," Lia answered. "The real question is, why are *you* here?" She poked her finger into his chest.

"To keep an eye on my brother," he said, and warning bells pealed in my brain.

"Brother?" I asked, and I already knew the answer.

"Marcus Humer is my brother," he explained. "I'm here to make sure he never leaves this place."

I'd never been conscious enough to make the connection whenever I'd seen Manes before, though now I doubted that was his true name. He had the same hair color, the same eyes, the same perfectly straight nose, and a similar build. Manes didn't have quite the same charisma as his brother though.

"Why don't you want him to leave?" Lia asked.

I was too busy connecting dots to ask the millions of questions I had.

"Because he's a monster," Manes said blatantly.

"He's your brother," Lia pointed out.

Manes sighed, "Yes, we've established that."

"And you helped him torture me," I reminded him, and he dipped his head. Rage burned in my gut. He didn't deserve forgiveness for the part he'd played in my torture.

"I'm sorry about all he did to you. I didn't want to help him, but I didn't have much choice. I was sixteen and had

nowhere else to go. I believed in him, at the time. Now I know what he did was horrific and wrong."

My brain latched onto *sixteen. Sixteen,* I repeated in my mind. I'd thought he was at least twenty to be able to carry me like I was nothing. Although, at that point, I practically *was* nothing with all the weight I'd lost from being held in captivity.

No. Not nothing. You aren't and never were nothing, I reminded myself. A bad habit I'd picked up was believing I meant nothing to the world because no one came for me for so long. I'd convinced myself that if I were to disappear, it would change nothing. I knew better. I had people who cared about me and loved me.

"If you truly are sorry, then take us to your brother so we can talk with him," Lia said.

"What's your real name?" I asked before Manes could turn around.

"It's Jared Manes. We don't have the same last name," he said, before turning on his heel and leading us up the stairs.

Jared Manes. I had a name to put to the face of the man who had carried me in and out of Humer's exam room each week. It did nothing to help me let go of the pain he'd caused me.

Jared led us to Humer's door. In the maximum-security area, all the doors were solid metal, no bars. There was a window in the door that he opened so we could see inside. It had only been twenty years since I'd seen him last, but he seemed to have aged fifty.

Lines had set into his face, giving him wrinkles on his wrinkles. His blonde hair had begun to gray at his temples and hung shaggy and snarled. His beard had gray streaks and it too had become unruly.

For a few seconds, I imagined the handsome face he'd had when we met outside that bar in Asmara. Before the image was replaced with reality. My mind couldn't make sense of such a fragile man having held so much power over me for so long.

"He's been a bit unstable since coming here," Jared said.

I scoffed, "Like he wasn't before?"

"Well, you'll see."

Knocking on the glass that separated us from Humer, Jared slid open another part of the door, revealing a slot where food could be sent in.

"Marcus." Jared's voice seemed to reanimate his brother. Humer's head rose from where it had rested on his chest and his once bright eyes were now dull and lifeless. I took a step back as he laid his eyes on me and a spark of intrigue lit his expression as he stood and approached the door. Fear took control, locking my muscles and halting my breath.

"Look what you've brought me, Jared," Humer's voice came out rough and crackling, likely from disuse. "My favorite patient."

Lia put her arm around me.

"Breathe," she whispered in my ear.

"Why have you come here?" Humer asked, pressing his hands to the door, and leaning in close to peer through the window.

Closing my eyes, a memory surfaced unbidden.

"Vivianne, be a good patient and stop squirming so much," Humer said, his grip on my arm tightening as he shoved a needle into it. "There. That will help."

"Vivianne," Humer said my name like a caress, and it sent unpleasant shivers down my spine. "Open your eyes and look at me."

When I did, he cackled and pointed at me through the window. "As obedient as ever," he said, and I cursed him inwardly. My hands shook and I lifted my chin, trying not to let him see me waver.

"We need to ask you a question," Lia spoke up, moving to block me from Humer's direct line of sight.

"Hm, hm, hm." Humer clapped his hands as he pondered. "A question?"

"Yes. About an object of power that the siren queen wants."

"Still looking for that old thing, is she?" He laughed again, and it grated my nerves. He hadn't used to laugh so much when I'd known him. I was beginning to sense why Jared had said he was a bit more unstable now.

"Yes, and we are hoping you might have information on it," Lia said.

Humer stepped away from the door and paced. Every time he passed the window, he found my gaze and held it until he was out of sight again. A shiver ran through me.

"An object of power to rule the sea," he said in a sing-song voice. "A necklace, a trio, one two three."

"See what I mean?" Jared grumbled, pinching the bridge of his nose with his thumb and forefinger. "He talks in riddles and stupid rhymes now."

"A necklace?" Lia ignored Jared and continued talking with Humer. I stepped closer to the door so I could see him better, though I'd rather never see him again.

"Others have said it's more likely to be a scepter or crown," I said.

"Oh, no, no, no." Humer stopped his pacing and slammed his hands against the door making us all jump. "The jewel is the power. It can be put in anything."

"So, it might not be a necklace then?" Lia asked.

"An object of power to rule the sea," he repeated, and I groaned. "A necklace, a trio, one, two, three!" He threw his hands in the air and cackled.

"Okay, so for arguments sake, we'll say it's a necklace. What do you mean by 'a trio?'" Lia asked, her fists clenching at her sides. I could tell she was becoming frustrated trying to talk sense with Humer.

"A trio, a triad, a trinity," Humer muttered, resuming his pacing.

"Those are all synonyms, yes," Lia said through clenched teeth. I put my hand on her arm.

"Give me a minute," I said, taking her place in front of the door. "Humer," I started, and he stopped to stare at me. I rolled my shoulders, trying not to let him intimidate me.

"Yes, Vivianne?"

"This necklace of power, is it on an island?" I asked, thinking about the map.

"An island?" he questioned, tapping his finger to his chin. "An island..."

"Maybe in a cave?" I tried again.

"The island, the cave, and the monster protect the power," Humer ticked each thing off on his fingers. "A trio," he grinned.

"Yes. A trio," I said. "Do you know where the island is?"

"Hidden," he said in a hushed voice as if suddenly wary someone might be listening in.

"Where?" I asked again.

"Hidden," he repeated.

I sighed, "How is it hidden? Magic? Fog? A hoard of demons?"

Humer narrowed his eyes at me. "I never liked your sassiness, Vivianne," he said and for a moment his old self shone through. "The island is hidden by the same ones who hold the key to finding it."

I nodded. "Okay."

A crackling sounded overhead and then a voice came on an intercom. *"Times up, Manes. Get to work cleaning those pots."* There was a click and then nothing more.

"Sorry, but we have to go," Jared said, sliding the metal coverings back into place on the door and sealing Humer off once more.

We stepped out of the prison and the fresh air revived me. As we walked toward our horses, I turned back to see the prison one last time. I felt as if I'd left a piece of myself there.

My thoughts were cut short when an explosion tore the world apart.

Lia

I grappled for Viv as I lay flat on my back. My ears rang from the explosion. Smoke painted the sky in grays and whites. Sirens blared somewhere to my right, and Viv groaned to my left.

Someone picked me up, half dragging me toward the edge of the cliff.

"What's happening?" I asked.

"The queen will reign for all time," a woman said almost as if it were a chant.

"Don't touch me!" Viv yelled and I whipped my head toward her. I was too disoriented to fight off my captor, but I watched Viv struggle against hers. I'd never seen these people before, but I could smell the salt and seaweed on them from the ocean. They were shifters, and from the vivid red hair of my captor, I'd guess mermaids.

"Traitors," I hissed, squirming in her grip.

"She is the one true ruler of the sea," she said before shoving me over the side of the cliff. A scream escaped me as I fell, slapping against the water hard, knocking the air from my lungs.

I regained a sense of self slowly, instinctively shifting into my Mer form. Before I could swim away or to the surface to search for Viv, something grabbed my tail.

Bubbles rushed by me as I was dragged down, down, down, to the bottom of the sea. I struggled against whoever had me in their grip, but they held on tight, refusing to let go.

Finally, I came to a stop and pitch-black eyes lit up before me, illuminating the siren queen's face as her tongue ran over the points of her teeth.

"Aurelia. So, we meet again." The siren queen's words sounded perfectly clear, as if we were above water. "I'm finding it a bit flattering you care so much about me and my plans."

"I will stop you," I tried to say, but my words could barely be heard. Instead, I reached out in my mind, but couldn't break through the barrier the queen had around her own mind. So, I aimed for someone else.

Viv, are you there? I pushed out with my telepathy, trying to find Viv's mind, but there was no answer.

The queen laughed. "Oh, but you've already failed. I'm simply here to distract you for a moment." Her smile was feral.

My heart clenched. "What did you do?" I screamed into the water. My head whipped up as if I'd see Viv being dragged down with me.

"I've simply taken what I want. Humer will be of great use to me, just wait and see."

My heart pounded as I struggled in the grasp of the queen's tentacle. I had no idea what she planned for Humer, but if she had Viv as well, I knew it wouldn't be good.

"Now, as flattering as your attention has been, it's hindering my plans. I needed to show you how serious this is, since my first warning clearly wasn't enough. People will get hurt

if you continue pursuing me." The queen's hand tightened around my throat. "*You* will get hurt."

My gills were trapped beneath the queen's palm, and I clawed at her arm, trying to free myself. The queen laughed and released me.

"I'll give Viv your regards." She cocked her head as if listening for something. "But right now, you're coming with me."

I shook my head, refusing to believe what the queen was saying.

"Why not kill me?" I asked.

"I'm not trying to start a war with Thalassia, silly girl. I will get what I want, and I will rule the sea. Until then, your mummy and daddy dearest can stay tucked away nice and safe in their little bubble."

Using one of her tentacles to keep me at her side, we moved through the water at speeds I'd never been able to travel.

We made it to Asmara in a matter of hours. It gave me time to try to plan an escape, but I truly had no hope of succeeding. Viv was gone. The sirens had taken her to Neros knew where, along with Humer.

"They finally left port. I hear the captain has a proposition for me," the siren queen crooned, chuckling darkly as she slowed. "Do you think I should make a deal with him?"

I ground my jaw, refusing to give in to the queen's taunts.

"You see all those sirens waiting underneath there?" She pointed to where they lay in wait beneath Brom's ship. I imagined Jami waiting with Brom for the siren queen to arrive so they could attempt to make their bargain.

No other shifters had entered the water, so I had no idea if Khali had convinced any of them to help us that day.

"I wonder what would happen if I gave them the order to destroy the ship? How long do you think it would last?"

“Don’t,” I hissed, a stream of bubbles the only indication I’d spoken.

“What was that?” the siren queen tilted her head as if trying to hear me. “Oh, that’s right. You’re not a real creature of the ocean. You don’t deserve a place in my domain.”

I thrashed against her, trying my hardest to break free, to no avail.

“Let’s see what bloodshed we can cause.” Keeping me tight in her clutches, she dashed through the water, headed straight for Brom’s ship.

Jami

I couldn't sleep on Brom's ship. He'd given me Roland's old quarters and I'd spent the night going through his belongings. It was strange, seeing a different side of him. There were love letters in one of his desk drawers from a woman in Sylvane. I hadn't read past the first one, not wanting to invade Roland's privacy that much, even if he was dead. Though I was tempted, I hadn't believed Roland capable of love.

There was a picture of our parents above his desk, tucked into one of the wooden boards so it hung crooked. No pictures of Charles or myself.

When the ship rocked more than usual, I headed above deck to find us leaving port.

"Is Finn back?" I asked one of the crew.

"Don't know. We're just following our orders," he answered.

A hawk flew overhead, dropping down onto the deck and transforming into Marley. She hurried to my side.

"They just got back. Finn's on the beach with Khali and the other shifters. The king isn't willing to help, as Lia said. His only interest was in the magic object because he wants it for himself," she explained.

"Sounds about right," I said. Finn had a higher opinion of King Danforth than I did, but I'd also never worked for him.

"We haven't heard anything from Lia and Viv yet, but they should be at the prison." Marley walked over to the side of the ship, and I followed. We both peered down into the water. I half expected to see sirens swarming us, but there was no sign of them yet.

I rubbed my lucky coin in my pocket, thinking about how I should be with Lia. But if we ever wanted this war with the siren queen to end, I had to play my role in it.

"Jamison!" Brom barked from the upper deck near the helm. "Get up here."

I gripped the rail as I made my way up the stairs. Being back on a ship made my heart sing. I'd missed the ocean breeze against my skin, and the sea spray misting my face.

Taking a deep breath, I let it settle in that we were about to face off with the siren queen. If we were lucky, she'd take the bait and make the bargain with Brom. I didn't want to think about what would happen if we weren't lucky.

"Captain Brom," I said as I approached him.

"This is as far out as we'll go," Brom said. "If you're friends are right, and the siren queen is as desperate for the map as they say, it will be enough."

"So, now we wait," I stated.

"So, now we wait," he repeated, staring out at the open ocean.

It was quiet for a while, but soon, there was a hum in the air, as if the sirens were singing their song underwater, but until they sang it above water, it wouldn't affect the crew.

Peering over the rail, the sirens could be seen gathered beneath the ship. Fear clutched me, but I didn't turn away. They stared up at us, waiting for something.

"I've made my intentions known," Brom said. "That I wish to make a bargain with the siren queen." He spoke loud enough that everyone would hear him, even any sirens who were above the water.

The sound of churning water came from behind me, and I turned slowly, dread bubbling in my stomach and making me queasy.

"Here she comes," Brom murmured. "Prepare yourself."

Brom stepped behind me, grabbing my arm and pushing me toward the rail where the siren queen rose on a wave. Her depthless black eyes stared into mine, and a terrifying grin split her face in two.

"What a turn of events," she said, her voice as sharp as her teeth. "I almost feel like this is...fate. Yes."

"I want to make a bargain with you," Brom said, his voice loud and clear. "I have a man here who is immune to your song."

Her eyes stayed on me as she said, "Is he now?" Moving her head like a snake, she scanned me with great interest. "I would like to know what you think you have that would mean anything to me." Finally, she turned to Brom.

"A map. The map you attacked my ship for," Brom said.

She pursed her lips. "And what do you wish for in exchange?"

"All I want is to be able to sail on the sea again. I request safe passage from you and your sirens," Brom explained, dipping his head to the queen slightly. It was a good show, I had to admit.

"I have a better deal," she said, her eyes widening as she grinned again. "I shall grant you safe passage on the sea, in

exchange for the map, and for *him.*" She pointed to me and my heartbeat faltered.

"No!" I heard someone yell from below the siren queen. Breaking free from Brom's grasp, I peered over the side and cried out as I saw Lia dangling from one of the siren queen's tentacles.

The siren queen laughed as she pulled Lia up and placed her on the deck.

"As I said, this meeting with you was fate," the siren queen said. "Lia here needed a reminder of what I can do to destroy her life if she continues to defy me."

"Don't give her what she wants," Lia said through her tears. The siren queen had a tentacle wrapped around her, though her arms were free.

"New deal," I said. "Take me and the map, leave Lia and give Brom safe passage."

"It's not happening!" Lia said, trying to fight her way out of the siren queen's grip. "Don't do this, please." She sounded so dejected, I hated doing it, but I needed her to be safe.

"What say you?" I asked, fighting against the bile in my throat at the thought of being dragged underwater by the queen.

"Getting exactly what I want *and* leaving Lia to watch her world crumble? Deal." Thrusting herself forward, she held a hand out to Brom. He shook her hand, though his lip curled in barely disguised disgust.

Dropping Lia on the deck, the siren queen turned her focus to me. I grabbed my lucky coin from my pocket and flicked it over to Lia before a tentacle wrapped around me.

"Hold onto that for me, beautiful," I said, the words catching in my throat.

Finn

Standing on the beach alongside other shifters, we waited as Brom's ship began to rock. A few sirens jumped out of the water, but none seemed to be directly attacking the ship.

Nix and Korra had gone into the water with a group of mermaids and other sea creature-type shifters so they could be ready in case the sirens attacked.

Garrett flew overhead, while Marley was on the ship with Jami. I'd sent her out there to fill him in on my meeting with King Danforth.

"It's her!" someone yelled from my right. "The siren queen!"

A gasp left me as I watched her rise on a wave to meet with Brom on the top deck of the ship. I couldn't see Brom or Jami from where I stood, but I assumed they were there now.

Pacing the beach, I waited, praying to Viv's goddesses that everything was going okay.

After a few minutes, the siren queen dropped back into the ocean, and I swore I saw someone dive over the side after her.

"Get out there!" I yelled at everyone around me. "I don't care how the deal went, if the siren's start attacking, we need to be ready!"

Thankfully those who remained on the beach listened and ran into the water, shifting into their animal forms.

I hated not being able to see what was happening beneath the surface where the real action would be taking place. Even if I shifted and swam out there, I'd be of no use, unable to see the sirens coming.

The churning in the water beneath the ship told me there was *something* happening.

Shifters started returning to the beach, though.

"What's going on?" I asked a shark shifter who returned first.

"The sirens are retreating. The siren queen made a deal with Captain Brom."

"Then who went overboard?" I asked. Panic seized me that Jami had gone in after her, or worse, that Brom had *pushed* Jami in. I wouldn't put it past him.

The shark shifter shook his head. "I don't know."

Thankfully, I saw Marley flying toward me from the ship. She would fill me in on what happened out there.

She shifted immediately upon landing and ran to me. For the first time in a long time, I saw fear in her eyes, and it sent me to my knees.

"Don't tell me," I said, putting my head in my hands. "It was Jami? He went after her."

She hung her head and closed her eyes as she knelt in the sand before me. "It was Lia. Jami made a deal with the queen, himself for Lia. The map for Brom's safe passage."

Confusion took the place of my disbelief for a second, before pure panic took over and I tried to ask all the questions racing through my mind, but I could barely breathe.

"Viv," was all I managed to say.

"I don't know. The siren queen had Lia, no one else. And she left with Jami. Lia jumped in after them and didn't resurface. No one said anything about Viv," Marley said, her words coming out fast and almost as panicked as I felt.

"She's okay. She *has* to be okay," I said, wiping my nose as it ran from the tears pressing against the back of my eyes.

"She took him," Marley gasped out, dropping her head into her hands. "*Jami.* He's gone. What are we going to do without him?"

"Don't think like that," I snapped. "We'll get him back. We have to."

Lia

Diving over the side of the ship after the siren queen, I collided with the water and shifted. The siren queen was nowhere to be seen, but I would take out my rage on her lackeys. I watched the sirens closely as I aimed for them.

It felt as if a vital part of me had been cracked open, stealing any sense of purpose or happiness from within. An entire future had been laid out before me with Jami. One where we would have shown each other our homes, and then built one of our own. I'd been ready to spend the rest of his human life with him, knowing that the short time he'd be able to offer would never be enough.

The sirens bared their razor-sharp teeth, and I could have sworn they were smiling. Hatred rose up in me as I collided with the first siren, driving the dagger I carried straight into their heart.

It wouldn't kill the monster, only slow them down. Sirens could live without a heart. Whether that made them incapable of feeling, I wasn't sure, but I'd never met a siren who cared about anyone other than themselves and their queen.

The siren screamed in pain, lashing out with its claws and raked them down my side. I echoed the siren's scream,

though it was muffled by the water that surrounded us. Blood tainted the sea.

I wrestled with the siren, trying to gain the upper hand. If I could stab the siren in the throat or the back of the neck, I could end its miserable life.

The image of that had nausea roiling in my stomach, bringing back the image of the man I'd killed in the alley. But I'd had no choice. It was either us or them who would be leaving this battle. Something collided with the siren from behind, sending us both hurtling through the water.

I took advantage of the distraction, fighting to regain a sense of where I was, and lashed out with my dagger again, striking home in the siren's throat. Bubbles streamed out of the wound, along with blood. The siren's hands released me and scrabbled at her neck. I wrenched the dagger from the wound, making sure to do more damage on the way out.

With my jagged dagger, it *always* did more damage on the way out.

The sirens retreated, but I wasn't finished with them yet. Before I could go after them, though, Nix swam in front of me, pushing me back.

Let me go, I yelled at her in my mind.

Stop this, Lia. You're accomplishing nothing. The siren queen is gone. Her words did nothing to quell the storm raging inside of me.

She took them. Jami and Viv. She took them from me. I screamed into the water, bubbles erupting from my mouth. Putting her arms around me, Nix pulled me to the surface.

"Stop this!" she said. "We will get them back, but not like this! The only thing you'll accomplish is getting yourself killed."

"She has Humer, too. What if he hurts Viv again? I promised her I would never let him... I promised her..." My words failed me, and I lost myself in a fit of sobs. Nix wrapped her me in her arms.

"Viv is strong. Whatever happens, we will find her, and we will bring her home," Nix said, stroking my hair. "Come on."

She towed me to the shore. I shifted into human form. My eyes snagged on Finn kneeling with Marley, and I ran to him, nearly tripping over my own feet in my haste. Finn's face was pale, and he seemed to be in shock.

"Where is she?" he asked when I reached him.

I dropped to my knees beside him as my world closed in on me.

"The queen," I began. "She took Viv."

Finn's eyes widened and he jumped up, running to the water. I followed, grabbing his arm.

"Not here. She took her back at the prison, after we left. There was an explosion and... She took Viv and Humer."

The remainder of our group surrounded us. Korra, Nix, Marley, and Garrett.

"No," Finn's voice came out as a whisper. "Why would they take her?" He growled, his lion side coming out as he scraped his hand through his hair.

"I don't know. It must have something to do with the experiments, I can't think of any other reason they'd take *her,*" I theorized, my mind reeling.

"Why would the queen care about the experiments?" Finn asked.

"Humer, the man who kept her captive for two years, did experiments on her and a bunch of other shifters. Viv is the only who survived, so maybe the queen thinks that means something and wants to use Viv somehow."

Rage bubbled up inside me. *She escaped, only to be taken once again...*

"You said they took her, though, which means she's still alive? She's okay?" Finn asked.

"Alive, yes. Okay?" I left the rest unsaid. The siren queen wouldn't be gentle with her.

"So, we go after them. We find her," Finn said as if it were so easy.

I scoffed. "The siren queen has never been located within the ocean. Her home base, or whatever you want to call it, is a mystery." Grinding my jaw, I stared out over the water to the ship that remained unscathed.

"So, we find it," Finn demanded. "Nothing can stay hidden forever."

"We find it," I echoed. "*We find it,*" I said a bit more excitedly. "We find the necklace! Or whatever it is. The power she wants, we give it to her. In exchange for Viv."

"That's insane," Nix argued. "We can't give the queen anymore power."

"Nix is right. Viv wouldn't want us to risk the fate of the entire sea for her sake," Korra added.

I whipped my head to Korra. "You don't know that. I know Viv better than anyone else, and I'll make the call." I turned back to face Finn. "Are you in?"

"I'll do whatever it takes to get Viv back," he said, his fists clenching at his sides. "Even if I have to kill the siren queen myself."

"Good. Then we're doing this."

"You're condemning the entire sea to the siren queen's reign if you do this!" Korra exclaimed.

I turned a cold gaze on her. "So be it."

About the Author

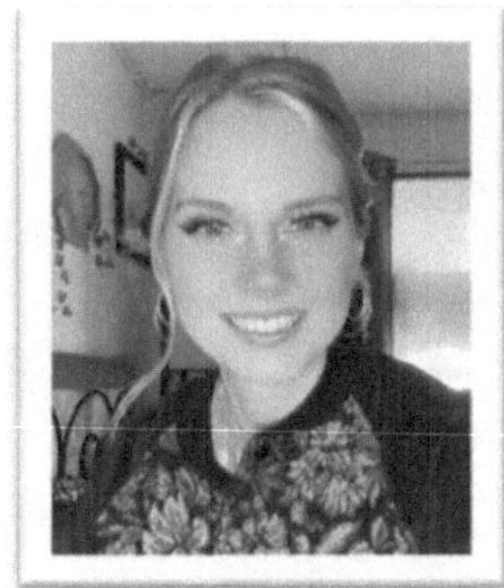

H. M. Huntress is a self-published author and content creator. She has been writing stories since grade school and is driven by the desire to share her writing with the world while encouraging others to do the same. All her books are currently available on Amazon. If you want to connect with her on social media, find her at the handle below!

TikTok & Instagram: @authorhmhuntress

I'd love if you left a review for *Forbidden Waves* on Amazon, Goodreads, or social media!

Scan here for updates on future projects and events!

Check out my other books!

Haunting Memories

The Forbidden Waves Series:

Forbidden Waves
Ruthless Tides

Beneath Venomous Sails

The Broken Angel Series:

Broken Angel
Condemned Angel
Forsaken Angel

The Unbound Series:

Unbound
Disgraced
Awakened
Ruined

www.ingramcontent.com/pod-product-compliance
Lightning Source LLC
Chambersburg PA
CBHW030238120726
47903CB00005B/1535

9798999637604